THE KING OF THE CON MEN
PUTS UP HIS DUKES

Six Wilson staggered, and a roar of excitement and dismay went up from his men; and the girl heard a man shrieking: "Six, Six, what's the matter with you? You can break the shrimp's back. What's the matter with you?"

But Speedy like a wildcat had followed in; and they whirled together. The legs of the boy seemed wound into those of the gaunt outlaw, but by his left hand he kept his best hold, and that hold was on the throat of the big man. She saw both their faces, ghastly in the moonlight; one killing, one dying.

But it was not ended, yet. Six Wilson had not come into the battle prepared to trust all to fair combat. Instead, his free hand now jerked up high, with a blade gleaming in it.

Mary Steyn screamed, but only half the scream was uttered as she saw the knife descend...

Books by Max Brand
from The Berkley Publishing Group

THE BIG TRAIL
BORDER GUNS
CHEYENNE GOLD
DAN BARRY'S DAUGHTER
DEVIL HORSE
DRIFTER'S VENGEANCE
THE FASTEST DRAW
FLAMING IRONS
FRONTIER FEUD
THE GALLOPING BRONCOS
THE GAMBLER
THE GARDEN OF EDEN
THE GENTLE GUNMAN
GOLDEN LIGHTNING
GUNMAN'S GOLD
THE GUNS OF DORKING HOLLOW
THE LONG CHASE
LOST WOLF
MIGHTY LOBO
MONTANA RIDES
ONE MAN POSSE
OUTLAW BREED
OUTLAW'S CODE
THE NIGHTHAWK TRAIL
THE REVENGE OF BROKEN ARROW
RIDERS OF THE SILENCES
RUSTLERS OF BEACON CREEK
SILVERTIP
SILVERTIP'S CHASE
SPEEDY
THE STRANGER
TAMER OF THE WILD
TENDERFOOT
TORTURE TRAIL
TRAILIN'
TRAIL PARTNERS
WAR PARTY

SPEEDY

BERKLEY BOOKS, NEW YORK

SPEEDY

1

WHEN JOHN PIERSON had a dog and a gun, he felt as though he owned the entire range of the Rocky Mountains from head to heel. And he had the gun and the dog with him, and there were still two days of clear vacationing before the moment when he had to turn back towards his home. He loved his home and he had made it worth living. He loved his work, and he had made it worth loving. But still his heart was half the time running out the window of his office and plunging off among the blue peaks that he could see.

It was not often that he got there in person. A week end here, and a fortnight in the slack season of the year were about all that he could afford. But he took what he could in the way of mountain days.

He was on foot. He had been raised on a horse, but when his time was so short, he generally felt that one got closer to the heart of things by walking. And so he walked now, with a good, free, powerful stride, in spite of his closeness to fifty years of age. He went uphill with a strong drive; he went downhill on springs. He was a big fellow, built like a rock, bull-necked, brown-faced. The tan on the back of his neck had been built up layer by layer since the days when he was a tow-headed boy riding range on a Texas ranch.

He was given a slightly professional touch, perhaps, by the short cropped mustache that he wore; it was still jet black, and glistening, though his hair was very gray. And in the keen, straight-looking blue eyes was the soul of the acquisitive man. Even the glance with which he surveyed the mountains he loved was almost that of one estimating their acreage, regretting that sheep were not browsing on the difficult patches of upland grass, or that cattle were not dotting the lower valleys.

In one of those lower valleys he paused so long that the

dog lay down in the grass and began to roll and play with itself, as though confident that the day's work and sport were over. For the master was lost in delight.

It was not much of a valley. It was a little broken ravine with a twisting, singing line of silver water thrown along the length of it. But it had groves along the banks, or single big trees thrusting out at a slant, holding green sunshades, as it were, over picnic grounds. And there were thickets of blooming shrubbery, and here a patch of rocks thrust up through the soil, glistening, the bony knees of Mother Earth breaking through a threadbare place. But mostly the water was enchanting. For sometimes it roared over a little cataract and multiplied itself with shadows, and in all ways tried to imitate a real river. And again it shot down a steep flume with a hissing sound of speed; but finally, it paused entirely in a large pool.

The very soul of John Pierson had paused there, also, and while the dog rolled in the grass, he was probing the mirrored mountains, the sky, the white blowing clouds that were quickly lost in the shrubbery along the banks, like sheep; and then the quick shadow of a soaring hawk skimmed across the water.

Down there below, where the water broke down from the pool and began to wrinkle as it gathered speed—there ought to be fish in that spot, among the rocks—good brook trout, basking there, loving their shadows and scornful of man! He saw exactly where he could stand, first here and then there, doing his casting. It was not long before lunch. He had shot nothing. And he determined that he would eat fish this day! It was one of his boasts that when he adventured into the mountains, he never took with him more than his rifle and his fishing rod and salt. Nature had to provide for all his needs—nature and his ability to harvest her gifts.

He screwed the pieces of the rod together and then tried the balance and whip of it with an expert hand. He was proud of that hand; the wrist was steel-strong, even now, when he was deep in middle age. And his touch was delicate, and his eye was sure. He would be able to fish that stream as no one had fished it before, as no one might fish it again. The trout that escaped from him would die of old age, he assured himself, as he selected his fly.

He whipped out a sufficient length of line, smiling with

delight as he listened to the sharp, small whistling of the thread cutting the air. In the cañon above, he could hear in the distance the talking of the little river, a musical, excited conversation. Farther down the stream, there was the harsh crashing of the water as it tripped over a ledge of rock and smashed itself into foam and spray on a base fifty or sixty feet below.

But though this sound was both steady and ominous, it was not loud. It needs only a little distance of the thin air of the mountains to muffle noise. Indeed, to the ear of the lawyer, there was just enough sound to make him conscious of the voice of the mountains; there was enough sound to make him dream in the upland quiet into which he would be plunging, before long. He would lift above the valleys before the midafternoon. He would be shouldering among the peaks, where only the wind talks, and the insects sing and whisper in small hushing waves of sound.

He was content. He was mightily content, and now he made his first cast—the line flew far, and flicked the water as straight as though its length had been ruled.

He admired that cast, the accuracy of it. Like the true fisherman, the fish were only in a corner of his mind, and his way of catching them was all that mattered.

He had dropped the fly just on the verge of the shadow that sloped down beside a big rock, and he had half finished reeling in his line, when the strumming of a guitar, nearby, smote his ear like the roar of trains, the disputing of voices, the whole angry noise of civilized, hurrying, foolish man.

And then a voice, pleasant enough, a man's baritone voice, rang through the glade, singing:

> "Julia, you are peculiar,
> Julia, you are queer;
> Truly, you are unruly,
> As a wild, western steer.
> Sweetheart, when we marry,
> Dear one, you and I,
> Julia,
> You little mule you,
> I'm gunna rule you,
> Or die!"

The lawyer finished reeling in his line and then put the rod, for a moment, over his shoulder. He looked for the singer with an air of personal insult. He had been snatched back too suddenly into the follies and vanities and idiocies of the youth of the world.

And now he found the musician, just finishing, his mouth wide on the last note. He was lying on a grassy ledge not twenty feet from the fisherman; the guitar was in his lap, his coat was rolled to support his head comfortably against the bank at his back.

The wrath of the older man overflowed. For he could see worthlessness in the tattered clothes of this boy, and in his too-handsome face. Good looks, when they pass a certain point, always appear a trifle effeminate, a weakening of the true male character. And this lad was made with the scrupulous care that should better have been bestowed on the making of a reigning beauty. He was slim, delicate, dainty. He had big, brown, sleepy, indifferent eyes. His rather swarthy skin bloomed with color. And he was set off, with the vanity of one who knew his good point, by a necktie of flaring yellow and blue.

The lip of John Pierson curled with wrath and scorn.

"Young man," he said, hotly, "d'you know that these mountains are not the place for young ragtime fools?"

He wanted to thrash the boy. He wanted to make him jump and howl. There was in him a great possibility of the family tyrant, though as a matter of fact his only child was a daughter who ruled him with an easy and impertinent adroitness. He knew that she was the monarch of the house, and yet he loved her all the more. But his sense of failure with her, made him a little more absolute in his dealings with others in the world.

The musician, pushing himself languidly up on one elbow, first plucked a blade of grass and began to bite at it absently, studying the stranger.

"Is this a reservation for tired lawyers, sir?" said he.

And as though to point the insolence of his remark, he raised his hat and bowed a very little to John Pierson.

The wrath of the latter flamed higher.

He could hardly say what irritated him most in this speech—the air with which it was delivered, the goodness of the English and the enunciation, or the happy guess which it contained as to his profession. Everything combined with the place and what had gone before to madden Pierson.

He said, "Your kind of nonsense ought to be kept for Mexican cafés. Are you a Mexican, young man?"

"No such luck," said the boy.

He resettled the coat under his head, so that he could regard Pierson more comfortably, without quite sitting up.

"No such luck," snapped Pierson. "You rather be one, eh?"

"Oh, you know how it is," said the other, yawning a little, and covering his mouth with a graceful, slender hand. "You know how it is, Mr. Lawyer; one grows a little tired of hearing the eagle scream, because it's usually yipping about work. 'Work, work, young man. In work is salvation. The kingdom of God is in the muscles!' And that sort of thing."

It was the most offensive statement that Pierson had ever heard. He guessed that a philosophy of indolence lay behind it, and vice is never so damnable as when the vicious justify their actions.

"You, I take it," said he, "are a fellow who doesn't care what the eagle screams?"

"Not a bit," said the other, "except when it turns me out of bed. I came up here to rest a little, but I see that the eagle has spotted me. He's screaming in my ear, again."

At this not too subtle reference to himself, the heat of Pierson increased.

"If we were a little nearer my home town," said he, "I'd find a more secure place for you to rest, my friend. Where you wouldn't spoil a landscape. They'd find something for you to work at, for about thirty days."

"No, no," said the youngster.

He showed his hands, smiling.

"For here," said he, "you see hands which have never yet been stained by work or feel!"

2

NEVER IN HIS LIFE had John Pierson met with a human being who so thoroughly irritated him in every way as did this lad.

"How old are you?" he asked.

"Twenty-two, sir," said the boy, with a false humility.

"College, eh?"

"Part way, sir."

"Stop calling me 'sir!' "

"Very well, sir."

Now, in his own town, throughout his community, and in many ways it was a large one, Pierson was a man of great influence and power. His word was respected, his advice followed. Throughout this same mountain district, there were few people, no matter what their position, who would not gladly have bowed to him. Here was the exception, and a most unpleasant one it proved. He was even angry with himself because a worthless waif moved him so much.

"My boy," said he, "I will make a bargain with you. This place happens to suit me. There must be a thousand others where you can lie on grass just as soft as that. I'll give you a dollar if you'll stir along."

The boy nodded, not as one assenting, but one considering.

"That's a matter," he declared at last, "that needs a lot of considering. In the first place, there's the question of the way this bank fits my back. Nature isn't such a handy cabinet maker, you know."

"Humph!" said the lawyer.

"Then there's the fish to consider," said the boy.

"The fish?"

"I've been seeing the glint of 'em down there in the

water for some time. I'd hate to disturb 'em as long as the sun is shining like this."

"But after it stops shining?" suggested the lawyer.

"Oh, then I'd eat a dozen of 'em with a lot of pleasure, thank you."

"A very good speech for the perfect opportunist," said the man of the law.

"Finally, and the thing that seems to close the question," went on the handsome tramp, "there's the matter of my profession."

"Ah-ha," said the lawyer. "And what might your profession be?"

"Acting," said this brazen-faced lad.

"You're an actor, are you? What parts do you play?" demanded Pierson.

"Sometimes," said the boy, "I'm a son who's been disinherited by a cruel father. Sometimes, I've been robbed by greedy lawyers."

"Stuff!" said Pierson. "You mean that these are the tales you tell to credulous fools?"

"Sometimes," went on the boy, "I'm about to go to work to earn enough money to finish my school course. Sometimes I'm recovering from an attack of the great white plague."

"Consumption, my foot," said Pierson. "You're as healthy a specimen as I ever saw."

"When one plays many roles, one needs makeup," said the boy.

He seemed pleased as he related his roguery; whatever annoyed the older man seemed delectable to him.

"Then again," said the boy, "I've been the son of a rich American owner of mines in Mexico. He and the whole family murdered, myself knifed and shot almost to pieces by Mexican brigands, I have fled north out of the country, and so I find myself destitute, but determined, one day, to return to the land where I have been wronged, and revenge my dead father and brothers and sisters upon the murderers!"

The lawyer nodded.

"In fact," said he, "You're a professional beggar."

"If you heard one of my yarns," said the boy, yawning, "you'd give it a more complimentary name. I ought, in fact,

13

to be a writer; but even writing, in short, is a form of labor."

"I suppose it is," said the lawyer. "Tell me, my young friend, do the dolts to whom you tell the Mexican story ever ask to see your scars?"

"I have even stripped to the waist," said the boy. "It's something that I don't like to do, but if I find, say a Texan who doesn't like greasers, I've stripped to the waist to show where the bullets struck and the knives cut. That is generally worth several hundred dollars."

"You're a thorough rascal," said the lawyer.

"It's my profession," answered the boy. "You can't blame a man for what he does inside his profession."

"Profession? Stuff! You make up the scars that the idiots think they see on your body?"

"You know how it is," said the youngster. "When one is shouldering his way around the world, one bumps into various obstacles that are capable of making wounds."

"Such as the toss of hobnailed boots," suggested the lawyer.

"Yes," answered the boy, without appearing to take offense, "or it may be the iron-framed lantern of a shack."

"You work the railways a good deal, I suppose?" said Pierson.

"Horses are usually too slow for me," said the boy.

"Yes," nodded Pierson. "I dare say that when you leave a place you usually have to leave fast."

"And go far," remarked the lad.

"Now and then," said the lawyer, "you will meet up with a dupe of a former day, too?"

"Now and then," agreed the boy, cheerfully. "But on the whole, this is an amazingly large world."

"You're young," said the lawyer. "As you get older, you may find more thorns on the bush."

"As I grow older, I grow more expert," said the lad.

"Tell me," said the lawyer, "what you call yourself?"

"An entertainer," said the boy.

In spite of himself, Pierson was forced to chuckle.

"And what name do you work under?"

"I've been called a good many names," answered the tramp, "some of them long, and some of them short. I've been called more one-syllable names than almost anyone in the world, I suppose. But the one I prefer is Speedy."

"Speedy?"

"You will see how it is," answered the tramp. "I sometimes give people a fast ride, and they generally have quite a bill to pay at the end of it."

"If you come into my community," said Pierson, "you won't take many for more than a short ride."

"No?"

"No," said Pierson.

"What's your town, if you please?"

"Durfee."

"I've heard of that place. How many people?"

"About ten thousand."

"Ten thousand? That's plenty. Ten thousand is a whole world of opportunity, to me. When do you go home?"

"In about three days."

"Very well," said Speedy, "I'll guarantee to be there. I'll guarantee to call on you at once, and let you know where I am, and whom I'm working on. And in spite of you, I'll promise that I'll come away with a good slice of coin."

"Impossible, you impertinent young rat," said Pierson, swelling more and more with his anger.

"Well," said Speedy, "I'll make you a bet."

"Very well. I'll take the bet."

"You give me odds, of course?"

"I give you odds? Why should I give you odds?"

"Because I hope that you're a fair sport. Here I am putting my cards on the table. I'm the mouse entering the lion's den. I'm going to go to your home town, where the celebrated legal power and brain, Mr. John W. Smith, is like the very blood brother of God Almighty, and there—"

"My name is John Pierson," said the lawyer, coldly. "I'll bet you three hundred dollars to one hundred that you don't make enough in Durfee to pay your end of the bet."

"Good," said the boy. "That's only an evening's work for me. The day I tell you on whom I'm intending to work, I'll guarantee that I get the money in hard cash. I'll collect from you the next morning."

"The next morning you'll be in jail for vagabondage," said the lawyer.

"I'll accept another bet at evens, on that account," said the boy.

"Perhaps you've never even been in jail, my lad?" suggested Pierson.

"I've been there," said the boy. "Once I even rested for a week, but that was because an unlucky Mexican had put a knife through my leg."

"Through the leg?" asked the lawyer, doubtfully. "Mexicans don't stab people in the leg!"

"This one started his knife for my heart," admitted the boy, nonchalantly, "but I kicked him in the face, and that rather spoiled his aim."

"I suppose," said the lawyer, frowning, "that you're an expert gunman, yourself?"

He maintained his scowl for a time. After all, there was a light in the boy's eyes that might not be altogether effeminacy.

"I never carried a weapon in my life," said Speedy. "It's not my way. Guns? Horrible things. They shoot men into prison. No, no, I never carry weapons."

"You carry the weight of a good many beatings, then," said the other.

"Now and then I've had a stick broken over my shoulders," admitted Speedy. "Now and then a bullet grazes me. Now and then a knife is stuck in me. But you know how it is—this is a world of sweets and sours, and—"

"You worthless, hypocritical—" began the lawyer.

And then he checked himself.

"I apologize," he said, ironically. "I forget that you simply are one who works inside his profession."

"Exactly so," said the boy, "and also—"

He also stopped.

For this time an interruption came from the little brown and black mongrel, whose wits and nose served Pierson.

It had started up a rabbit among the rocks. The rabbit had jumped the stream, and the brave little puppy had unwisely attempted the same feat. The result was that it fell plump into the middle of the stream, and was now whirling round and round, barking a call for help, as the water swept it rapidly down towards the brink of the waterfall.

— 3 —

THE LAWYER LOVED all animals, but above all he loved this little brown and black mongrel. He had used thorough-bred pointers, before, and now he had been amazed by the ability of the cur to do as much as any of the others. It was, perhaps, a little overeager. That was its only fault, and it is the best of all demerits in a young dog. For the rest, it was picking up the right education to a surprising degree; and it loved hunting as much as its master did.

Now, when he saw it spinning on the brink of destruction, he uttered a great cry, that choked short off in the middle, so furiously was he running to the rescue. But he knew, before he had taken ten strides, that he would be too late. It was a bitter moment for John Pierson, and the more so when he saw, or thought he saw, the appealing glance of the dog fixed specially upon him as it was carried down to destruction.

Then a slim form went by him, the tramp, the lazy and worthless sponger, Speedy. He ran like a deer, with a sprinter's high action, with a sprinter's long and powerfully reaching stride. It seemed that his toes barely tipped the earth as he fled towards the danger point.

The lawyer shouted hoarse and short in appreciation and amazement. For how had the boy managed to get down from his higher perch so suddenly and appear in this fashion in front of the race?

Even the tramp would be too late, however. That appeared clear. But, reaching the bank of the little stream, he threw himself headlong in, with a long, beautiful, flat dive.

He struck the water below the dog, well beneath it down the course. The power of the current jerked at him, and yet

17

he found his feet with a wonderful dexterity, and instantly scooped the puppy out of the current and flung it well to the shore.

In that effort, he overbalanced. The smooth, powerful sheet of the current was striking him above the knees, and curling to his waist. Now, as he staggered, it seemed to rise in a wave and strike him with a renewed power. Over he went, fighting with his arms to regain his poise, but fighting in vain. Over he went, and though he turned in the water like a snake in the effort to regain his feet, the force of the water had him at too great a disadvantage, and he shot over the brink of the cliff.

The lawyer stood stock still. The moment, the dreadful picture, was burning into his brain, never to be eradicated. And he remembered one thing that would never leave his mind. It was the fact that the boy had not cried out. Silently, like a hero, he had left this life, and left behind him, his wretched trickeries, the thousand deceits of his profession. But his heart was great. John Pierson swore that, from that moment, his heart would be enlarged to look upon rogues with a tenderer understanding.

Then he saw the mongrel standing on the verge of the bank, below the rim of the fall, and barking furiously.

"He has seen the body!" thought Pierson, grimly, and strode forward to see.

What he saw made him cry out like a madman with joy.

For there was Speedy hanging by his hands from a projection of rock just under the lip of the waterfall. He kicked his feet above fifty feet of empty space which lay between him and the cruel teeth of stone on which the stream was shattering.

But even now, the boy swung his body like a pendulum and shifted his grip to another jutting bit of the stone.

What a handhold to swing by over the lip of destruction! The spray from the falls had covered the stone with moss and with green slime. And one slip of the fingers would be the last slip on this earth for Speedy!

Yet, as he swung there, he deliberately turned his head and smiled and nodded at the lawyer.

It swelled the heart of John Pierson to the bursting point.

How could he help? He got out farther towards the ledge, lay flat, and stretched out his hand. But there was still a good distance between him and the place where the boy was working slowly, from point to point.

Now one hand gave way. The boy hung by the grip of the other, only, and at that moment, inspired by the devil, a contrary gust of wind cuffed a sheet of the falling water aslant and struck it heavily against the body of the boy.

"The end!" said Pierson.

But it was not the end. With a desperate effort, his body convulsed by it, Speedy managed to reach out to a fresh hold with his left hand, and now behold him, under the very hand of the lawyer.

"Here!" shouted Pierson.

His arm was strong, his wrist was steel, his body was anchored by a very solid and substantial weight. In a moment he had both of the boy's wet hands in his. And what a grip they gave him! He was amazed at the strength in Speedy, the idler.

Then, heaving up with all his might, he swayed the boy high as the armpits up to the edge of the rock.

Speedy was in a moment lying on his back on the grass. He lay with his arms thrown out to the side. He lay like a cross upon the green. There was no working of the face, no exaggeration. Only the flare of the nostrils, the stern straightness of the upper lip, the heaving of the breast in long breaths, told Pierson of the strain through which Speedy had been passing.

For his own part, he was shaking from head to foot. He sat down by the boy and pulled out his feet and watched a thing that oddly pleased him, but that oddly touched him in a raw spot.

It was the little mongrel, Brownie, making his demonstration of joy and of gladness of living, and of gratitude, not to his master but, rightly enough, to his deliverer from danger. And now, sopping wet as he was, he lay curled on the not less soaking breast of Speedy's coat and licked his face, and beat his tail frantically, whining.

Yes, it was very right that he should make a fuss over the boy. He certainly had earned Brownie's devotion. And yet the heart of John Pierson was a little sore. He was ashamed of this secondary emotion. It made him feel smaller than ever.

At last the boy sat up, held himself there on the stiff of

19

both arms for a moment, and then rose to his feet. The lawyer watched him, but said not a word, for there was not a word to say.

And, calmly, deliberately, Speedy peeled off his soaked clothes, wrung them out, and laid them on shrubs to dry. Pierson noted, with interest, that if the outer clothes were shabby, the underclothes were scrupulously clean. Moreover, the body underneath them was clean, and brown as if from long seasons on beaches—the rather scrawny body of a young boy, but outfitted with stringy muscles that explained at a glance how the athletic feats under the brink of the waterfall had been accomplished.

Well, many an idler might be an athlete as well, trained by swimming, by tennis, by dancing and riding until he was as tautly stringed with power and muscle as any football player or day laborer.

These things occurred to the somber eye of Pierson, as he considered the boy.

He had filled his pipe, and now he was smoking and thinking of many things—and, for the first time in a good many years, not of himself.

Said Speedy:

"That's the coldest water that I've seen in a long time."

He turned his back to the sun, that it might dry that part of him more quickly.

"That's snow water," said Pierson.

He thought it odd that these should be the first words interchanged between them, after the boy's heroism. But, the more the event receded in time, the more impossible it was to speak of the thing. What made it perfect was that the cause for the courage was so small. If it had been a child say—well, it would not have been half so admirable.

He looked back at the spot of the bank where the toes of Speedy had gouged deeply into the ground as he took his header into the stream.

It seemed to be at the very edge of the falls. And he, Pierson, would never have been able to attempt such a feat. Furthermore, if he had, by this time he would be a pulpy, smashed and broken corpse, pounding to pieces among the rocks where the water shattered itself in volley after volley.

"Speedy," he said, "I want to say something to you."

20

"I'll tell you something first," said Speedy. "Don't you say it. Let it be, please. You're going to give me some good advice and wind up with calling me a lot of pleasant names; you're going to apologize for telling me a few home truths, just before this, and you'll probably offer me a place in your sun. But don't you do it."

Even now the lawyer could be a little vexed by the cool insight of the boy.

But he said: "I wish you'd listen to me, Speedy."

"I won't though," said the boy. "It's happened a couple of times before that people have got a wrong idea about me. Hell, I know that I'm not all bad. But I know that I'm a damned long ways from all good, too. I don't get away from that, Mr. Pierson. And it makes me sick to cash in on a foolish impression, unless I've worked to make it, professionally. And just now," he added, with a smile, "I wasn't being professional."

"No," burst out the lawyer, "you were being—"

He checked himself before the extravagant word. It had been well enough earned, but something told him that it was not wanted. He could see the relief spread on the face of the youngster as he made the pause.

"What do you call making a fool professionally?" he asked, at last.

"I'll tell you," said the boy. "We're all men, we all have a share of brains, we all want money, we all want an easy time. Well, your dollars are your treasure; your wits are the soldiers that guard it. If I can put your soldiers to sleep, I take your money. That's my game, and it's a good game. It beats chess all hollow."

"You hate to make a false impression," grinned Pierson, "unless you've intended exactly that thing. Is that it?"

"That's it," said the boy. "That's part of it. Now, you and I understand each other a good deal better. Brownie and I are friends. And I warn you—if I take that three hundred—no, it's four hundred dollars—off you in Durfee, I'll dance on your front porch and laugh in your face, Mr. John Pierson!"

—4—

THE HOUSE OF JOHN PIERSON in Durfee was not pretentious. His wife and daughter were often at him to build a much finer place because, as they pointed out, his income and his fortune both warranted such an outlay. But he continually refused.

"If I build a big house," said he, "people will be afraid to come to me. They'll know that the fees they pay are what support me. They'll begin to figure out my income. As it is, they can't tell. I take a good many charity cases. They never know just what I rake in. Believe me, my dears, there is nothing that makes a man unpopular in a small Western town so quickly as a large income which they know he bleeds out of the town without producing anything."

"Producing!" said his wife, on this evening of his return from the mountains. "Producing indeed! I should like to know what man in Durfee produces more hard work than you do!"

"That's very well," said Pierson, who was at heart a very fair man, "but you must understand that after all, what I produce is only words. I don't raise grain or cattle, or dig minerals out of the ground, or turn trees into lumber, or make cloth, or do anything else that has a concrete value in the eyes of the world."

"Stuff!" said his wife. "You keep the affairs of people straight!"

"There is nothing," said Pierson, "that men hate so much as paying for advice."

"There's no use talking any more, Mother," said Charlotte Pierson, the daughter of the family. "Father is beginning to philosophize, and you know that when that happens neither of us can argue with him."

"I know," said Mrs. Pierson, "and it's tiresome. I'm

going into the house and let you sit out here with your philosophy and your thoughts about that tramp in the mountains. I should like to see that boy, though."

"You probably will," said Pierson, "when he comes to try to win his bet."

"I never heard of such nonsense as that bet," said Charlotte. "Of course he can't do that. Because you'll even have a chance to warn the proposed victim."

At this point, a slender man walked down the street, paused, and then turned in up the path towards the Pierson veranda. He walked with a leisurely step, and when he came to the foot of the steps, he said: "Is this the house of Mr. John Pierson?"

"It's Speedy!" said Pierson, springing up in excitement. "Charlotte, call Brownie, will you? Come up here, Speedy. I'm glad to see you. Mary, this is Speedy, about whom I was talking to you."

The boy paused again, a step from the top, and bowed to Mrs. Pierson. Charlotte could be heard calling Brownie from the back porch of the house; and presently there was a scampering of the dog's feet as it tore through the house, barking with excitement.

"He'll know you, Speedy," said Pierson, half kindly, half jealously. "The little rascal—"

Here Brownie knocked the screen door wide open with a blow of his forefeet, and sprang up straight at the stranger and then began to leap and whine and bark as though his real master had just come back.

"There you are," said Pierson. "I told you so. Brownie, let him alone, now. Down, sir, down!"

There was some impatience in his voice. He could not be altogether pleased when he saw his favorite hunting dog making such a demonstration over another man.

Then Charlotte Pierson came out on the porch. The lamplight caught in her blonde hair and set it shining about her face. She was twenty, straight as a string, brown as leather and pert as an unbroken mustang, running wild.

"Charlotte," said the lawyer, "this is Speedy. I told you that he'd turn up!"

Charlotte did not hesitate. She went forward and thanked the stranger.

She even let her hand linger in his, while she looked

23

more closely into his face; for he was so dark that, in this light, it was hard to see him with any accuracy.

Her father was somewhat angered. He did not see why his girl should be so familiar with a tramp, no matter what good qualities that tramp might have.

So he broke in: "How did you get here so soon, Speedy?"

"Why not?" asked the boy. "I came on the same train that brought you."

"The deuce you did," said Pierson. "You couldn't have done that, Speedy!"

"That's the train I came on," persisted the tramp.

"I had an idea that you might try that trick," said Pierson, "and so I warned the conductor, and he warned the brakeman. I know that both of them watched for you every minute."

"It wasn't an altogether easy trip for me," admitted the boy. "I started on the coal tender, and then I had to shift to blind baggage. They chased me off that, and it was the rods for a while, and then the top of the last coach, and, finally, I got pretty tired, so I came down and sat in a seat, and finished the ride on the cushions."

"What!" exclaimed Pierson. "Didn't they see you?"

"Sure they saw me—with my coat off, and a smudge of soot across one eye and the bridge of my nose—that's as good as a complete mask, you know. And I had my sleeves rolled up, and a plumbing wrench in my hand. The conductor just thought that I was going back to Durfee from a railroad repair job down the line."

Pierson lay back in his chair and laughed heartily. So did Charlotte. But Mrs. Pierson said that she could not understand what it was all about.

"It means that he beat me," said Pierson, frankly. "And now, my lad, what's your next step in Durfee?"

"My next step is to win the bet," said the boy.

"To win the bet? You mean that you're really going to try?" asked Charlotte.

"Why," said he, "the bet's made, and so I'll have to do my best."

"Oh, but Dad would let you off," said she.

"Oh, but I wouldn't," said the lawyer, hastily.

"Dad!" cried Charlotte, in reproach.

"Certainly not," answered Pierson. "If he can't win the

bet, he'll have to go to work to make the hundred dollars that he'll owe me. Because if I win, I want an honest hundred, young man! Two hundred, in fact, is the whole bet, if I put you in jail for this job! And I think that thirty days in jail would give you a good chance to think your life over!"

"John, you're letting yourself go. You're brutal!" said his wife, angrily. "After a poor boy has—"

"It's all right," said Speedy. "I just wanted Mr. Pierson to name the man he wants me to try for the hundred dollars."

"Great Scott," said Pierson, "you mean to say that you'll try anyone I name for you?"

"Certainly," said the boy. "A man's not a real musician unless he can play a good tune on a bad instrument."

Pierson began to laugh.

"Of all the brazen-faced—"he began.

His own laughter stopped his words.

"All right," he said. "And I'll tell you what I'll do. I'll pick out the hardest man in town. Wait a minute. Mary, who's the tightest man in town?"

"Old Tom Jenkins," she answered, without hesitation.

"He never gave a penny away in his life," agreed the lawyer. "But there's someone tighter than he is. Charlotte, what's your choice?"

"Mrs. Hilton," said the girl. "She's given away so much that she—"

"I beg your pardon," said the boy. "I can't try a woman, because I never make them professional clients of mine."

"Hello!" said Pierson. "You limit yourself with a lot of self-made rules, it seems to me. But I'll tell you what, my boy, I'll name a harder subject than either of the ones the ladies have suggested. I'm going to send you to a man who works on every charity committee and never spends an infernal cent. He never gives to beggars because he says that no man needs to go hungry in a country as full of honest work as ours. I don't think that he ever spent a cent in his life, except on himself. He's never married, because he never could bear the thought of buying a wedding ring! That's the kind of a fellow he is. I'm not exaggerating."

"You mean Mr. Chalmers," said Charlotte, breaking in. "But, Dad, that's not fair. He's the district attorney."

"What of that?" answered her father. "He's the district attorney, and he's as keen as a hawk. The moment he begins to suspect the nature of your profession, as you call it, he'll have you in jail so fast that your head will swim. But that's my choice. Mind, I can't hold you to it. But you asked me to name the hardest man in Durfee, and you see that I've done it. Now do as you please."

"I'll try Mr. Chalmers," said the boy, nodding. "He sounds like a promising fellow, to me."

"You'll find him a hard nut. I haven't exaggerated about him!"

"Well, I believe that, too," answered the lad. "But you know that the hardest nut is packed with the sweetest meat. Will you direct me to Mr. Chalmers' house?"

"It's three blocks straight down that way, and a block to your left. You won't miss it. It's a big white house, with a lot of trees in front of it. The reason he's living in such a big place is because his father gave it to him. I'm always wondering that he doesn't take in roomers to fill up the spare corners of the house."

He did not like Mr. Chalmers. As a matter of fact, he had run against him at the last election.

"Very well," said the boy. "I'll go to Mr. Chalmers' house."

"You'd better not go straight off," warned Charlotte. "Mr. Chalmers will be at dinner, now, and if you disturb him—"

"No fair, Charlotte," said the lawyer.

"That's all right," said the boy. "People give better from the table than they do from the street, I suppose. Goodbye!"

He started down the steps.

"Hold on!" said the lawyer. "How long a start am I to give you before I come over and warn him?"

"Well," said the boy, "whatever you'd call a sporting start. I don't care. You can come over with me, if you want."

"Tut, tut!" smiled Pierson. "I'm not that sort of a fellow. But I take it that you're a fast worker, and I'll give you only fifteen minutes."

"Oh, shame, Dad!" cried Charlotte.

But the tramp was already halfway to the gate.

– 5 –

SAMUEL P. CHALMERS was giving a dinner.

He rarely gave a dinner to more than one man at a time; this evening he was saying to his guest: "Two people can talk, discuss, sir. Three makes the development of a subject impossible. I wanted to have you alone with me, tonight, Mr. Chase. Because you are the man in Durfee whose opinion counts most with me. I wanted to consult you quietly, and personally, about certain matters of policy."

Mr. Chalmers affected a grand style, not only in his speech but in his clothes. He wore tails and parti-colored waistcoats, with a double loop of bright golden chain draped across it. His neckties were the joy of the matrons and the despair of the men of Durfee. Anyone other than Chalmers would have looked foolishly overdressed in such cravats; but they seemed to go well with the broad sweep of his blond mustaches, which he kept well and cleanly away from his bright pink lips.

Mr. Chase was a large rancher; and his support had, practically unassisted, elected Chalmers over Mr. Pierson. That, added to the fact that people felt that Pierson already had held the office long enough. They had nothing against the latter.

And Mr. Chase was flattered.

He said: "Yeah, when you come to think of it, there ain't any way so good of settlin' things as to go and have a good talk with a man. Seems like trouble gets all ironed out pretty slick, before long."

"It does," said Samuel P. Chalmers, "and therefore I thought that I would have you alone, Mr. Chase. Your experience in the world, and the brilliance of your achievements as a business man—"

"Askin' your pardon, Mr. Chalmers!" said a timid voice.

27

The district attorney had a piece of meat on the end of his fork. He turned rather wildly and saw a timid face, a great, frightened pair of eyes at the window. He turned farther, with a growl.

"What the devil is this?" he said.

"I tried the front door," said the timid voice, "and they said that you was busy. And then I tried the back door, and they up and said there that you was still busy. And they said that they'd take and throw me over the fence if I didn't get away, but I kind of had to see you, sir. So I just looked in through this window and——"

"Who are you?" snapped the district attorney.

"I'm Mort Waley's boy, sir."

"Mort Waley? I don't know any Mort Waley. Where do you come from?"

"I come from over in Grant County, sir."

"I have nothing to do with Grant County," said the district attorney. "Run along, my lad. What's brought you here, anyway?"

"It was Pa that sent me, sir," said the boy. "He's kind of laid up, or he'd of come himself. He said there was one place to find justice in the world, and that was from Mr. Chalmers, down here in Durfee. So I just walked down, sir."

Said Mr. Chase, his fat face reddening a little: "You gotta reputation, Chalmers. Doggone me if it don't warm me up a good deal, to see how folks come to you for a square deal."

Mr. Chalmers expanded. It was true that he knew few people in Grant County, and that he never had heard of a man named Mort Waley. But a compliment is never paid uselessly to a vain man. His own heart warmed. He cleared his throat.

"Come in, my lad," said he. "Come in, come in. I'll have the front door opened. Not exactly my business hour, Mr. Chase," he added, with a deprecatory laugh, "but the law demands all the time of its servants!"

Said Chase, the rancher: "You go right on. I'd rather be hungry than see folks stay in trouble when they might be helped out."

"Don't you bother about the front door, sir," said the boy. "I could climb right in here."

28

And straightaway, he put his knee on the window sill, and climbed through.

He made a sad picture. He had no coat. His trousers were badly tattered. The shirt was missing, and had apparently been wound around the bare feet of the boy. The rags of the shirt were bloodstained! Blood spotted the floor with darkness where the youngster stepped.

Mr. Chalmers was a man of strong expression.

"By the Eternal God!" he exclaimed. "What outrage is behind this?"

The boy shrank as from a blow. He raised a hand to protect his face. He shrank shuddering back against the wall.

"I ain't meaning no harm, sir," said he. "I'll clean up the blood on your floor."

"*You'll* clean it up?" said the district attorney. "*You'll* clean it up? My poor lad, who has done this to you?"

He advanced and laid a fatherly arm about the shoulders of the lad. Humped shoulders they were, with the bones thrusting out a little.

Then he turned towards Chase, whose broad, rather heavy face was pinched with pain and with pity.

"Shaking like a leaf, poor child," said Chalmers. "Sit down here, my boy. Who did this to you?"

"Nobody, sir. I dunno what you mean?"

"You don't know what I mean?" cried the attorney, his voice rich and ringing with indignant sympathy. "I say, who reduced you to wander barefoot through—"

He was about to say "wilderness" and suddenly realized that the term was a shade Biblical for the stomach of Mr. Chase.

So he paused on "through."

"Dad was laid up," said the boy. "And this here was the last day. He told me to come runnin' to you."

"Not another word," said the district attorney, "until you've had food and drink. Sit down here, if you please! Sit right down here—yes, at the table, by God! I beg your pardon, Mr. Chase. I should have asked your permission, first, but—"

The rancher stood up.

"Don't be a damn fool, Chalmers," he said, bluntly. "The kid's sick. He's wobbly. Bring him over here and shove some food into him."

"You have a good heart, Mr. Chase," said Chalmers, gratefully.

"Hell, man," said Chase. "It's your house. I'm doggone glad to find out that they lie that called you a proud man, Chalmers. All I gotta say is that you're gunna have my vote every time, and the votes of all my friends."

The effect of this speech was to make Chalmers bless the day that brought this youthful vagabond to his door.

By this time, he had brought the lad to the table, and now he forced him to sit down. But the boy looked in terror at the long, bright board, and at the heaped plate which the Chinaman now brought in and set before him with a pleased grin. For every cook loves to set forth his best before the truly hungry.

"Go on," said Chalmers, bursting with Good Samaritanism, his eyes stung with tears brought by the sense of his own virtue, "eat, my lad, and afterwards I'll hear you."

"If you please, sir," said the lad, shrinking in his chair, "I wouldn't feel none too good eatin', when Pa ain't had a bite for two days, since he was laid up."

"Two days, eh?" said the district attorney, darkly. "And what laid the man up, my lad?"

"It was three days back," said the boy. "He didn't count the shots, right, and when he went into the shaft the next morning, to clean out the broken ground, the last shot went off. It kind of tore off his left leg at the knee."

"My God!" said Chase. "The poor devil! I remember seeing—go on, boy! How did you take care of him?"

"I come when he hollered," said the boy, "and he was layin' on the ground, with a good holt on his leg above the knee, with both hands, and there wasn't no leg to be seen nowheres below the knee—"

He paused and shook his head, his eyes blank with wonder, still, as he recalled this strange moment.

The two men interchanged glances. The lad was a good lad, it appeared, but a little lacking in the wits.

"Pa told me to go and start up the fire and heat a stove lit till it was red hot, which I done it, and then brung it to him with a pair of tongs and—"

His eyes withered shut. He clenched a fist and raised it before his eyes.

Sweat was streaming down the face of Mr. Chase.

"We know the rest, son," said he. "We know the rest. It's all right. You don't have to tell me. I remember seein'—but that don't matter. Go on and tell me how your old man is resting now?"

"Why, he's restin' pretty good," said the boy, his stopped voice coming back with a gasp. "He's restin' pretty good, I guess. I partly drug and he partly hitched himself along until we got him to the cabin and into a bunk. He says that one day he'll walk better than ever on one wooden leg. He says that a wooden leg, it sure saved a pile of wear on shoes. I reckon he's right."

Chase laughed, shortly.

But the district attorney shook his head.

"A picture of a brave heart, told in a few simple words," said Chalmers.

"He's a fellow with guts," said Chase, through his teeth. "Then two days without food, eh?"

"He was gunna go down to town, that same day, and try to borrow some flour, because he'd run out of money. And then he hoped he'd make a good strike in the mine, and in the two days that would be left, he'd get out enough gold to pay back Mr. Pierson and—"

"Mr. Who?" exclaimed the two men together.

"Mr. John Pierson, of Durfee. Pa was pretty broke about six months back, when Mr. Pierson come along on a huntin' trip and seen the mine, and looked it over, and liked the color that was showin'. Pa said there was a big vein about to open up, and Mr. Pierson, he said somethin' I didn't mostly understand about development, and capital, and words like that; and he would lend Pa a hundred dollars for six months, and if Pa didn't pay back the money by the end of that time, he was to give the mine to Mr. Pierson, and—"

"By the Lord!" cried Chase, "I never knew why I didn't like Pierson, before. I know now."

The Chinaman came into the room.

He announced that Mr. John Pierson was calling.

"BRING HIM IN!" said the district attorney, scowling as if with hatred, at the boy. And the lad shrank from the grim eyes.

"And you walked down here in bare feet?" he asked.

"Mostly I run, sir," said the boy. "Till I kind of give out in the feet."

"You tore off your shirt and wrapped it around your feet, and you kept on running!" said the district attorney, through his teeth.

"I reckon you seen me!" said the boy, his great eyes opening in the simplest wonder.

Chalmers smiled bitterly at Chase.

"A poor, simple, honest lad!" he said to Chase. "I'll see justice done to him even if he doesn't live in my county. I'll see justice done to him if it's the last act of my life!"

Just then, the cheerful voice of Pierson said at the door: "Is this right, Chalmers? Shall I come in here? Sorry to disturb your dinner, but—"

Both Chase and Chalmers were upon their feet. They turned on the intruder with thundering brows.

Chalmers, in place of answering, pointed a long, heavy arm at the boy.

"Pierson," he said, in a terrible voice, "this is your work!"

It was a little difficult for Pierson to recognize Speedy in the tousled hair, the shrunken, bowed body, the haunted eyes of this youngster.

But now he chuckled, easily.

"By the Lord, Speedy," said he, "your making a mighty good play for your money!"

And he laughed, more loudly.

"It's a hundred dollars he wants, isn't it?" he asked.

Chalmers was taken somewhat aback; but Chase exclaimed: "Yeah, a hundred dollars—of blood money! Blood that you're takin', Pierson."

To the surprise of the district attorney and his first guest, the lawyer laughed cheerfully again.

"This is a great dodge," said he. "The little rascal says that I'm extracting blood money from him, does he? Is that the dodge?"

"Yes," said Chalmers, fiercely. "I'm not to be laughed down, Pierson. I tell you, this thing is going to be sifted to the bottom!"

"Oh, rot," answered Pierson, with a sweeping gesture. "This youngster is making a fool of you—two fools. He's a professional swindler and loafer. I bet him three hundred to one hundred that he couldn't wheedle a hundred dollars out of you. Another hundred at evens that I'd have him in jail before morning."

The first doubt struck Chalmers a hammer blow.

He turned on the boy.

"What's this about?" he demanded.

The boy merely gaped. His eyes were greater than ever.

"You've scared the youngster to death," said Chase. "Leave him to me. Son," he added, gently, "you understand what Mr. Pierson says?"

"No, sir, I dunno that I quite do," stammered Speedy.

Then he started up and clutched the arm of Chase.

"Oh, my God," he said, "doncha go and let him put me in jail, or Pa'll starve. He'll lie waitin' for me, and starve to death! If you're gunna jail me, go and send some flour and bacon to Pa. *You're* a kind man; you got a kind face. Doncha—"

"Oh, what rot," said Pierson. "Are you two going to be taken in with this play acting? I tell you—"

"Wait a minute," said Chase. "How long before this money is due to be paid?"

"Pa said it was due by midnight," answered the boy.

"There you are," said Chase. "And Pierson, I'll wager, would stand here and argue till the time was up. But by heaven, I'm convinced right on the spot. Look here. So, here's a hundred dollars and—"

He put the money before Speedy. The latter drew back from it. Bewilderment spread on all faces.

33

Only Pierson cried out: "You see? I told you that the agreement was that he should get the money out of *you*, Chalmers!"

"Pa didn't say nothin' about askin' help from anybody but Mr. Chalmers," said the boy. "I couldn't be takin' money from nobody else."

Suddenly he rose and stood stiff and proudly before them. But his voice was quiet as he added: "The Waleys ain't beggars, I reckon. I didn't come here to ask for no money. Pa, he sent me down to ask Mr. Chalmers for justice. I ain't gunna take no money from nobody! The Waleys, they ain't beggars. They never *been* beggars!"

The speech had its effect.

Mr. Chase gathered up his sheaf of money and sat down, heavily.

"Now, then," he said, "I wanta see you two smart fellers, you two lawyers, figger out this thing together!"

And he waited, scowling up at them, alternately, under his brows. The boy began to tremble violently.

"I'll be goin' on," said he, and turned towards the door.

Chalmers caught him and forced him back into the chair.

"Justice is what you're going to have, my poor boy," said he. He lifted his voice until it had the electioneering ring in it. "I thank God that Samuel P. Chalmers can work for naked justice rather than for golden fees!"

He was proud of that speech.

But Mr. Chase said, rather shortly: "Well, let's do something about it, then!"

"Wait a moment," said Pierson, who was gradually turning a bright red.

"I've waited long enough," thundered Chalmers. "Your disgraceful piracy and—"

"Oh, shut up, man," said Pierson. "You explain to me, if the boy's cock and bull story is the truth, how I could know that he was here at this minute, bulldozing you, Chalmers?"

Chalmers gasped. He turned again to the boy.

"You heard that question?" he asked.

"I dunno how he would know it," said the boy. "I dunno how he would know that I was comin' here. When I seen him tonight, I just begged him to let Pa have a mite more time, account of his leg being blowed off, and I said that the

34

only other hope I had was to try to get Mr. Chalmers to help us—"

"There you are, Pierson," said Chalmers. "Now tell us what rat hole you'll next try to dodge into to mask your infernal greed, your brutal, grasping knavery. There is a law somewhere that can be called down on your trickery. At least, there is honest public opinion that shall be called on. The people shall know of this, Mr. John Pierson!"

Pierson was a violent crimson. Sweat streamed down his face. He stared at the boy as though he wanted to throttle him. And then he broke into a choked, wild laughter.

At last, turning sharply around, he exclaimed: "Look here, you two madmen!"

"He calls us madmen, now," said Chase, sourly, bitterly.

"Look here," said the other. "If the boy's story is true, his feet are worn almost to the bone—to judge by the rags on them. But I'll tell you. If you look close, you'll see that the red is red paint, or red ink, and his feet are as sound and whole as the feet of any of us."

"Very well," said Chase, with the sneer of one who submits to a last test, but whose mind is already made up. "We'll look at the poor youngster's feet. Boy, take off those rags!"

"Yes, sir," said Speedy, with amazing willingness.

And he slowly unwound the rags, making a little face as he got the first one off his foot, with a tug at the end as though it were stuck to the raw flesh.

And they saw—and Pierson with the rest, his face agape with bewilderment—a foot covered with clotted blood. The toes were choked with mingled blood and mud. Yes, fresh blood, freshly oozing, for it newly stained the hand of the boy.

The snort of Chase was like the challenge of a wild stallion. Yet his voice was carefully controlled.

"I reckon that's about enough proof," he said.

"This damns you forever, Pierson," said Chalmers. "This will drive you straight out of this town!"

"It will," said Pierson, savagely, "unless I can prove that there never was a man named Waley, that he never had such a mine, and that this boy is what I called him before —a professional humbug."

"Pierson," said the district attorney, dramatically pulling

out his wallet, like a revolver, from his breast pocket, "from this time forward, I hope that your form will never darken my doors again! I must say that I've always suspected you of sharp practices, but now I know what you are!"

He counted out a hundred dollars and placed it in the hand of the unwilling lad, who drew back from it, protesting.

"No, my boy, no, my young friend," said Chalmers, "this is not charity, neither have you been a beggar. This is only justice—the beginning of a wave of justice which, I hope and pray, will wash you onto a happy shore of—"

He was about to pause, for he hardly knew what word should follow "of," but here Pierson cried: "Well, you've let yourselves in, you two. Now I'll tell you what's going to happen—I'm going to have you laughed out of the town, Chalmers. I took you for a man of sense. And now you've been cheated out of your eyeteeth by a clever young rascal. By the Lord, I still can't believe it—though I see the money in his hand. I can't believe it! You pass for men of sense. And yet there he stands with the money in his hand. All right, my lad, you've won. You've got the bet won. But now, Mr. Wiseman, Mr. District Attorney, I call on you to arrest this boy for swindling."

Mr. Chalmers stood spellbound. He was partly white and partly purple, for of all things in this world, he most dreaded ridicule. And there was a certain ring of savage triumph in the voice of his political rival.

But now the boy said: "All right, Mr. Pierson. You admit that I've won the bet. I won't have to jump through the window. I have the hundred. Now I return it to you, Mr. Chalmers. I thank you. I apologize for taking up so much of your time. But I hope that the entertainment has been worth while."

And he bowed, and smiled, and glided towards the door.

– 7 –

BY THE TIME JOHN PIERSON reached the front door of the Chalmers house, he was beginning to think that perhaps this little adventure might be worth all of four hundred dollars and even more. He was reasonably sure of it, when the district attorney followed him, and from the front porch shouted: "This is a damnable trick on your part, Pierson. This is a trick, a low, deceiving trick, to appeal to my foolish and soft-hearted humanity. But I see through you, Pierson. I've always seen through you. You won't be able to make me a laughing stock through this, as now I demand your assistance to lay hands upon the worthless puppy who was your tool, in this matter."

Pierson stood still, near the front gate of the yard. He was counting from his wallet, four hundred dollars into the hand of the boy. And, as he finished, he turned with a chuckle:

"You're a laughing stock already, Chalmers," he said. "This business will roar you out of town. People will learn from this just what a windy joke you are, and always have been!"

This was language brought home with a smash, but Pierson's heart was still sore because of his political defeat. And he relished mightily this opportunity to get a little of his own back.

So he went on laughing, while Chalmers began to roar again and again from the front porch. At last, Chase came out, and taking his friend by the arm, told him bluntly not to make a further fool of himself, and so got him back into the house. Already neighbors were opening doors and murmurs of interest came drifting through the air.

The lawyer at the front gate was saying to the boy:

"Come along with me, Speedy. I've several things to say to you."

"I can't go along," said Speedy. "I have to stay here to do one thing more."

"Then answer me one question."

"Certainly."

"How did you make your feet seem to be bleeding?"

"They didn't seem to be. They were."

"Tut, tut," said the lawyer. "Don't tell me that!"

"It's true, though," insisted Speedy. "After all, a tablespoonful of blood makes a pretty big stain."

"But where did you get the blood?"

"Out of my feet, man! I simply made a small cut behind the ball of each foot, where the skin's tender and the blood's near the surface. The movement of walking kept the drops of blood leaking out. It isn't painful, but, as you saw, it makes a good lot of blood. And a bit of sticking plaster on each cut will make it as sound as ever. You should have asked me to wash my feet. Then they could have seen through the sham. But people get excited and careless, at times like that. They're apt to believe their eyes, and eyes are almost never right, you know."

John Pierson paused in thought. There was much in the last remark of this odd youth. Finally he said: "I want to see you again, Speedy. Shall I?"

"I'll be in the town long enough to get a new suit of clothes," said the tramp. "And then I'll go on again. I need an outfit. I was trimmed down almost to my guitar, when I luckily met you, and since then I've been thanking my stars."

"Will you come to my office tomorrow?" asked Pierson. "It's been growing in my mind almost ever since I met you."

"Thanks," said the boy. "You don't mean that you're going to try to reform me?"

"No. Not that. You have a pretty thick skin, I take it?"

"I don't pride myself on it," said Speedy. "But I suppose that I have a pretty thick skin, all right."

"Now, then, listen to me. I have some work in mind that will need the thickest skin in the world. It's not dishonest, but it's a gamble and a chance, and a good chance. I want to put it up to you. What do you say?"

"I always liked chances," said Speedy. "And I always

liked long ones. I'll come in tomorrow at the end of the morning."

"No, come early in the afternoon, because our talk will take a long time," said Pierson.

So it was agreed. They shook hands, and Pierson went up the street, while the boy waited behind until the door of the Chalmers house opened, and Mr. Chase came down the front steps hastily, making rumbling sounds in his throat. It seemed certain that among other things, Mr. Chalmers had not cemented his friendship with Chase any more firmly on this night of nights!

At the gate, the boy stepped out from the shadow of a tree.

He said: "May I speak to you for a minute, Mr. Chase?"

"It's the young whippersnapper, again," said the rancher, stopping short. "I want nothin' to do with you, friend. And you want nothing to do with me, if you know what's good for you. Goodnight!"

"I want to talk to you for half a minute," replied the tramp, quickly. "I went there to make a joke of Chalmers. Not of you. I'm sorry you were there, because you're real, and he's only a sham. I couldn't make a joke of him; he's a joke already."

Chase sputtered for a moment, and then he exclaimed: "By the jumping lord jackrabbit, if you ain't right. You got a brain in your head, young man. It's all right, the way you pulled the wool over my eyes. I ain't one that pretends to sharp sight with men, anyway. I can see a hoss, a cow, or a sheep. But that lets me out."

"Goodnight, then, Mr. Chase. And no hard feelings, sir," said the boy.

"Why, boy," said the rancher, "doggone me if you ain't pretty clean speakin', too. I take a sort of a likin' to you."

"You ought not to go on trusting your impressions of me," warned Speedy. "You've already found out that it doesn't pay."

At this, the other chuckled.

And he said: "It's been worth more than me bein' made a fool of tonight—worth a lot more, because I've had a chance to see through one special kind of varmint. I'm gunna make a change in lawyers right pronto!"

He waved goodnight, and went with a firm, heavy stride

up the street, a rather weaving step, such as one often sees in men who have spent most of their lives in the saddle.

The boy watched him for a moment; then he went to the smallest hotel in Durfee, down by the railroad track, and got a little room, and turned in. He was very tired. He simply wrapped himself in a blanket, and without taking off a stitch, he fell asleep as soon as he had closed his eyes.

He slept smiling, as one whose conscience is absolutely whole; and when he wakened in the morning, he was singing in five minutes. Ragged and unkempt he went down to buy his breakfast. But when he had finished a busy morning, a very neat young man sat down to lunch, dressed in a natty brown suit, with a broad-brimmed hat of tan color, and a tie to match. There was nothing showy about him, but he looked as though much money had flowed through his hands, and as though he expected the future to deal kindly with him, also.

After lunch, he went to his room for a siesta. And then, fresh and wide awake, he found the office of the lawyer. It was in a small wooden shack; and the "shingle" of John Pierson was not in large letters. But the building was itself a relic of the old, early days of Durfee, and the people looked upon it with affection, and with respect on a man who was willing to content himself with such quarters. It made Pierson seem more an intimate part of the town's life, and in the West, townsfolk like to see men who identify themselves with the life of the community.

Chase walked out from Pierson's door, as the boy came to it.

He himself reopened the door.

"Here's another client for you, Pierson," he called. "And I reckon that he'll keep you busier than I do!"

But he shook hands with the youngster, and then closed the door after him as Speedy went inside.

There was triumph in the eyes of Pierson, as he took the boy into his inner room.

Said Speedy: "I imagine that it was worth four hundred dollars, after all, Mr. Pierson?"

The lawyer laughed.

"Worth ten times that much," he said, brushing back his short black mustache with a nervous gesture of thumb and forefinger. "And still more than that. It pried Chase loose from Chalmers—that wind-bag! And it put him in my hands. You've made your peace with Chase, it seems! How did you manage that?"

"I stayed behind to apologize to him," answered the boy. "You know, Mr. Pierson, I don't live off honest men—unless they make bets with me!"

The two of them smiled at one another, with understanding. It was a bright day for Pierson, and he could endure remarks far more stinging than this one. Then he sat down, waved the boy into a chair, and leaning his elbows on his desk, he plunged into his idea.

He said: "Speedy, there's a big ranch on the Rio Grande. Thousands and thousands of acres. You don't measure a place like that in acres. You measure it in miles and leagues. You don't walk over it. You ride. And you ride hard, and change horses in the middle of the day, if you want to get around the land and back to the main ranch house by nightfall."

"I've seen a couple of places like that," said the boy. "Spanish landgrant somewhere at the bottom of 'em, usually."

"That's what's at the bottom of this one, too," said the lawyer.

He paused, and cleared his throat.

"Now, then," he said, "in the house on that ranch lives a man eighty years old. He lives alone. His wife is dead. His one son died a good many years ago. He thinks that he has no heir. But he's wrong. He has a granddaughter, and I can prove her claim to the place—the whole estate—all of those millions! Unfortunately, other people also know her claim. And they're trying to get her married to one of themselves. She doesn't know that she's an heiress. But what she does know, apparently, is that she doesn't want to marry. They've wooed and sued her, but they've all failed. Now, then, it seems to me that you're the sort of a fellow who succeeds best when the work is the hardest. Half the brains you invested in winning four hundred dollars from me, would be enough to bring that girl into camp. You'd find yourself a rich man. And then I come in. Not for a split. I simply want the regular legal fees for handling that property when the old man dies, and the land goes into

41

your hands. That's my case as simply and shortly as possible.

"Now tell me whether you want to remain a hobo, or marry a fortune?"

Said the boy, without hesitation: "Thanks a lot. But the fortune can go hang!"

— 8 —

THE LAWYER ROSE A LITTLE, as though somebody had lifted him in his chair by the collar. In fact, his coat bunched loosely and wrinkled between the shoulder blades.

Then he settled down again.

"You're playing for time. You don't mean what you say," he replied, bluntly.

Said the boy: "Maybe I didn't tell you before, but in my games, I leave the women out."

"Why?" asked the lawyer.

"Because I don't like to fool with them," said the boy, and he frowned.

"Because you think that they're too easy?" insisted John Pierson.

Speedy shrugged his shoulders.

"I'm not ready to marry, even if I could," said he. "I prefer a free life."

"Every man has to settle down some day," argued Pierson.

"That's what the anchored ones say," replied the boy. "It's put the white on your head. Why d'you want me to turn gray, also?"

At this, Pierson laughed a little.

"You have a way with you, lad," he admitted. "But here you're wrong."

Speedy waited, but with the manner of one who is polite, though he considers that the subject is closed for further discussion. The lawyer, silently, got out a box of cigars from a drawer of his desk, offered them vainly to Speedy, and then cut off the end of one and lighted it.

Through the smoke he squinted towards the boy, seeing him only in part, concentrating on his serious problem.

At last he nodded.

"I think you're right, after all," he said. "I jumped at a thought that came into my mind, but I begin to see, now, that you're right."

Speedy agreed, silently, with a gesture. He made himself a cigarette with adroit speed, and not a grain of Bull Durham fell to the floor. He lighted the cigarette, flicked out the match and placed it without a sound on the ashtray. The lawyer noted the singular graceful dexterity of every act.

"No," went on John Pierson, "I was thinking of your cleverness, and the way you accomplish the things that you want to do. However, this is something that you couldn't manage."

The boy raised his head a little: "No," he said, "I'm not a ladies' man."

Pierson looked down, scowling to cover a smile. Very little except the handsome tramp had been dinned into his ears by his daughter since the night before.

But he looked up as solemnly as ever.

Then, shaking his head, he went on: "Whether you're a success in the eyes of the ladies or no is not the question just now in my mind. No, not at all. Your cleverness could jump that hurdle, I think. No, it's a matter of the men that fence her in. No, it would never do. They'd kill you out of hand, my lad!"

In the brown deeps of the eyes of the boy appeared a glimmering light. For that light the lawyer had waited.

"Oh, they'd kill me out of hand, would they?" said Speedy, gently.

"We'll talk no more about it," said Pierson. "The fact is that I thought of you because, Speedy, in spite of your profession, I like you. Because of Brownie I have a reason. Because of yourself I have a reason. Most of all, I think I admired the impudence with which you made a fool of me, last night. And I have an idea that once you gave your word, you could be trusted to the end of the world!"

The boy waved these compliments aside, with a saintly, rather pained smile.

"But about the man-eaters—" he began.

"No, no, no!" said Pierson, shaking his head. "Now that I think the thing over, I'm horrified because I ever dreamed of dragging you into the business. No, I was entirely wrong. Utterly and entirely wrong, of course. I wouldn't dream of it. Here you are, a fellow who never carries weapons, even—no, the thing would be murder."

"But—" began Speedy.

"I'd have your death on my conscience all the days of my life!" said Pierson, resolutely. "Let's talk of something else, Speedy!"

The tramp sat forward in his chair.

"It may seem odd to you," he said, "but you know that even bare hands and bare brains have handled gunmen before now!"

Pierson raised the flat of his hand and pushed the subject away from consideration.

"I understand," said he. "The idea of a difficulty to be overcome—that rather attracts you, doesn't it? But I wouldn't draw you in. You think that I'm talking of a few reckless border ruffians, but you're quite wrong. No, no! Devils! That's what they are, my lad. I've been down there and looked them over, myself. I've seen fellows who could fan their guns so accurately that they could blow the lettering off a sign a hundred yards away. I'm not simply talking. It's a thing that I saw with my own eyes!"

"Sign posts are not men, after all," suggested Speedy.

"I know what you mean," agreed the lawyer, sympathetically. "But the fact is that they're a chosen lot of devils, down there in the place I refer to. A chosen lot, by heaven! They'd as soon kill a man as a rabbit. And they do. Constant shooting scrapes, d'you see? And a man who tries to make eyes at that girl is marked down in a moment!"

"Then they must be killing one another off at a rate that will make the place safe for strangers, very soon," said the boy.

"You'd think so, but you don't understand the angles of the game," replied Pierson. "No, no, my boy! All of those ruffians have long ago found out that she won't look twice at any of them. They're sure that she won't elope

44

with one of the old hands. It's strangers that they watch."

"Is the girl a half wit?" suggested young Speedy. "If the whole countryside knows that she's an heiress, do you mean to say that she has no inkling?"

"The whole countryside doesn't know," said Pierson. "Only two men down there have the facts in hand. They're both ambitious, but they're both likely, one of these days, to tell her the truth, because each one of 'em will be afraid that somebody else will pick the plum. You see, I've sketched the thing in very crudely. Only, believe me that I don't exaggerate. The finest shot in the world be taking his life in his hands if he went down there with the purpose I suggested. As for you—it would be plain suicide. You'll wonder that I didn't think of all of this before. But you know how a dream jumps into a man's head, and he tries to realize it when he wakes up. Well, the mist has blown out of my brain, now. Let's talk of something else, Speedy."

The tramp stood up, restlessly, and turned towards the door. Then, hastily, he came back again, and dropped his hand on the edge of the lawyer's desk.

"Down there on the Rio Grande—down where the girl is—that's a real dropping off place, is it?" he asked.

"You bet it is!" answered Pierson, heartily. "The men in the spot I'm talking about are born with a knife in their teeth, and they learn to shoot the eyes out of running jack-rabbits before they can walk."

The boy drew a great breath.

"I never thought much of the Rio Grande," he said, "but that's because I never took a good look at the country around it, Mr. Pierson. But from your description of the scenery—why, I see that it's the very next place where I'm to go."

"Come, come," said the lawyer. "You don't mean what you say! Forget all this, Speedy. I beg you to forget it."

"Ask a man to forget the lungs he breathes with!" said Speedy.

"You mean that you seriously have the thing in mind? No, but then there's the question of the girl. She's not the sort you would like."

"No?" said Speedy, mildly.

"No," answered the lawyer. "She's a pretty thing, but she's a shrew. A man wants a gentle woman around him.

Something to work for. But she's a wild caught mustang, if ever there was one!"

"Mr. Pierson," said the tramp, "may I ask you a favor?"

"Certainly," said the lawyer, putting much heartiness in his voice. "I'll do anything for you that I can!"

"Then give me the name and address of this man-tamer!"

Pierson jumped up.

"Don't ask me to do that," said he. "I've promised—but don't hold me to my word, Speedy!"

"I do hold you," said the boy.

"Confound it!" exclaimed Pierson. "You mean that you'd go down there and try to marry her?"

"In spite of the guns, I'd like to try it. And as for the girl, well, wild horses have been gentled, too!" said the tramp.

Pierson strode to the window. He turned his back on the boy and spoke loudly, angrily, without turning his head.

"You've cornered me, Speedy," he said. "But if I have to tell you, I have to! Her name's Mary Steyn, and she lives near Villa Real."

"Mary Steyn—Villa Real," murmured the boy, thoughtfully. "I'll look her up as soon as a train can get me down there!"

Suddenly he crossed the room and stood at the shoulder of Pierson. The latter, little by little, turned. A grin was on his face, triumph in his eyes. For a moment they stared at one another fixedly.

Then Speedy nodded.

"You took me in, that time, Mr. Pierson," he said. "It was all a little game to bait me, eh? A red flag for a bull. Was that it?"

The lawyer broke into ringing laughter. He dropped a hand upon the shoulder of the tramp.

"Speedy," he said, "you know that turn and turn about is fair play, eh?"

"Yes, I know that," said the boy, soberly, "but this was a good, full turn, after all. Well, I've told you that I'll do it. And I will. But you tell me what strings you have on me!"

Pierson shook his head.

"Not one!" he said. "Suppose that you should win—and honestly I think that your wits may give you one chance in three—you may care to remember John Pierson, and remember that he's a lawyer capable of dealing with estates. But there's not a string or a hold that I have over you. But, by the way, I'll be glad to finance you for any expenses that—"

The boy grew suddenly crimson to the roots of the hair. He said not a word.

But Pierson took a quick little step back from him.

"I beg your pardon!" said the lawyer.

–9–

THE HOUSE OF Art Steyn was not a beautiful one. It was just a sprawling shack of a ranch house, with three rooms in it. In one room, the punchers ate with the family, which consisted of Mary, the adopted daughter, and Steyn himself. Mrs. Steyn, who had taken the waif in, those years ago, had long since died.

Neither was the situation of the house charming. It was simply backed against a bald, brown hill. There were no trees near it. Even the water had to be carried a hundred feet from the corral troughs. And the sunburned grasses that covered the rolling country for leagues around wore into well-defined trails near the place—though there was no real road—until finally the ground was beaten bare by many hoofs all about the immediate vicinity of the shack.

And yet, every Sunday morning, cow punchers from distant parts of the range were sure to come trooping. What attracted them? Perhaps it was the music which Mary pounded out on a rattling piano that stood in a corner of the long dining room. Perhaps it was Mary's lively tongue. Perhaps it was Mary's brown, pretty face. At any rate, they came like bees to honey. And Art Steyn used to sit behind the veil of his seventy years and smile dimly at "the boys."

Those Sunday meetings served more purposes than merely to see and hear Mary, or to eat the liberal cold lunch which, with beer, was regularly served to all guests, and no questions asked. In addition, the place was a sort of no-man's land, where weapons were never drawn since the day when poor Jay Minter was shot to death by the outlaw, Sam Willys. Mary Steyn was only fifteen, then, but she was already a cause for war among men, and after the death of Minter, an unwritten law declared that no man⁻ should either wear or use artificial weapons at the Steyn house. When a rider arrived, he hung up his belt and guns on a peg on the dining room wall. That was his first act; afterwards, he spoke to those present.

And, because of this good custom, it came about that sometimes deadly enemies met under that roof and regarded one another coldly, but without either violent words or violent actions following.

That was not all. Hatred is generally based on ignorance of the other man. And many a hatred softened and mellowed into actual friendship in the good-natured atmosphere of the Steyn house.

On this Sunday, for instance, Rudy Stern, when he came through the doorway, stopped with a shock, for he saw the face of a puncher who had recently come off a more northerly range. It was Alf Barton, big, powerful, solemn of speech, a fighting man. He was not sure death, like Rudy Stern, but he had been man enough to stand up to Rudy in a memorable battle, long ago. And Rudy had been looking for him ever since the two of them were discharged, on different days, from the same hospital.

The story was well known, and when the pair eyed one another, a silence swept in a wave across the room. The girl who was rattling the piano, noticed it, and spun about on the stool.

She saw the cause at once, and did something about it. She went to Rudy Stern and took him by the elbow.

"You come along with me, Rudy," said she. "Hey, Alf!"

Barton turned, lumberingly, and glared at the girl's companion. However, slowly, step by step, he went to meet them. The two men eyed one another as though they were hunting for places to strike.

Said the girl, as she halted Rudy close to the larger man: "What's the matter with you two fellows? You shot each other up once. Isn't that enough? Now, you quit it! You're throwing a chill into the whole party. Rudy, Alf Barton's a man, and a real man, and you ought to know it. Alf, you know that Rudy has an edge on you in a gunplay. You may be brave enough to die, but why die today? Rudy, you're a bully by nature, but you're not going to start your tricks in this house! Look here, the pair of you. A pair of better punchers never forked a horse. Now, you either get out of here, or else shake hands, now!"

Alf Barton stood rigid and formidable, even then. For it was true that Rudy was the better gunman of the two, and Barton for that very reason would not give way. But Rudy, perhaps a little conscious that his great reputation made it possible for him to bend from his high position, suddenly thrust out his hand, with a smile.

He said: "Alf, old boy, you certainly socked me in Miller's place. But Mary's right. This is no place for us to wrangle. Besides, for my part, I'm glad to forget all about that. I've got nothing against you except that day; and the only thing that I've got against you on that day is that you shot too damn straight. Let's shake and call it quits!"

Barton colored a little. But he took the hand of Rudy in a great, honest grasp.

"I'm a mighty happy man to forget everything, Rudy," he said. Then he admitted, in his straightforward way: "I'm gunna stop payin' life insurance, now!"

The whole room laughed at this sally, and the laughter swept away the last iota of bad feeling between the two. They marched up to the piano, arm in arm, and bellowed loudly in discord in the next chorus that Mary played. The whole room was singing.

Under cover of that song, a grizzly veteran of the range entered, hung up his guns, and went to a corner, where he sat down and smoked a pipe. And presently another of the same type came in, and followed suit. He even drifted into the same corner where the first one had gone.

And it was he who said, half an hour later, lighting a second pipe: "Listen, Jack. I wanta talk to you."

Said Jack, "Damn your ornery hide, that's the only reason that I'm here—is to listen!"

"If you talk like that, Jack, I'm gunna take you outside and slam you!"

"Shut yer fool face, or the girl'll hear you."

"Ay, I forgot about her."

"I wanted to talk to you about that steer. It's a lie that I picked it off your range. That runnin' iron brand must of been the work of—"

"Hold on. I ain't here to argue. I ain't been close enough to you, since that day, to ask you face to face. It ain't been safe to get within rifle shot of you. But now here I set and I ask you, man to man, is it the truth that you're telling me?"

The other stared at him out of keen eyes.

Slowly, bitterly, he said: "No, it ain't the truth. I've lied to you, partner."

"Lie or no lie," said the other, with a sudden heartiness. "It shows the man you are to admit it. Son, we'll fix that matter up peaceable. And the load off my shoulders will be worth the price of twenty steers."

Said the other: "It wasn't the price of the damn steer. It was just that I wasn't gunna be outsmarted by you. Partner, you'll see I'm square. I'll settle it right here and now!"

This small conversation meant much, but it passed almost unnoticed. There was hardly a Sunday when two or three old enemies did not meet in this extra legal court and settle difficulties. And if a very moot point arose, old, faintly smiling Arthur Steyn would be called in to act as the judge. Quietly, in five minutes of talk, he was generally able to straighten out everything.

Now, it was when the merriment was in full swing, and at least twenty men or more were in the room that from outside the house came the sound of a guitar, and a ringing, clear baritone voice which accompanied the piano and the singers inside, a voice that cut through the others by the purity of its rounded tone in spite of the distance of the singer.

"Hello!" cried Mary, as the piece ended. "There's a real musician floating around here! Wait till I get him. This is going to be a party!"

She ran to the door.

And there she saw the player of the guitar standing.

She stopped with a frown.

"Only a tramp—a lowdown hobo!" she exclaimed with a cruel loudness.

For the boy before her was dressed in rags; his toes thrust out at the ends of his shoes; his necktie was askew;

a tattered hat was on his head. The sling which supported the guitar from around his neck proved, as it were, that he was a professional mendicant, singing for his living. Now, in an equally professional manner, he lifted his almost brimless hat and bowed to her, and then straightened with a smile on his brown, handsome face.

"Miss Steyn," said he, "I've come a long way to see you. I hope there's something to eat in your kitchen!"

"Look here," said the girl, sternly. "We don't like hoboes, around here. One of your kind burned down the barn, a couple of years back. We want no more of you. Get off the place! Or if you really are just down on your luck, you'll find a woodpile around there behind the house. Go on and tackle it, and we'll feed you when you've earned your meal."

He kept his hat in his hand. The wind waved his tousled hair. His smile did not grow dim.

"Nothing that I'd like to do," said he, "better than to chop some of that wood and get the good hard exercise. But I've a vow that keeps me from it."

"You have a vow?" she asked, disdainfully. "What sort of a vow have you made?"

"Never to raise a callus, ma'am. You know that when a musician wants to keep his touch——"

"Musician? You low hobo, I'll give you five minutes to get off the place!"

And she turned abruptly back to the piano and played the next piece which was being clamored for.

She had scarcely ended when the mellow voice of the tramp broke in upon her, singing:

> "Julia, you are peculiar,
> Julia,
> You are queer.
> Truly,
> You are unruly
> As a wild western steer.
> Sweetheart, when we marry,
> Dear one, you and I,
> Julia,
> You little mule you,
> I'm gunna rule you,
> Or die!"

There was laughter from the crowd, laughter from the girl, also, but she said: "He sings pretty well, but he's a hobo. I gave him five minutes to get off the place. Say, Fat, you go and throw him off, will you?"

—10—

FAT GINNIS WAS a hardy fellow who hardly deserved his nickname. His face was fat; the rest of him was as hard as wrestling with mustangs and beef could make a man.

He merely said: "Say, Mary—where d'you want me to throw him, and how far?"

"Don't hurt him," she called over her shoulder. "Just start him on his way. That's all."

"I'll start him, all right," said Fat, with the tone of one who would finish him, also.

And he disappeared through the doorway with long, determined strides.

The merriment grew, inside the house. Beer was served in the following manner. Two kegs were carried in and hoisted onto the long central table, and over each was appointed an overseer and bartender, who filled the glasses in turn and tried to keep the liquid from dripping on the floor.

However, as Mary said: "We can get another floor, but we can't get another crowd together as good as this one!"

A series of toasts began, and the first, as usual, was to Mary. It had hardly been downed, and she was laughing, and the first roaring of cheers had died a little, when the voice of the singer floated clearly though faintly in from outside the house:

"... You are peculiar,
Julia,
You are queer,

52

Truly,
You are unruly,
As a wild western steer . . ."

The words seemed to have a peculiar aptness, at the moment, and the face of the girl flushed with anger.

"Will one of you fellows go and see what Fat Ginnis is doing out there, to let that hobo hang around and spoil the party for us?" she demanded. "Will you go, Doc?"

Doc waved his hand. He rose, shifted his quid—he had been taking his beer without removing the quid from his mouth—and tightened his belt. From a peg on the wall, he took down his hat, carefully adjusted it on his head, and then stepped out into the glare of the sunlight.

Someone laughed, looking after him.

"He'll kill that hobo!" suggested someone.

The girl was singing out after him: "Don't break the kid up for life, Doc. Just slide him along on his way."

But Doc gave no sign that he heard, and his wide shoulders, muscled as only a lumberman's shoulder may be, had a resolved swing to them, and he was leaning forward in his stride.

Other men in the place envied him. There was not a fellow there who did not ache to win a smile from Mary Steyn.

However, Doc would handle the business very well, no doubt. If he did not let himself in for a manslaughter charge, or some such thing, it would be well. There was an ugly story, somewhere current, about a certain Canuck who had died in the grasp of Doc.

Now the fun began again, under Mary's supervision. She loved these Sunday parties, and all week she looked forward to them, but her chief care was that the pleasure should be distributed, and that no one should be slighted. She had her favorites, of course, but the vast base of her popularity was composed of two elements—one, that no man could have her, and two, that she was equally nice to everyone.

When a girl makes a choice and shows a preference, the rest of the world of men promptly turns its face from her and cares not a whit if it never sees her again. Mary Steyn never had made that mistake. And if a too importunate wooer appeared, she simply winked at any of a hundred bold-handed ruffians, who promptly showed him that the air was better in other parts of the country.

Now Mary was busy for a time in moving through the corners and the distant angles of the big room, finding the oldsters, sitting beside them for a moment, making their grim eyes light up and smile back at her. And it was in the midst of just such a moment that she was suddenly aware that the entire rest of the room had fallen silent, while through the open doorway streamed the words of the infernal song:

> "Sweetheart, when we're married,
> Dear one, you and I;
> Julia,
> You little mule you,
> I'm gunna rule you,
> Or die!"

It was the hobo singer again, and his voice was raised and more powerfully ringing than before.

Amazement had stilled all sounds in the room. Amazement stilled the very heart of the girl. And into her mind's eye, once again, stepped the powerful form of Doc, as he had gone out to battle, a man in a hundred, a man in a thousand, even, when it came to physical combat.

Had she made a mistake about the boy?

No, she remembered the almost loathesome beauty of his face, his brown skin and ruddy color in the cheeks, the deep, soft brown eyes, the femininely flashing smile—

No, she could not have made a mistake about him as a man. But whatever little mystery it was that detained both Fat and big Doc should be looked into at once.

Said one of the men in the room: "Ma'am, what kind of an hombre did you say this hobo looked to be?"

"He's a worthless, shiftless tramp whose pride is that he never had a callus on his hands. A guitar-playing loafer and hobo. That's what he is. He looks like a girl in disguise! But I wish that something could be done about him!"

Ready faces surrounded her. But they were graver faces, now, she noted. Whatever the mystery was that lay in the disapperance of both Fat Ginnis and Doc, it was plain that a real man was required to handle the hobo now.

Her eyes picked up the men, one by one, and discarded them. Gentleman Joe Wynne was not there. She was beginning to miss him more and more, when he absented himself from one of the parties, or came dashing up very late in the evening, when most of the others had gone. He was the Achilles who could do all things—beat a Mexican throwing a rope or a knife, and shoot the eyelids off the hardiest gunman that ever pulled a Colt and fanned it.

There was Rudy Stern, as good as Gentleman Joe, when it came to gunwork, but not such an able man of his hands. A terrible and efficient warrior was Rudy, but if he undertook this battle he would probably invent a weapon offhand and kill the young tramp.

She wanted no more killings around the Steyn house!

Then she saw Alfred Barton. Alf was the biggest and the strongest man in the room. They said that he knocked a mustang down one day with his bare fist, and that the mustang stayed down for half an hour. A glance at him made the story appear easily credible.

So she said: "Alf, I hate to bother you. You've hardly more than come in. But I wish that you'd go out and see if Fat and Doc are shooting craps, or watching a hawk fly, or what. D'you mind?"

Alf Barton laughed.

He could pull a gun and he could shoot it, but he never was thoroughly at home with weapons. His hands were his medium. Whether it were catch-as-catch-can, or fists, or a roughhouse combination of the two, he was at ease and at home. He spread his elbows at the board and smashed bones!

And to do this little favor for Mary Steyn?

So he laughed, for an answer, and started for the door.

"Don't be rash, Alf," called the girl. "The hobo has some trick, maybe!"

He waved his hand over his shoulder without so much as turning his head towards her, and continued until the sunlight flashed upon his blond head. Then the edge of the door cut him off from view.

Every man in that room yearned to follow; but no one would break up the party, except at a sign from Mary.

She said: "If we followed along, it would make that tramp feel too important, even while he's taking his licking."

Straightaway, the buzz of talk began again, but this time there was only one theme; what had happened to the first two; what would big Alf Barton do to the stranger?

And the buzz grew denser, but softer, as the minutes slid by. Mary Steyn, to be sure, noted the passage of the time, and her amazement and her anger grew.

What was behind the whole thing?

All three were men; the last two were carefully picked men, worthy to fight a battle with ten. But—none of them came back!

And now, in the midst of her bewilderment, the thing she dreaded, which had become a pulse of sound at her ear, sounded just outside the door:

> "Julia,
> You are peculiar,
> Julia,
> You are queer . . ."

And there stood the hobo in the doorway!

He had not altered.

If he had had three encounters with three formidable men, no one could have guessed it. His rags were the same. The same remnant of brim adhered to his hat. His face was unmarred, and, for all that she could see, his breathing was not interfered with by any recent violent exercise.

Women hate mysteries and problems. And Mary Steyn was preeminently a woman.

She stamped on the floor.

"If one man can't handle him—" she cried out.

And then she paused, for a quiet voice called from the farther end of the room:

"Come in, lad!"

That voice took the case out of her hands. It rarely interfered, but when it spoke, it was absolute. For it was the voice of old Arthur Steyn himself.

"Come in, lad," he said, "and sing us another song. I like your style!"

The hobo took off his hat and bowed. It was a deep and graceful bow.

"What will you have, sir?" he asked.

"Something old," said Steyn. "Some old darky song would please me best. Mary, play something at the piano and—"

But Mary had suddenly disappeared from the room.

—11—

SHE HAD SLIPPED OUT through the door, and turning the corner of the house, the first thing that she saw was the form of Doc loosely sitting in the saddle, slouched over to one side, with his head hanging on his chest, and the air of a man who has been shot through the body. He held onto the pommel of the saddle to support himself. His hat was off. It remained somewhere unheeded behind him, even the sombrero sacred to a cowpuncher.

His head flopped up and down, as the horse began to trot.

"Doc—has been beaten—within an inch of his life!" she gasped to herself. "And he's going home, shamed!"

Well, Fat Ginnis might have done the same thing. But where was the great Alf Barton?

He was not in the woodshed nor was he behind it. He was not behind the great corded pile of wood which was waiting to be cut.

Had he disappeared from the face of the earth?

No, running on, breathless, beside the barn she found him lying face up in the glare of the sun. His face was running crimson. One eye was open, but it looked up at the terrible sky without sense. The other eye was closed; it would remain closed for some days to come, she could guess!

His very clothes showed the signs of struggle. His coat was ripped almost from his back. His shirt was torn open across his breast.

What monster, part grizzly bear and part mountain lion, had dropped upon poor Alf Barton?

Not that slender, worthless hobo, with his singing voice and his guitar, surely! Such a thing was impossible!

She kneeled beside Alf, putting her body between him and the cruel sun. She took his head on her lap and with her handkerchief, she dabbed at the blood upon his split and swollen lips.

Then a flicker of life came back into the fishy, open eye —It winked. Alf Barton pushed himself slowly to a sitting posture, where he supported himself upon trembling arms.

His head hung down, not in shame but in sickening weakness and in pain.

She, still on her knees, laid a hand upon his shoulder; she could feel the big muscles dissolved to pulp, and shuddering under her touch.

"Alf," she said, "it's Mary speaking. Tell me what on earth happened. I'll take care of you. Not a soul shall know. What did the scoundrel do? Did he strike you from behind with a club?"

He looked vaguely at her. His breath rattled in his throat, but he seemed to be recovering little by little.

Then he raised a hand to his head, and fumbled at the crown of it.

"No," he said, "I reckon I half remember that part of it. That was where he slammed me up agin the barn, and my head socked the edge of a plank. That was kind of towards the end."

His thick mumbling voice horrified her. But she was fascinated more than she was shocked.

"D'you mean," she said, "that the hobo did it—all by himself?"

At this, he raised his head higher, inspired by a rising heat of indignation.

"All by himself?" he echoed. "He ain't all by himself. He's got a whole bag of tricks for company. He ain't never alone. He's got more legs than a spider, and three pairs of hands."

"He—did—these things—to you—with his hands?" she cried.

"I didn't say that," answered Alf Barton, shaking his bleeding head. "It was my hands that he used."

58

"Alf, you're crazy," she said. "How could he use your hands?"

"Ask him!" he replied, angrily. "Don't you go and ask me. How do I know? When I reached for him, I just seemed to hit myself. That's all that I know about it. When I rushed him, I just tripped on the place where he'd been standing, and sailed right on and lit on my face. When I stood off and sparred at him, he picked a straight left out of the air like an apple off of a bough and turned around, and bore down, and just about dislocated my arm at the shoulder. After that I didn't have nothing but a right, left to me. But a right was enough—if only I could of pasted him once."

"He's a professional prizefighter?" exclaimed the girl.

"He ain't," said Alf Barton. "I've seen plenty of them. I've met 'em in camp when they'd just got through with the ring. And plenty of ex-pugs I've poked in the chin and watched 'em drop to sleep. But I couldn't poke this kid. He never was where I wanted him. I tried to rush him and wear him down with weight. That was when he slipped me over his shoulder and heaved me into the side of the barn, and after that, everything begun to get kind of dim. That's all that I know."

"Alf, tell me this. Did he ever hit you with his fists?"

"Him?" muttered Barton. "I dunno. But towards the end, it seemed like I remembered something small and light tapping me on the chin, and my brain going black. Something like the tapping of a tack hammer. It put my brain to sleep. It turned me all numb. Then I forgot the rest, till I heard you talkin', Mary. I'm gunna go home."

"Wait till I've fixed you up," she said.

"I won't wait for nothin'," he said. "I ain't gunna run the risk of any of the boys seein' what he done to me! That shrimp! I'll break him in two like a stick of wood, one of these days, I tell you!"

"Of course you will," said she. "But first, let me go and get some water and adhesive tape and—"

"I won't be here when you come back," he said. "I got my hoss right here in the barn. But tell me something before I barge along."

"I'll tell you anything I can, Alf."

"Did you have something agin Doc and Fatty and me that you elected the three of us?"

"Alf!" she cried, in painful protest. "Every time that one of you went out, I was ashamed to send such a man after such a worthless splinter of a boy."

"He ain't a splinter, unless it's a splinter of steel," replied the other. "A splinter like him could slide into a man's heart or brain and leave him dead and not knowin' that nothin' had struck him. I'm gunna go home!"

He heaved himself to his feet. She herself accompanied his unsteady steps into the barn. She was deeply hurt, but she knew that nothing she could say now would persuade him. It was plain that he still nourished a doubt of her honesty in this matter.

And, when he sat in the saddle, he muttered at her through lips increasingly thick and numb:

"Magician, that's what he is. One of these here, now you see it and now you don't. One of them kind of fellows he is. And you knew it, Mary Steyn!"

She started to protest. He merely shook his head, and rode off at a rapid gallop down the slope, a gallop which he was not yet able to sit out easily, for he swayed and reeled wildly in the saddle as the horse raced along.

She looked after him with the feeling that the ground had been cut from under her feet.

And just then she heard the heavy pounding of the piano in the house. She recognized one of the three tunes that Bill Sanson was able to play, and now and again, she heard whoops and stampings, and single yells of joy going up from a delighted crowd.

That was the stranger at work again, no doubt!

She wished that the hobo could be buried in the center of the earth.

She had ordered him from the place; now he had fought his way in, as it were, made a fool of her, shamed her, and established himself in the graces of the crowd.

And she, Mary Steyn, the queen of those ranges, had to go back and try to face him in her own home!

She groaned, the sound making her throat quiver.

Of only one thing was she sure, and this was that she detested the tramp more than she ever had dreamed before that she could loathe any human creature.

60

However, she had plenty of nerve and courage, and she forced herself to go back to the door of the dining room, where the party was in progress. And there she saw the crowd standing huddled against the walls of the room, while up and down the center of the open space flickered and whirled and bounded the form of the hobo, now doing a buck and wing, and now a soft shoe step or two whose silence threw the crowd into an ecstasy of delight.

Bill Sanson himself, hammering out the tune on the piano, over and over again, could hardly contain himself. He was almost falling from the stool. There was her father also, who rarely even smiled, now wiping tears of childish pleasure from his eyes.

And now the dancer, fiddling with soft shoe steps at one end of the room, announced his imitations—a tipsy man going upstairs in his house, startled by noises on the way, and finally confronting his wife at the head of the steps, and falling all the way down to the starting point.

How realistically it was all done; she found herself smiling, though grimly.

And then, a cat crossing muddy street—earnestly looking and in vain for dry spots, leaping here and there, pausing an instant to shake mud and water from the dainty feet, and finally, with a great bound, coming at last to the safety of the dry sidewalk.

Then he did other things—a boy passing a group of girls gathered on a front porch—with a disastrous stumble in the midst of the passage. An old horse on the trail; a young mustang fighting against the rope; a wise old outlaw bucking with science and yet with an apparent sense of humor, which he showed when the rider was slung to the ground.

At last the boy stopped.

Why, they howled and raised the roof, begging for more; and the tramp, smiling at them, seemed to thank them for their appreciation, and seemed willing to go on forever.

But first he turned with his bow, heels together, and head inclined low, towards the girl.

"Do you want me to go on, Miss Steyn?" said he

"I know you're tired," said she, grimly.

And then, sullenly, listened to the roar of protest, heard the volleyed entreaties that he should go on. And she watched him delicately, tactfully, declaring that he was really worn out.

It seemed to her that the youth had come there on purpose to discredit her friends and to discredit her. She hated him with far greater bitterness than ever.

—12—

ALL THE OTHERS had come and gone. Even Gentleman Joe Wynne had been there and had departed once more.

She sat, in the tired dark of the evening, after supper, in the kitchen. The dining room was too great a confusion. It would take her half the next day to put it to rights. This should have been a quiet moment, a restful time for her alone with old Arthur Steyn.

But they were not alone. All the others, the old and tried friends, were gone away, but there remained—the stranger!

There he sat, at the right hand of her father, sipping his third cup of coffee and talking on, in a gentle, half dreamy voice.

How consummately, more and more, she hated him!

What was he saying now?

For the waves of her detestation now and then stopped up her ears and prevented her from following the sense of the words. This was where she picked up the thread of the narrative, and the boy was saying:

". . . and when I saw him lying there, and realized that he was dead, I knew what I had to do."

"You went to your father and told him the truth about the blackguard, I hope," said old Steyn, earnestly.

"I couldn't do that," said the boy. "You see, Uncle Tom was a lot younger than my father. He'd raised Tom like a son, and he cared for him a great deal more than he cared for me. It would have broken his heart to think that Tom was really—"

"You mean to say," exclaimed Steyn, "that you let your father think that you had *murdered* your uncle?"

"That was the easiest way for Father," said the boy. "He never thought much of me. I was too much like my mother, and they had separated a few years after their marriage. He never spoke of her, not even after her death. He's a stern man, is my father. He loved only one thing—Uncle Tom. I knew that. And Dad was very ill. He had a heart that wasn't worth a feather. It's better now, I understand."

The girl fixed a stern, doubting gaze upon the boy. And his glance met hers.

Could she believe her eyes?

He deliberately winked at her! Yes, in an instant he seemed to admit that he was talking nonsense to amuse Arthur Steyn and to win the old man's confidence.

She almost gaped with open mouth at the boy.

"And you, my poor lad," said Steyn, his voice troubled, "what did you do?"

"Well," said the boy, "I left home."

"Did they follow you?"

"Yes—I'm sorry to say that Father told the law everything. The police hounded me to the end of South America. Then I managed to slip them and I've worked my way this far to the north."

"And you're bound where?"

"To see Father again, before he dies."

"Suppose that he gives you up to the law?"

"He might," admitted the tramp. "But his face haunts me. You know, since I've been roughing around the world, I've had my share and a little over, of hard knocks. And in the worst times, I've begun to think the most of my father. A man has to grow up a bit before he realizes what a father means."

"It's true," said Steyn, in a voice greatly moved. "It's terribly and profoundly true. My lad, I'm going to help you to—"

"Mr. Steyn," said the boy, pushing back his chair a little from the table, grasping the side of it as though he intended to leap to his feet and leave the room.

"I want to help you," said Steyn, warmly.

"If I'd thought that," said the boy, "I never would have

said a word to you. If you think that I've been adroitly begging—"

"No, no," said Steyn.

"It was only," said the hobo, sadly, "that something about you reminded me of Father as he'll be when he comes to your age, if God lets him live that long."

And again, in the midst of this semi-tragic speech, his eye caught the stern glance of the girl, and he winked at her again!

"And so you go on your way," said Steyn, gloomily. "It's a terrible story that you've told me. I want to thank you for speaking as you have. I want to thank you for the confidence that it shows—"

"Mr. Steyn," said the boy, "I imagine that half the world takes its troubles to you!"

And the eyes of Steyn softened and brightened at once.

"There *are* some people who trust me," he admitted, gently.

Then he added:

"You haven't told me your name. Can you do that?"

"You'll see that I can't do that, sir," said the tramp. "My traveling nickname, though, if you want to hear it. They call me Speedy, because I'm never long in one place."

"Hounded as you've been," said Steyn, hotly, "how *could* you remain long in one place? Speedy, if that's what you want me to call you—"

"I'm used to the name," said Speedy.

"Speedy, I want you at least to spend the night here in my house. You know where the bunks are. It's rough hospitality. But I want to have another chat with you, tomorrow."

Speedy hesitated.

Then he said: "I'll stay. I'm glad to stay. You don't want to talk to me half as much as I want to talk to you. You know, Mr. Steyn, that a man who's lived his life knows what life is. And youngsters can't."

Steyn stood up and grasped the hand of the boy, and shook it firmly. Already he had overstepped his usual bedtime by an hour.

"Your story will be with me all night," he said. "In the morning, I hope that I'll have something to say to you."

He kissed the girl goodnight.

"When Speedy wants to turn in," said he, "give him a lantern, there—or a lamp, if he prefers it."

And he left them alone. The girl closed the door after him.

Then, turning, she rested her shoulders against the door and stared with open hostility at Speedy.

"You don't mean that you're going tomorrow," said she.

"No, I don't," said he.

He sat down by the stove, made a cigarette and tilted back in his chair to smoke it, grinning at her through the smoke.

"If poor Dad could see you now!" she exclaimed.

"He won't, though," said Speedy.

"You're intending to settle down and sponge on him for a while, are you?" she demanded.

"Yes, for quite a bit," said the boy. "I like the Sunday parties. I was always partial to beer."

"How long do you think you'll stay in the house after I've told him the truth about you?" she asked.

"He won't believe you," said Speedy.

"He!" she cried. "You mean that he won't believe what I solemnly tell him I know?"

The boy shook his head.

"I wish that you'd explain that," said the girl.

"No man will ever admit that he's been turned into a perfect fool," he answered her.

She could not help admitting that there was much truth in this. But rage was working in her like a ferment.

"Your wretched impudence!" she said. "You won't be here tomorrow night, Speedy!"

"Are you betting on that?" he asked.

"If you were thrown out, you might steal back and break in—to win the bet!" she suggested, contemptuously.

"I won't break in, because I won't be thrown out," said he.

"I'll make a wager on that!" said she.

"What will you bet?" he asked.

"As much as you wish," said she.

He drew a large roll of bills from his pocket.

"Here's something over three thousand," he said.

"You know I haven't that much," said the girl. "You sham, wearing rags, and carrying that much cash!"

"I'll bet you a thousand that I'm here tomorrow night," said he. "If you lose—you go to the first dance that's given around here—with me."

"With you?" she exclaimed. "Go to a dance with *you?*"

He merely smiled at her.

"Yes," said he, "with me. That's the bet I offer. You have all of tomorrow to work on your father. If you win, I leave a thousand dollars behind me."

"I can imagine you doing that," she sneered.

At this, the smile disappeared from his face.

"I'm the world's champion liar," he admitted, "but my promises are as clean as a hound's tooth."

And she wondered why she knew that now he was telling her the complete truth.

She studied him in a growing bewilderment that almost overclouded her detestation of him, but she added: "You know, Speedy, that if you begin to pay a lot of attention to me—there may be trouble ahead for you?"

"I know the legend," he said. "The gunmen, and all that —but what do you suppose brought me all this distance, my dear?"

"Don't call me that, if you please," said she.

"You are, though," he said. "I'll tell you, Mary. I came for you, and I'm going to take you."

She laughed; but her teeth hardly parted to let the sound out.

"You're going to marry me and carry me away, are you, young Lochinvar?" said she.

He laughed in turn, easily, confidently.

"That's what I'm going to do," said he.

"Do you know," she replied, quietly, "that I detest you more utterly than I ever have detested a human being in my life? Your lies, your tricks, your vanity—your everything!"

"But I've broken ground with you, Mary," grinned Speedy. "In your whole life you never have thought so much about any man in any one day."

She could not deny it. And her inability to do so choked her. Suddenly she flung from the room, and ran to her own chamber, and there dashed herself down on the bed and lay trembling with fury, her brain spinning, her face hot.

– 13 –

Words which have been brooded over during an entire night are powerful words; and the speech of Mary Steyn was filled with hot strength when she saw her adopted father the next morning. Her eye was cold and straight as a bar of steel, and it fixed and held him.

She told him the story in few words.

"Speedy, as he calls himself, is an imposter. He's a sham. He told me so last night. He's the most horrible man that I ever met. He's come here to sponge on you, and to try to marry me. He—he actually told me so!"

Arthur watched her in her fury.

Then he said: "Where's Speedy now?"

"He's outside. I don't know just where—not far from the kitchen, I suspect!"

Said Steyn: "Go call him in here, and you come, too."

She was fired with joy at the prospect. Swiftly she went, and found the boy with his hands in his pockets under the eaves of the woodshed, whistling to a blue jay which alighted on the rooftree. Once, twice and again, as she watched, the blue jay, in alarm, started flapping its wings. Once it actually rose a foot or so for flight, but always it settled down again and regarded the enchanter with one eye and then with the other, amazed, horrified, fascinated to helplessness.

The scene seemed to her neither clever nor common, but horrible; there was some sort of power in this handsome youngster which both beasts and men felt, and she wanted with all her soul to be far from it.

Her voice broke the spell. The blue jay fled in a straight, flashing line through the air, wavering a little up and down in the excess of its zeal to get away. Then Speedy turned to her, and took off his brimless hat, smiling.

"Good morning, Mary," said he. "What is it?"

She looked at him with scorn, and with rage, and with contempt. There was a definite fear in her, also.

She said: "Father wants to talk to you."

"About last night, eh? I hope that you'll be present."

"Oh, I'll be present all right," she answered, grimly. "You don't need to think that I'll miss that little party. When you're unveiled before him, Speedy, I want to be there. I wouldn't miss the picture."

"Poor Mary!" said he. "You'll wish to heaven, afterwards, that you never had told him a word about it. But if I have to go in there, I'll split you and Arthur Steyn a mile apart."

"You'll split me—and my father—apart?" she said, furiously. "*You* will—half a day after we've first laid eyes on you?"

"Oh, I'm a fast worker, Mary," said he. "Didn't you notice the blue jay, even?"

"You took the blue jay's eye with your tricks for a minute. He'll never come back to lay eyes on you again, so long as he lives."

"You're wrong," declared Speedy. "In half an hour he'll be back there on the crest of the woodshed, wondering what happened, and what it was all about. The same with you, Mary. If I left you, before a day was out you'd be sorry that I had gone away!"

Her angry denial did not reach her lips, since before she uttered it, she saw that he was mocking her with laughter, in expectation of her fury.

Instead, she led the way to where Arthur Steyn now sat, as always, on the eastern side of the house, to enjoy the first brightness of the morning, before the heat became too great.

The boy took off his hat and went cheerfully up to his host.

"Good morning, sir," said he.

"Good morning, Speedy," said Steyn. "Mary has been telling me a tale about you. What's the truth of it?"

"A tale about me?" asked Speedy, good-naturedly, smiling still. "What sort of a tale, sir?"

"Let me say it over again," urged the girl. "Let me tell him, before your face, Father."

"Very well," said Steyn.

He was not excited. He was merely a little stern, but his old eyes reserved judgment. And Speedy saw this, with relish.

"When you were talking to Father telling him the cock-and-bull yarn about your trouble with your father and the 'murder' of your uncle, you winked at me across the table. D'you deny that?"

"I winked at you?" said the boy.

Her anger almost was stifled by the blank amazement in his face. For an instant she doubted her ability to count against such consummate acting. But then the strength and outrageousness of her case came over her. She went on: "Do you deny it?"

He glanced at Steyn.

"I don't know what to say to this, sir," said the boy. "If you don't mind, I'll hear out what she has to say. There seems to be more behind this."

"That ought to be the best way," said Steyn. "Mary, don't let your emotions run away with you. Let's have everything as clearly as possible."

"I'll be as clear as glass!" she exclaimed. "Don't doubt that, for a moment. I'll let you look right through his black heart. When you were gone out of the kitchen, Father, he made no attempt to conceal anything. He talked straight out. He's a loafer. He's an idler. You know when he came that he boasted he never had raised a callus by honest work. He admitted that he had arranged everything just in order to sponge on you for a while. He told me in so many words that he had come here for that purpose. He even told me— the contemptible—"

She checked herself.

Then she exploded: "That he would manage it so that he would marry me!"

She paused again, gathering her breath, controlling a tomboy desire to smash her hard, small fist against the blank amazement that was shown on the face of the boy.

"And when just now I told him that you wanted to see him, he said that I'd regret calling him, because he'd split you and me a mile apart—you and me, Dad!"

She ended, trembling; still her eyes shot fire at Speedy. And he looked back at her; his lips slightly parted. His eyes were big, but that eye which was concealed from the sight of Stern now suddenly winked at her.

It was the crowning touch; she grew half blind with fury. She could not speak again.

Then Steyn was saying: "Speedy, will you look at me?"

"May I ask her one thing, first?" asked the boy.

"By all means," said Steyn.

And he said: "Mary, is this a practical joke?"

"A practical joke?" she cried. "A practical joke? Oh!"

Then Speedy turned to the wise old man, and met his straight eye.

"She seems to mean it," said the boy. "People dream things pretty vividly, sometimes, but this isn't a dream. I don't know what to call it."

"Neither do I," said Arthur Steyn. "Did you say those things?"

The boy looked at the ground, frowning, seeming to make an effort of memory.

Then he said, as though to himself, slowly, softly: "First, I winked at her, as much to say that my uncle hadn't died and—"

He paused.

He turned from them and walked a few paces away; then he came back. He raised his head and looked at Steyn.

"After that," he said, "I waited until you had left the kitchen, and then I told her that I was a tramp, and a sponger, and that—that I was going to marry her."

He looked back at Mary.

"Wasn't that it? You *did* say the last thing, too, didn't you?"

"You know very well what you said!" she answered.

Arthur Steyn said nothing. He was leaning a little away from his chair, staring steadily at the face of Speedy.

And Speedy said: "People grow hysterical, and I suppose that she was upset by what happened yesterday. I'm sorry that I stayed on. Good-bye, Mary. Good-bye, Mr. Steyn. I'll not be forgetting you, for reasons that I told you last night."

He held out his hand, but Steyn shook his head.

"You can't go, Speedy," said he.

"I *have* to go," said the boy. "No, if you want to hear

her berate me some more, I'll stay and listen to it. But that's no good, really."

"Mary," said Steyn, "look at me, my dear."

"Dad!" she cried. "Is it true that you're doubting me?" He drew a soft, long breath.

"I want to make a list of the things you say that he told you, Mary," said the old man.

Then he enumerated them:

"First, that he winked at you, while he was telling me the terrible story of his breach with his father.

"Second, that after I left the room, he admitted that he was a sham.

"Third, that he said he had come here to sponge on me.

"Fourth, that he finally declared that he intended to marry you!

"Now, Mary, that makes a queer conclusion. It doesn't sound like ordinary wooing!"

She was desperate, but out of her desperation she cried: "I didn't add that he swore he would bet me a thousand dollars that I couldn't persuade you to send him away from the house. And I like a fool took the bet. If I lose, I'm to go with him to the first dance in the neighborhood! Will you believe *that*?"

Steyn, after a moment, said gently: "I've thought for a long time that these Sunday parties have been growing too much for your nerves, Mary dear. Now I know it. We've had the last one—for a long time, at least. I hope you'll spread the word around that we've stopped receiving everyone on Sundays."

She cried out in an agony, for she saw how completely she had lost. It was the totality of her true story that had undone her. Part of it might have been believed, but not the staggering whole, and now she exclaimed: "Tell them yourself—let *him* spread the news! I don't care! I don't care! I'm going away from here and I'm never coming back —ever!"

And, with that, sobbing choked her. She turned and fled.

SHE PAUSED IN HER ROOM long enough to get into boots
and spurs, and to jam a hat on her head, jerk a bandanna
around her neck. Then she raced on to get to the barn.

But no one was waiting there to prevent her departure.

That was the work of the tramp, too! That was the work
of the devil-inspired boy! She turned at the door of the
barn and shook her fist at the house.

Then she ran on, snatched a rope from a peg and hurried
into the pasture.

She whistled for the gray mare, Whimsy.

Whimsy came to her like a favorite dog to a hunter, as a
rule, but this morning she threw up her head, stared at her
and fled with a snort.

For a sweating half hour she had to work, the sun
growing higher and higher, before she finally caught her
in a corner, and as she mounted, finally, with Whimsy
under the saddle, she looked back towards the house and
saw—

This strange picture: of the tramp done up in one of her
own faded blue gingham kitchen aprons in the back yard,
holding a small armload of wood, and looking after her?

No, not that. She might not have existed, so far as he
was concerned, it appeared. He was lifting his head a little
and above him, on the rooftree of the woodshed, was a blue
jay, fluttering its wings but never rising into the air, as
though held in a trap.

That was too much for her.

She had been consumed with rage before, but now despair, shame, bewilderment all rushed over her, and she
sobbed loudly, like a child, as Whimsy carried her headlong
over the trail.

She hardly knew what trail it was that she had taken; she

only knew that the brown forms of the hills were sliding behind her, and growing bigger and bigger before her, and then, rounding a turn, she almost rode the foaming mare straight into Gentleman Joe Wynne's big-striding black horse.

She swerved Whimsy in a flash; she bowed her head to conceal her tear-stained, swollen face, and cried in a muffled voice: "Hello, Joe!" as she darted by.

She knew that he had turned behind her. She heard the long, rolling beat of the hoofs of the black horse. She was in despair of a new kind, for she knew that Whimsy, even carrying her light weight, could never get away from the long-limbed black racer that Wynne bestrode.

He would think that she had fled to him for help!

Well, and perhaps some instinct had forced her down that trail, urging her towards the one man in the world she came nearest to loving. Certainly he was the one who had her entire and whole-hearted respect, her admiration. To his wisdom and to his power, both, she could look up. He was not rich, but the whole range esteemed Joe Wynne as the first of men!

He came rushing up behind her. Now he was riding at her side. He did not catch at her bridle rein, as any fool would have done.

"Joe, go away! I don't want to talk to you, I don't want to see you!" she shouted.

Even speaking against the wind and the beating of the hoofs his voice remained gentle and controlled.

"I'll go away in an instant," said he. "But you're in trouble of some sort, Mary. I wish you'd tell me what it is!"

She saw, now, that having come this far, she would have to go farther. So she nodded her head. And when their horses were halted, and they faced one another, she was amazed to discover that she really could let him see her reddened face, her swollen eyes, without too much shame. For there was nothing smiling, or sneering about him, there was no concealed air of superiority. He was not looking down at her. He seemed merely waiting, honestly anxious to face her worry with her and help to bear the burden of it.

Suddenly her heart flowed out to him.

73

"Oh, Joe," said she, "you're the finest fellow in the world. I love you!"

He flushed, but he made no move towards her, even after he had heard the last word.

"Thanks, Mary," said he. "It means something to hear that."

And he was waiting again.

What a man he was! Truly, the lions are gentle in their ways! Like a glorious lion he looked to her, with his wind-bronzed face, his tawny hair and his flawless, clear blue eyes. No shame had ever come upon him, no shame ever would come. True, there was that terrible fighting rage which drove him berserk, more than once, and made the gunmen shun him like the shadow of Satan. But that was the only flaw in the character of Joe Wynne.

Gentleman Joe, the range called him, and there was not a shade of irony in the expression.

The fullness of her problem came over her. It was more than she could deal with. She needed help. She had to have help. And where could she turn, except to Joe Wynne?

And so the story poured out for him——from first to last. When it ended, he did almost exactly as Steyn had done. He enumerated the points one by one.

And, as he ended, she cried out: "Joe, you don't believe me!"

He answered her, without hesitation: "If anybody else had told me such a yarn, I'd call him a liar, but you've told it—and therefore it's gospel. I believe every word of it."

"God bless you, Joe," said she.

"Now, what shall we do?" he asked her.

"I don't know, Joe," she answered. "I'm trying to think. My mind simply whirls. When I last saw him, he had one of my aprons on, and he was whistling to a blue jay. I suppose it was the very one that he had whistled to before. He was bringing in wood. I think that he's done what he said he would. He's separated Father and me forever. I know that's true! I can't go back, ever! I can't go back!"

"What could he want?" asked Joe Wynne.

"I don't know. Just to make trouble. He hates me because I sent the three of them out to handle him, one after another."

Said Joe Wynne: "A man wouldn't hate you for that.

74

You simply gave him a chance to show his mettle. And there's a lot of mettle in him. That's clear."

They both paused. A mournful lowing came to their ears, and looking up the side of the hill, Mary saw a cow, her head down, standing by a Spanish bayonet, and pouring out her melancholy soul in the foolish way that all cows have, from time to time.

And the whole world seemed tawdry, silly and complicated to her.

"You've got to go back, of course," said Wynne, finally.

"I won't go back," said the girl, "while he's there. Not while that creature is there. I tell you I won't, Joe!"

"You'd better think about your father," said Wynne. "You don't want him left with a trickster like that."

"Poor Dad! But he sided with Speedy against us. He wouldn't listen to me!"

"Your story is pretty hard even for me to swallow," said Wynne, frankly. "I don't know what else to say to you, Mary. But I think that I'd better ride on and see this Speedy. I saw him dancing, the other evening. I couldn't make him out. You say that he smashed up Fat Ginnis and Doc, and even Alf Barton?"

"Yes."

"Alf Barton was one of them?"

"Yes, Alf was one of them."

"Barton is a good man with his hands," said Wynne, shaking his head.

"It's all trickery that Speedy uses," said the girl. "Of course you understand that. It's trickery that gets him along in the world and that's put several thousand dollars in his pocket! He's nothing but cowardly deceit and—"

"Deceit, all right," suggested Wynne, "but not cowardly deceit."

She beat her hands together.

"I'm half mad," she said. "I don't know what can be in his mind. Perhaps there's something about the ranch that he wants. Perhaps he's found pay dirt somewhere in the rocks among the hills. I don't know. I *am* half mad, because I can't understand anything about it!"

Joe nodded at her.

"Perhaps it's something like that," he agreed. "I don't know, either. He's no common hombre. That much is clear as the nose on my face. But I'll tell you what—you're all heated up, Mary."

"I know it," said the girl. "I can't quiet down. I'm shaking."

"Look here," said he, after a moment, "I want you to get down off Whimsy—you've ridden her half to death—and sit down in the shade of the cactus—thank the Lord it's good for something once in its life—and then you're going to stay here a half hour and think things over."

"I don't want to stay here, Joe," said she. "I want to be a thousand miles away from that—that thing—that devil —that Speedy, as he calls himself!"

He sighed. And then she saw that his face was growing sterner and more set. A ring came into his voice.

"You'd better do what I say," said he.

"Joe," he cried, "are *you* turning against me, too?"

"I?" said Joe Wynne. "Never while I live. But sit down here, will you, Mary? Sit down here and think things over. You need to be alone. Not even with me. I'm going to leave you and come back in a few minutes. Then we can make some sort of head or tail of the thing, I hope."

She nodded. It was against her will, but she felt that if she went counter to his advice, she would be left alone in the world.

So down she slid from the saddle and sat obediently in the shadow of the giant cactus, while Whimsy, still panting and blowing, finally began to crop at the sun-cured grasses, and Gentleman Joe rode up the side of the hill.

At last, the peace of the hills began to pass over her, gently and softly. The familiar touch of the wind on her cheeks, the very sun-drenched blue of the sky, and Whimsy, cropping and snorting nearby, jerking up her head now and then to study the wind against enemies—all of these things soothed the girl.

At last, she was suddenly aware that the half hour had passed, and more than the half hour. For the shadow had moved far beside the cactus, and still Joe had not come back. What did it mean?

Understanding leaped and caught her by the throat.

She had said that she would not return home until the boy was gone; and Gentleman Joe had gone to clear the way!

It meant murder; there was no other way. The tramp

76

would be shot, surely; or Gentleman Joe at this moment lay still in death!

—15—

ONCE OUT OF THE GIRL'S sight and hearing, Wynne had ridden as fast as the great black horse would carry him, straight for the house of Steyn.

He was not one to waste time over delicate problems. If tact, straightforwardness and honest dealing could not carry the day, there was always the power of the strong right hand, naked—or with a weapon in it.

And he had the strong hand and he had the weapon to fill it. Whether with the bowie knife which was at his right hip, or the six-shooter on his right thigh, worn well down the leg, he was perfectly at home. He did not fight often, but when he did, blood was spilled, and it was not the blood of Joe Wynne. He was one of those proverbially slow, cool, almost sluggish people who, when aroused, are tigers.

He was half a tiger now as he rushed the horse over the hills, but time, and the wind cooling his face altered his temper before he came to the house of Steyn.

He told himself that there were certain factors clear in the case. The tramp was a criminal, and there for a criminal purpose, exactly what, no one could tell. By driving the girl away from the house, he had achieved the first step in his program. And now, God help poor Arthur Steyn, abandoned into such hands as these.

But to combat against such an enemy needed a cool and clever wit, as well as a ready hand and a strong one. So it was a very sober Gentleman Joe who finally arrived at the Steyn house.

As he came near, he saw Arthur Steyn riding down the trail towards town. He knew the man in the far distance by the straightness of his back, the set of his fine head and the gleam of his white hair beneath the hat and through the shadow of the wide brim.

He was glad of the absence of the old man, for what he probably would have to do this day wanted no witness!

So he dismounted, tied his horse to the hitching rack, and knocked at the front door. No answer.

He went around to the rear of the house, and knocked at the kitchen door.

"Come in!" called a cheerful voice.

He opened the door, and there he saw the tramp seated in a chair in front of the sunny window, with a dishpan in his lap, half filled with potatoes. He was peeling the potatoes with a dexterous speed, dropping the peels onto a sheet of newspaper on one side of him, and the crystal shining, naked potatoes into a pan on the other.

"Hello!" said Wynne.

"Hello yourself, Joe," said Speedy, with friendly familiarity. "Sit down and rest your feet."

"You're a cook, eh?" asked Wynne, taking off his hat to cool his hot forehead, and sitting down in an opposite chair that creaked a little under his weight.

"I'm half a cook," said the tramp. "Want the makings?"

"Don't mind if I do."

The boy dipped with the wet tip of thumb and forefinger into an upper vest pocket, extracted a package of Bull Durham and a sheaf of brown papers, and threw them across to his guest. Gentleman Joe made a cigarette, slowly. He was glad of the time it gave him to arrange his thoughts.

"I thought," he went on, as he folded one end of the cigarette and placed the other between his lips, "I thought that you didn't work, Speedy?"

He threw the papers and the sack of tobacco together towards the boy. They separated in midair, but with one hand, with two movements fast as the pecking head of a sparrow, Speedy picked the articles out of the air and restored them to his pocket.

"I don't raise calluses," he said. "I don't mind work that leaves the hands soft."

"Soft hands are good for cards," said Wynne, tentatively.

"Yes, aren't they?" agreed Speedy. "Or for sleight of hand."

"You know some tricks, I suppose," said Wynne.

"I'm only an amateur. Just a little working knowledge. I pick up a few pennies here and there."

"What I wonder," said the big man, "is that you waste your time here in the Wild West. A fellow like you, Speedy, could dance on the stage, and sing there, too. Easy work, and a lot of easy dough going along with it."

"I couldn't make the grade," answered Speedy. "I'm all right in a bunkhouse or at a schoolhouse dance. The boys and the girls laugh at my little tricks and my dancing steps. But I'm stale compared with the real masters. And you have to be a master to work on the stage."

"I suppose that's true," said Wynne, surprised to find himself rather liking the frankness of the other.

"Besides," said Speedy, "this is my country. That's why I stay here."

"Your country?" exclaimed the other, with surprise. "Born here?"

"Not born here," said the boy. "It's mine by adoption. I did the adopting," he explained, with a grin.

He finished the peeling of the potatoes, scooped up the paper loaded with peels, laid it aside, carried the pan of potatoes to the sink, and washed some water over them from a bucket that stood on the drainboard.

"Here, Joe, be a good fellow and pack in some more water, will you?" he asked.

Joe took the bucket, hardly thinking.

Was it Mary's blue gingham apron that compelled him?

"All right," said he, and strode off to the spring. He came back, wondering at his own docility, and put the bucket down on the floor with a thump; the tramp was building up the fire.

"Kitchen work is pretty snug," commented Speedy, turning.

"Yeah. It's all right when you have somebody to pack the water for you," agreed the other.

"That's right," said the boy. "Carrying water raises calluses."

"Going to keep this job?" asked Wynne.

"Only filling in for Mary."

"Where is she?"

"Where you left her, I suppose," came the astonishing answer.

Wynne rolled his eyes. No, the lad could not have trailed her and overseen anything. He could not have beaten the black horse so much as to get into these togs and this work in time. It was simply one of the lad's acts of mind reading. He must be full of such tricks. Wynne felt full of thumbs.

"What d'you mean by that?" was all he could think of saying.

"I mean," said Speedy, "that she ran to you and asked you to come back here and throw me out of the house. Isn't that right?"

Wynne said nothing. But he bent his brows, for such prescience annoyed him greatly.

"As a matter of fact," he said, bluntly, "you and Mary can't live in the same house."

"Oh, but we're going to," answered the boy.

"You are?"

"Why, yes," said Speedy. "Mary's in a sulk, just now. But she won't leave her poor old white-haired father to the mercy of a rascal like me. She'll come back here and settle down to work like a good fellow. She's not a bad girl. But you people around here have spoiled her a good deal."

Wynne gritted his teeth.

"You'll take that out of her, I expect?" he queried.

"In time," said the boy.

Wynne reached out a hand and laid it on the shoulder of the boy. He expected a mass of sinewy muscle; he was surprised to find that his fingers wrapped right around the bone and touched it. He felt that he could crush the joint, if he made an effort.

"It's time for you to start, son," said Gentleman Joe.

"Don't do it," answered the boy. "Don't start anything, Joe."

"Are you warning me?" asked Wynne.

"You've got a hold on me," said Speedy. "That's not a fair break. We're still inside the house, and that's against the rules."

"What rules hold with a rat like you?" said Gentleman Joe, the berserker madness surging suddenly up in him.

He saw the chest of the other heaving. Why, the fellow was a mere wisp, to be broken, or bent out of shape at will!

80

"Don't do it, Joe," insisted Speedy, with something like pleading in his voice. "Don't hurt me."

"Begging, are you?" said Wynne through his teeth.

"I'm not begging, Joe. I'm telling you not to hurt me. I've been hurt too many times before. I'm tired of it. If you manhandle me, I'll make you wish that you'd laid your hand on a chunk of living hell fire. I'll burn you to the heart!"

"I'm going to teach you a lesson, you sneak," said Wynne.

"Step outside and let go of me," said the boy, "and I'll read your lesson as far as it goes."

"Go outside, then," said Wynne.

And, stepping in—half maddened by his own sense of power, and with a peculiar relief that the magician had so far showed none of his powers of magic, he caught the boy with his other mighty hand, and heaved him above his head. Even then he wondered a little at the limp, unresisting weight that he lifted. Then he hurled the loose body against the door.

The shock tore the flimsy door from its hinges. Speedy crashed with the door on the porch outside, and then rolled headlong down the steps beyond.

Down them he tumbled, and lay flat on his back in the dust of the backyard.

A little whirlpool of wind came walking across that dust and passed the limp, motionless form of the boy.

Wynne, amazed at the success of his effort, realized now with how taut a sense of expectation he had attacked this enemy, small as he was.

Now he rushed on out, and leaned over the fallen lad.

Straight down into the face of the boy he stared, and suddenly the eyes opened, and one eye winked at Gentleman Joe!

It staggered him. He was so amazed that he was hardly aware of the rapid beat of horse's hoofs approaching, until Mary Steyn rushed up to him, crying out: "Joe! Joe! Oh, for God's mercy, have you killed him?"

"Killed him?" said Joe Wynne. "The rat has just winked at me. He's only playing dead, now!"

"Do you mean it? There's blood on his head! You *have* killed him, Joe!"

And she dropped to her knees beside the limp body.

16

WHAT PASSED THROUGH the mind of the girl, all in a flash, was murder, the trial scene, the witness which she and perhaps her father would have to give, and then, finally, the condemnation of Gentleman Joe Wynne, the blasting of the fame of herself and her father, and finally, the execution of Wynne himself.

For such a train and process of thought, it requires only a fraction of a second. All of the pictures flow through the agile brain, and there is time to spare.

She was convinced before she leaned and applied her ear to the breast of the fallen boy. And she heard what she firmly expected to hear—nothing!

The dreadful conviction almost beat her to the ground. She was barely able to raise her ghostly and accusing face towards Wynne:

And she cried: "You can't say that I told you to do it! You can't say that I wanted you to do it!"

He had practically forgotten that wink which, as it seemed to him, he had received from the boy. In his turn, he dropped to his knees and bent his ear at the breast of Speedy. Was it the surging of the blood through his ears, the nameless hammer strokes of terror that overwhelmed his sense?

At any rate, he heard no sign of a heartbeat.

He started back, aghast in turn.

He picked up a fallen arm of the boy—and it dropped with a convincing flop into the dust at his side.

"What have I done!" breathed Wynne.

He rose to his feet; he placed a hand before his face. He could remember, now, the brutal emotions, the triumph, the red rage that had been in him when he grappled with the lad and swayed him above his head like a catapult lifting a stone.

Yes, that was the sort of thing out of which murder flowed! Had he not been warned before? Had not his own father, in his childhood, taken him upon his knees, after one of his rages, and said: "Joe, one of these days, you may be stronger in your hands than you are now, and then God and good advice help you to keep that temper of yours!"

Now the thing had happened.

Desperate faces they turned to one another, big Wynne and the girl.

"Bring him into the house!" she gasped.

Wynne snatched up the burden. Head and heels hung down helplessly, and the arms trailed in a horrible way to the ground. The girl, with a low cry, supported the head and shoulders. And, as she did so, cast from her white face a look of horror and of reprobation towards the rancher.

So they struggled with the burden into the house, to her own room, and stretched young Speedy on her bed.

She was on her knees again, and pressed her ear against his breast. She could hear not the faintest beat, feel not the least pulsation.

"Do something, Joe," she exclaimed. "Help me to do something!"

"Brandy," he managed to say. "That ought to be good for something."

She fled on wings to get it, and Gentleman Joe looked about the room with the wild and haggard glance of one about to die, peering his last upon the fair world. He noticed the neatness of the white curtains, and the gay rug on the floor, and his own picture standing there on the dressing table beside the photograph of old Arthur Steyn.

Well, that was what he would have expected her room to be like, except that he had not dreamed that his picture would be there. No, he had not guessed that he had already stepped so far into her heart.

But what did that matter—to a murderer—a gallows-bird?

She was back, coming through the door with a rush. It was Wynne who raised the limp head—leadenly heavy!—while Mary Steyn parted the teeth and held the glass.

The lower jaw sagged exactly as she had left it. The liquor which she poured in streamed out again.

She groaned with horror!

Then, pushing the head back, it dropped with a jerk, as though the neck were broken, over the curve of her strong arm. And still the mouth gaped open! Into that mouth she poured the brandy.

"He's swallowed it! He's swallowed it! Oh, thank God, Joe!" she cried. "Put him down at once!"

Gently they lowered him to the pillow, and the loose head turned a little to the side, while the last swallow of the brandy leaked out again onto the cambric.

Mary Steyn collapsed upon a chair, her hands pressed over her face.

As for Gentleman Joe, he could do nothing, think of nothing, except that he had thought he saw the boy wink after falling to the ground—and that he was not dead—dead as a doornail!

Mary was up again.

This time, she caught a mirror from the dressing table, and held it before the ugly, gaping mouth of Speedy. After a few seconds, she withdrew the glass and looked at it; no trace of moisture appeared—the breath no longer passed those lips, it appeared!

She moaned with terror and grief. There was still another test.

She pushed up the eyelids—dull and glassy the eyes looked back at her—no, not at her, but at eternity, it appeared. And most convincing of all, when her touch was gone, slowly, little by little, the eyelids closed again, as though of their own weight!

Well, that was the final touch.

She turned upon her big companion.

"He's dead, Joe," she whispered.

"He's dead," said Wynne. "And I've got to run for it!"

"Yes," she said angrily, "run for it, and let the body lie here on my bed! They'll think that I struck him from behind with a club or something. They'll have *me* in jail!"

The selfish injustice of that remark stunned him.

"Except for you, he *wouldn't* be there," said Wynne.

"Ha!" said she. "Are you blaming me?"

"You ran to me and told me a yarn that you knew would

make me ripe to murder him!" answered Gentleman Joe, honestly enough.

She was honest, too, at heart, and she answered him: "I know that's true. I shouldn't have gone to you. I told you that, too. You saw I was hysterical. You shouldn't have listened. But you *did* listen. You didn't give him a chance. You caught him where he didn't have a chance to get away. You attacked him without warning there in the kitchen. Answer me! It's true! It's true, isn't it? You began to manhandle him before he ever suspected that you meant to touch him!"

His frank honesty made him answer:

"Yes. I got him by surprise. I knew that he was a tricky snake. Once I had a grip on him, I wouldn't let him go."

"Because you were afraid!" she taunted. "Oh, Joe, you've done a horrible thing! When I saw his poor little limp body flinging through the air and hitting the ground like a limp wet rag and the great bulk of you running out after him! Oh, Joe, when I saw the size of you and the size of him, I felt that he was dead already. That you could smash the life out of him with one stroke! And that's what happened! How could you do it?"

He pushed a hand across his brown forehead.

"I don't know," said Wynne. "I think it was because you'd told me what he did to Ginnis and Doc and Barton. Barton's as big a man as I am, and stronger, if anything. When I met the kid, I sort of expected magic, and tricks, and that sort of thing. I don't know what I expected. I just grabbed him and—"

He paused, shaking his head.

"What did he do?" she gasped.

"He begged me not to hurt him."

"I don't believe you!" she cried.

He looked helplessly at her. Much as she meant to him, there was something besides love of her in his heart, at this moment.

"He begged me not to hurt him," he said. "He asked me to let go of him and fight fair, in the open, outdoors. And he said that if I hurt him without giving him a fair chance, I'd wish that I'd sooner put my hand on a chunk of hellfire, because he'd burn me to the heart!"

"He'd say that. If he lived, he'd do that!" said the girl.

"I know he would. He was all fire—and devilish cunning—but he was brave and cool—he was a hero, Joe!"

He shook his head, looking hopelessly at her.

"You're going to get enthusiastic about him now that he's gone and out of the way," said he. "But he was a worthless tramp, when you met me over there on the trail."

"I was just plain hysterical," said she.

"He'd made you that way," insisted the other.

Suddenly she stamped.

"Joe Wynne," she exclaimed, "are you trying to *justify* what we've done?"

"I'm only telling the truth," said he. "You know the shape you were in, when I met you."

"I see," said she, coldly. "You're going to throw the entire blame on me!"

"I didn't say that," he answered her.

"You implied that," said the girl.

"It's not true," he answered, frowning blackly.

"What do I care what you think is true, or untrue?" she cried suddenly. "There he lies—dead! Such a man never came on this range before. Oh, Joe, you've done a terrible, terrible thing! And he was only half your size, too!"

"You've got it well centered on me," said Joe Wynne. "I'm a brute and a bully because I did the job you wanted me to do."

She grew red—then instantly white.

"You did the job that I wanted you to do when I was beside myself," she said. "Now go and save yourself. I've seen enough of you today, Joe Wynne."

"I'll stay here!" said he.

Her anger raged out.

"Leave me alone with him," she commanded. "Go wherever you please—but I don't want you in this house—when the law comes!"

His sense of outrage made him sweep up his hat and stride to the front door.

There he paused and turned.

"You mean it, Mary?" he asked. "You're sending me out of the house?"

"Yes," she cried, frantically, "and out of my life."

17

Joe Wynne strode out.

The flimsy door of the house trembled a little under the weight of his strides, but then the screen door slammed, she heard him go down the steps from the front porch, and then the jingle of his spurs, a small, ghostly sound, as he went to get his horse.

Last, the black horse and the gallant rider cut across her view through the window.

He had taken her at her word, and ridden out of this trouble, out of her life, indeed!

She was left alone there, with a dead man. And she heard the buzzing of a great blue bottle fly as it thumped audibly against the pane of the closed window, then left the light and went with droning flight, circling around the room.

She ran to the window and jerked it open.

Why did she do that? For reasons that she hardly could have put into words, but it was a ghostly feeling that she dared not remain there alone—imprisoned both with the dead body and the spirit of his vanished life!

Leaning on the windowsill, she drank in the open air with closed eyes—closed because she was seeing herself, turning the glance back upon her soul.

A frail and sinful creature she saw, full of pride, impulse and vanity. What good had she done with her days? No, all the good had been done to her, and she had merely accepted with an open palm!

Here was Speedy gone, because of her.

After all, she wondered, how had he really harmed her? It was she who had cast the challenge down to him, and he had answered her in such a way as she had not dreamed possible. He had beaten her champions, and struck down her strong men of battle. He had laughed his way into the house, and laughingly still, he had jested and smiled her out of the house. He had done as he had said he would do—placed a great gap between her and old Arthur Steyn.

Now, when the old, kind man returned, would he not remember that she was not of his blood, after all? Yes, he would remember that, and she could only blame herself.

She saw a wasted, foolish life behind her; she saw ruin and empty loneliness before her.

And then—a faint groan sounded from the bed!

Was it possible? She turned. She would have flung herself out of the window to the ground just below, except that there was a dreadful feeling that something would seize her from behind before she got through.

But now, she saw a movement in the horribly open mouth of Speedy; she heard the groan come from him.

She could have dropped to her knees, to give up thanks to God, for that change in the course of events. Straightaway, she ran to him. She took the brandy flask again. She raised his limp head, and as she did so, the eyelids slowly rose, flickering.

She poured a dram down his throat.

"That'll do you good, Speedy!" she stammered.

And again hot thankfulness swept over her as she saw the swallowing muscles of the throat languidly at work.

He coughed and stirred with his whole body. He gasped for air, and began to push himself erect with his hands.

But she put her hand against his breast, and held him down, easily—he who had crushed three strong men, one after another, unscathed by them all! Yes, he was really frail. She could feel the sharp angle of the collar bone through his shirt. He was only a slender boy, but the great spirit in him was what made him significant.

"Lie still, Speedy," she said. "You're all right. You're going to be better, God willing. Lie still, Speedy. You'll be all right—if only—if only—"

Her voice trailed away.

If only his fall had not fractured his skull! That was the sentence which she had been unable to complete!

His eyes were steadily open, now, and clearing. His breath came deeply, regularly.

Suddenly he started up from the bed, up from under her hand.

"You sneaking coward, Wynne!" he gasped.

And reeling, he put out his hands before him, and staggered.

She caught him under the pits of the arms. She steadied him. He was so weak, that his head sagged far over upon one shoulder.

"Joe Wynne has gone," she said. "He won't be back. You're all right, Speedy!"

"He grabbed me!" said Speedy, his breath whistling through his teeth. "And I'll burn him to the heart for it. He didn't give me a fair chance—I'll—here, here, what am I talking about!"

She could see full consciousness return to him, see him collect and gather himself, as it were. Relief and admiration mingled in her. Yes, once this lad took to the trail of great Joe Wynne, she would not give much for the chances of the larger man!

She said: "Are you all right, Speedy?"

"Why, hello, Mary," said he. "Are you back again?"

"I'm back again, Speedy," said she, her voice trembling.

He nodded, frowned a little, and then raised his hand to his head. It came away thick with blood. On her pillow the same bloodstain appeared!

"I remember, now," said he. "It was Joe—well, never mind. Does Wynne happen to be around here?" he asked, casually.

She saw the brightness in his eyes.

"He's not here," said she.

"Well—that's all right," he murmured.

She broke in: "I know all about it. I came riding up, just in time to see you fall, Speedy."

"Yes," he said through his teeth. "He slammed me, all right!"

"It's no shame to you," said she. "He had to admit that he didn't give you a fair chance. Speedy, tell me how your head feels? Is there a terrible splitting pain from your hurt?"

"My head's all right," said he. "As right as can be."

"I'll wash the cut," she said. "Let me do that, Speedy."

Said he: "Thanks, Mary. But my head's all right. If you

don't mind, though, I'll borrow a horse from you, if I may."

He was quite himself again. She could see that. And the truth came over her.

"You're going to find Joe Wynne," she said.

"Joe? Not at all. I'm just going out to get a little air. I want to see more of the hills around here, Mary. I want to have a look at things and—"

She barred his way at the door, feeling helpless, and therefore all the more desperate.

"You're going to hunt down Wynne," she declared. "And you're going to kill him, Speedy! Admit it! Admit it!"

"Not kill him," said Speedy. "He's a big man—and I suppose that he'll lick me again. But I've got to see Joe Wynne. Mary, will you stand out of the way?"

"I won't stir. I don't dare to stir, Speedy!"

"I'll slide out the window, then."

"Speedy!" she screamed.

He turned back to her.

"Yes, Mary?" said he.

She wondered at the quiet of his voice. The most terrible raging, roaring accents would have been less terrifying than his calm.

"Speedy," she implored, "listen to me one moment!"

"Certainly," said he. "There's no hurry—about what I have to do. It's simply on my mind, you know."

"If there's somebody who deserves killing, it's I," said the girl. "I went weeping and raging down the trail. I met Joe. I told him about things—the way that they seemed to me. I think I begged him to throw you off our place. And Joe came straight back to do what I'd asked him to do. It's my fault. You'll see that it's my fault? Speedy, for God's sake don't let any more harm come out of miserable, wretched me!"

He stood with his hand resting lightly on the sill of the window.

And he turned his head and looked gravely, considerately at her.

"You wanted to have me killed, Mary?" said he, in the gentle tone that dissolved her with terror.

"I was more than half mad," said she. "I didn't know what I was doing, Speedy. Try to believe that."

"But what had I done to you?" he said. "I'd joked and

laughed at you, and told some huge lies, and made a silly bet with you, and I thought that the whole thing was a game between us. And then—you go down the trail to find a man to—"

"To murder you!" she cried. "I know that was what I wanted. God forgive me, Speedy. I never dreamed before today how bad I am! Tell me that *you* forgive me, too! Try to tell me that, Speedy, or else—"

What could she say at the end of that futile sentence?

She heard him saying: "Joe Wynne means a lot to you, doesn't he? And—"

"It isn't Joe, alone. It's the whole wretched business that comes out of my fault! It's all my fault! I'm ashamed. I'm sick about it."

"If it means a lot to you," said he, "I'll stay here. I won't go trailing him. Only, if he comes around the house while I'm here today, or across my trail after I've gone tomorrow—"

His raised voice he checked suddenly.

She was running across the room to him and catching him by the hands.

"That gives me one day of grace," said she. "And now I'm going to try to make the most of it, and ward off trouble that's ahead of us all. Five minutes ago—if anyone had told me that I'd be hoping again so soon, I would have laughed. I thought that you were dead—I thought that Joe Wynne and I were murderers! Oh, Speedy!"

"Stuff," said the boy. "Forget about that, will you?"

"I shall. I'm glad to. Only, you won't go near Joe Wynne?"

"I've told you that I won't," he exclaimed, irritably. "And I mean what I said. I suppose I can swallow what Joe did to me. But now, let's fix things up so that your father won't guess there's been trouble, when he comes home. The back door was knocked off its hinges, as I remember it."

She shook her head, smiling faintly.

"I won't lie to Father," she said. "I've told him lies enough before, but never again, after today. I begin now to tell the truth. He's to know every black thought that was in my heart, and just what happened—every detail!"

— 18 —

THEY HAD SEVERAL THINGS to do together, however.

First, she washed the wound in his scalp, and found it a very shallow scratch, to her infinite relief. A sizable bump had grown up around it—that was all. There was not even need of adhesive tape to close the lips of the wound!

After that, they put the door back on its hinges, and tacked into place a panel which had been broken outwards by the shock.

"I'll tell Father," the girl said, "but there's no need why he should know."

They had barely finished this work, when a boy's voice shouted outside the house: "Hey, Mary, are you in?"

She opened the door. A freckle-faced lad slid off his horse and grinned at her.

"Hello, Billy," said she. "What's the news?"

"Ma wants to know will you and Mr. Steyn come over to our house Tuesday night. That's tomorrow. There's some sort of a doings."

She shook her head at once.

"I can't come, Billy," said she. "I'm sorry, but I can't come."

"Ma'll take it hard," said he, indifferently.

"Come in and have a cup of coffee," she invited. "Or some buttermilk. I have some good cold buttermilk, if you like that."

"Not me," said the youngster. "I've gotta get along, anyway. It's a long ways to the Jenkins place and to Wynne's."

"Are you going to Wynne's?"

"Yes."

"Wait a minute, Billy. I want to send a note to Joe."

She hurried to pen and paper and wrote:

"Dear Joe,

He came to a little after you left!

There's only a shallow scratch in the scalp, and a bump, thank heaven!

Forgive me for the way I talked and acted. Everything is my fault.

One thing more, and this is the most important of all. Speedy is going to be here for a few days, I think. And while he's here, please don't come near the place. You can guess why.

He seems to think that he didn't have fair play when he met you, and I think there's blood in his heart on that account. For everybody's sake, stay away.

Thank you with my whole soul for helping, or wanting to help.

Mary."

This she sealed and gave to the boy, who was talking busily to Speedy in the back yard, and Speedy was making five small, bright pebbles dance up from his hands, and shower down through the air again in a mysterious fashion, through many designs.

Billy shouted with joy, and exclaimed with wonder.

He hardly gave the girl a glance, when she handed him the letter.

Then into the saddle he whisked, and off he galloped, waving back at them, and yelling: "You know, Speedy, you don't forget that you're gunna teach me how to do that!"

"I won't forget," said Speedy. "You bet that I won't!"

And he turned and smiled at Mary.

"Billy's a good kid!" he said to her.

And the sudden answer jumped to her lips: "So are you, Speedy!"

All at once, they were laughing together, merrily; and a moment later, she wondered mightily at herself.

It was hardly half an hour or an hour before that she had still thought him the most complicated and complete scoundrel under the wide round of the sky. And now she found him the best of companions!

He was sitting in the kitchen window, later on, swinging his heels, chatting to her, as she went about her work.

"Why did you start doing the kitchen work?" she asked

him, looking down at the shining heap of newly peeled potatoes.

"Well, that was to make you suffer a little more. Make you think that the house could get along without you, pretty well. That was the idea, at least."

She nodded, frowning a little.

"And to drive in the wedge between me and Dad?" she asked, without looking at the boy.

"I'd threatened I'd do that," he admitted. "You'd made me pretty hot, Mary."

"Suppose," she asked, looking straight before her—though the wall was only a foot away. "Suppose that you don't feel so angry with me now—?"

"I'm all over that," said he. "Every bit."

"Suppose the other way—that you *hadn't* gotten over being angry at me?" she suggested.

She held her breath, waiting for the answer.

"Why, he loves you, Mary," said the boy. "And you love him, don't you?"

"Father? He's a saint. I worship him!"

"Well," said Speedy, "when two people love one another, they can't be kept apart, very long."

She looked askance at him.

"You haven't answered me, really," said she.

"About what?"

"About what harm you might have done—if you'd kept on being angry with me."

"I don't intend to answer," said Speedy. "Chiefly because I don't know. I never know very well, from one day to the next, what I'll do."

"I know," said she. "It's the strangeness of every day that you like to have around you."

"Yes, that's part of the idea," he admitted.

"And wandering, and new faces and all of that?"

"Yes, all of that."

"But you're a tremendous liar, Speedy," said she.

"About the greatest in the world," said he, with complacence.

She looked oddly at him. Truly, he was unlike all the other men in the world.

"Well," she said, "you're convincing, too. Even that cock-

and-bull story that you told Father last night about your Uncle Tom, and all that rot—"

"Did you believe it?"

"Yes, every word, till you winked at me."

"Yes, that gave things away," said he.

"But why did you wink?"

"I don't know," said he. "It just occurred to me that that would make the job harder and more interesting, to have you scoffing on one side of the table, and yet to make your father believe, on the other side of the table."

"More interesting because it was harder?" she queried.

"That was the idea."

"And afterwards, Speedy, when we were alone in the kitchen, here, and you made the bet—and you talked about—"

She flushed, but she looked straight at him.

Then Speedy laughed.

"You know how it is, Mary. I wanted to make you pretty angry, and I was succeeding. I wanted to pay you back for sending those three thugs out after me. That last one was a hard nut to crack—but he fought fair to the finish!" he added, scowling.

"You made me angry enough, Speedy," said she. "I think that I understand you a little better. Not well, but a little better."

"You know, Mary," said he, leaning a trifle towards her, "I don't understand. By the way, it looks as though I might win that bet from you, after all!"

She laughed with the utmost frankness.

"It won't be hard for me to pay," said she.

When Arthur Steyn rode back from town and put up his horse, he heard singing from the kitchen of his house, and coming in, almost on tiptoe, he found Mary working between stove and sink, and the lamp burning brightly on the table, and Speedy, in a corner, working hard at a churn, and keeping time with the strokes to the song that he was singing.

He stood by the door for a moment before he was noticed, for the girl had joined in heartily on the chorus.

Then they both noticed him, and greeted him cheerfully. And he smiled, standing there by the door, leaning his shoulders against the wall, standing as tall and as straight as any youth.

"Time is a great doctor, eh?" said he. "Speedy, you're working that churn too fast. The butter will be rancid, if you don't look out."

Late that night, Speedy sat by lantern light in the big dining-bunk room, and he wrote rapidly:

"Dear Mr. Pierson,

I've arrived, been introduced formally and informally, too, and looked the lay of the land over, and am now stopping for a few days in the Steyn house.

Steyn is a charm.

The girl is not a wildcat at all, but gentle as a lamb—when her claws have been trimmed.

As for the terrible gunmen, I see that you've exaggerated. People are not watching her, as you say, and it seems to be the general impression that she's to marry a big handsome fellow called Joe Wynne. Gentleman Joe.

I hope to do away with that impression in a few days.

As for the two thugs who know about the girl's fortune and want to marry her on account of it, I have only met one—Rudy Stern. He's a handy man, they say, with his starboard cannon and his port side, too. However, time will tell which one of us will drop. It will mean a fight to the finish, because he's a devil for punishment and has a long memory.

The second man you told me about, the worst of the lot, has not showed his face around here.

He's not popular. People shiver and look over their shoulders when his name is mentioned. So I'm waiting for him anxiously, and I dare say that he'll call on me when he knows that I'm staying here in the house. When Mr. Six-card Wilson, as they call him here, turns up, I appoint myself a reception committee of one.

I will keep you posted.

My regards to you, respects to Mrs. Pierson and love to Charlotte.

Sincerely yours,
Speedy."

–19–

Two DAYS LATER, Mary Steyn paid her debt and went to the dance in the Nixon schoolhouse with Speedy. He was to leave the very next day, he said, but odd words came from old Steyn just before they rode off towards the schoolhouse.

He came out and stood at the head of the boy's horse, a lump-headed mustang which was, nevertheless, well regarded on account of its rocking-chair lope.

Said Arthur Steyn: "Speedy, are you running on a very strict time schedule?"

"No," said the boy.

"Then promise me something."

It was exactly what the boy had wanted.

"I'll do whatever I can," said he.

"Then promise me to stay here another week," said Steyn.

There was so much seriousness in his voice that Speedy leaned a little from the saddle and through the dull twilight looked fixedly at the other.

"All right," he said.

The old man sighed. He seemed to feel such relief that his straight, rigid body drooped a little.

"That's good," he added. "Go have a good time, you youngsters."

They rode off together; the sunset grew tarnished and more dim, the stars began to come out, first Jupiter, blazing when nothing else in the sky had force to show, and immediately afterwards, steel-blue Sirius shone through the mistier lower air, then Arcturus to the east thrust through, and Orion, finally, was printed big in the west.

All things took life about them. The rocks wavered with the swaying lope of the horses, the Spanish bayonets became living silhouettes, like Indians at watch with war-spears raised and ready for the charge. In the air there was a faint smell of alkali dust mingling with the breath of spring flowers.

They came to a long rise, very dark, the horses stumbling among broken rocks. So they drew down to a walk.

"It's only five miles more," said the girl.

Speedy laughed.

"I can stand that," he said. "But you see that I'm not much good in the saddle."

"Nobody can do everything," she answered, philosophically.

But he could tell from her tone that it was hard for her to make the allowance. In her eyes, if a man could not ride a horse he was hardly a man. Through those first miles, she had been actually fighting to retain some respect for the figure which swayed and jolted even to the easy gait of the roan mustang.

"Horses take learning," said he. "I've ridden the rods or the blind baggage more than I've handled horses."

"You've beaten your way on the railroads?" she translated. "Speedy, why d'you do it? It's not right!"

"You mean," he corrected her, "it's not what most people do. But it's right for me."

"Is it?" she challenged. "Right for you to be a loafer and never lift a hand at work?"

"There are a lot of others like me," he responded. "And the ones who don't drift around a good deal—well, you know, they're apt to explode, now and then, and break things up. Travel is an outlet; safe-cracking, crooked gambling, all kinds of thuggery are outlets, too. I keep myself out of jail by keeping on the road."

She looked closely at him through the darkness.

"Why do you tell me all of these things, Speedy?" said she.

"Why shouldn't I?" asked the boy. "I want you to know me."

"You're only showing me a part of the picture," she insisted. "There's a lot more to the picture than what you tell me."

"Well," he answered, "you want to make me a mystery. That's what we do with everyone we first meet. But there's no mystery about me. All of us are a lot alike. You change the wrinkles in the face, or the pitch of the voice, put your high-stepper in a cowpuncher's saddle, or Europe and champagne in a puncher's system, and we all average out about equal."

She digested this thought for a moment.

He seemed serious enough, and yet she had a feeling that he was making game of her. She nearly always had that feeling, when he was talking, unless she could see his eyes, and that was impossible through this dim light.

Finally she said, "You're as different from the rest as a horse is different from a deer. You know it, Speedy. Don't pretend that you don't know it."

"You've known a lot of people," said he, as though making an admission on her side.

"I've known a few. I've seen a lot of punchers and ranchers, and such, about your age. Oh, you're different, Speedy. You know that you're different."

"The other night," he went on, changing the subject a good deal, "you hinted that people who've been fond of you have had a rough time of it. You remember?"

"I said a lot, the other night," she replied. "None of the boys ever gets serious about me now, Speedy."

"Because they're afraid to?"

"It's a hard thing to talk about," said she.

"I'd like to know," he persisted.

"I don't make you out, Speedy," she said with the utmost frankness. "But if you—"

"Why, I'm going to marry you, Mary," said he, and laughed a little, in a way that turned the words into a jest. "And the way to marrying you seems to be dangerous. If you're friendly, I'll expect to be told why."

"It's a queer thing to talk about," said the girl. "But I have to talk to you. I saw you lying dead, once. At least, it was the same to me as though you were dead. Ever since, you're like somebody out of the grave, to me. And I thank heaven that Joe Wynne hasn't a rope around his neck! By the way, Joe will be there tonight, I suppose. How'll you act towards him?"

"The way he acts towards me," said the boy, instantly.

She considered this, found it hard to comment on, and then continued:

"About people who've been pretty close to me—I mean, about what we were talking of—"

"Suitors, eh?" said he.

"Well, boys that took me a lot to dances, and that sort of thing," she answered. "Three years ago, Sid Winchell paid me a lot of attention. Sid was a good fellow—a little wild, but straight as a string. One day there was a shooting scrape at a crossroads. Sid was picked up half dead. When he got out of hospital, he left the country. He's never come back."

"And never sent you word?"

"He sent word to me, right enough," she answered, grimly. "He wrote me a note when he was out of the hospital. It simply said: 'I hope that I never lay eyes on you again, and God help the next man that gets interested in you!' That was the word he sent to me."

"He was a hound," said the boy.

"No, but he had his walking papers from somebody in a pretty high saddle," she said. "His people live ten miles from here; they've never seen his face since that day. He was told to go, and he went. I don't know who told him, but that must have been what happened."

"That's hard on him," said the boy, carelessly.

She was angered by his indifference.

And she went on: "Toppy Lancaster was pretty interested in me, about a year after that. We went around a lot together. I didn't think about Sid's disappearance so much. Toppy and I went everywhere. I used to see him two or three times a week. And—"

She paused.

"Got engaged?"

"No, but I liked him a lot. And then, one day, Toppy's father heard loud voices in the barn, and one of the voices belonged to Toppy himself. There were several shots fired, and Toppy came walking back to the house holding his right arm against his side; he was dripping blood. And the strange part of it was that he wouldn't say who had had the fight with him. But as soon as he could ride, he left the county—and he's never come back!"

"Hello!" said Speedy.

And he whistled.

"That was pretty bad," went on the girl. "And still I

didn't connect him with what had happened to Sid, until I had a note from Toppy Lancaster. He wrote that he was bound for Alaska, but he said that he was not intending to dig gold for me. He said that I'd cut his throat for him, and he only wished me bad luck. That's the last that I've heard from Toppy. Nobody else around here has heard from him, either, except his parents. And they don't speak to me, any more."

"That's two in a row," said Speedy. "Any more? Or were the boys beginning to be pretty suspicious, by this time?"

"They were suspicious," she replied. "Toppy's folks did some talking. They let people think that I was responsible, some way. But only about ten months ago, Red Sam Marvin showed up. I suppose that you've heard of Red?"

"No. Famous man?"

"He's a rough fellow," she said, "but he's all right. He's so rough and tough that he didn't care what the talk was about me. He liked me all the better because there might be some danger. And I liked him. He could talk about all sorts of places and people. He'd been everywhere and done everything. And so we went around together a lot. And then he had the same thing happen to him."

"Shot up?" asked the boy.

She paused. The silence weighted down the air.

Then she said, softly: "Red was shot dead in his own house. His body was found a day or two after the killing. That was the third man."

"And that was enough for the rest of the boys?" asked Speedy.

"That was enough," she agreed.

She went on: "They're nice to me. They dance with me. But nobody calls on me alone, you can be sure. I suppose that's why we've come to the habit of giving the Sunday parties."

They surmounted the slope.

Before them was the thin sickle of a new moon, and by earth shine the dim, small globe of the moon showed in the arm of the brightness.

"Well," said Speedy, quietly, "I'm putting in my claim, tonight, to be number four on the list!"

–20–

THEY GOT TO THE SCHOOLHOUSE at nine-thirty, when the dance was barely beginning. Such affairs have a late start; some of the people come thirty miles to them, over rough mountain trails. However, there was already a good number at the schoolhouse. Saddle horses stood at the hitching rack, drooping their heads, prepared for a long wait. Others were tethered under the shed where the schoolchildren put their ponies in the winter weather, and inside of the building, the orchestra had commenced; the scraping of feet could be heard at a great distance.

When they dismounted, Mary Steyn took a brush out of her saddle bag and brushed off her divided skirts. She passed it to Speedy, and he made himself as fit as he could. The day before, he had bought new clothes in the town, to take the place of his tattered rags, which had been part, and a necessary part, of his role on arrival at the Steyn ranch. Then they dusted off their shoes. Toilets did not have to be elaborate at such a dance as this. Good dancing and good nature were the two requirements.

But, on the way into the schoolhouse, she touched the arm of her escort, and looking vaguely toward the west, where half of Orion's splendor was sinking beneath the horizon, she said: "Why do you do it, Speedy?"

"Do what?" said he.

"Let yourself in for so much trouble? You don't care a rap about me, Speedy. I don't want you in trouble, anyway."

He said: "I care a lot."

"I know," she said. "You care for the game."

She nodded, and walked on again. And he followed her half a pace behind, watching the way she held her head, and the curving line of neck and shoulders. He noticed her

102

walk, too, and the easy spring of it. For his part, he was feeling those eight miles, but she was as fresh as though the day had just begun.

The arrival of a crowd of a dozen or so, all together, covered the entrance of the girl and Speedy, but not entirely. He was aware of bronzed faces of girls and youngsters turned towards him. It seemed to him that the orchestra gave an extra lift to its music, also.

There was a violin, a cornet, a slide trombone and a drummer who had all sorts of appliances for making noise, and for four people, no one could complain of the volume of that orchestra. It whooped and roared and rasped, and for high moments, there were solos by the violin, here and there, and from the nasal, whining cornet, also.

But that did not matter.

Mary Steyn stepped into a whirl of dancing from the start. And never had there been so much conversation with her partners. Sometimes they almost forgot their steps. It was Speedy they wanted to know about.

How long was he staying at the Steyn place?

Where did he come from?

Was he only a tramp?

What had he done to Fat Ginnis, Doc and Alf Barton?

Was he a "good fellow"?

She put these questions off with smiles and half answers.

The longer she watched Speedy circulating in the crowd, the surer she was that she had not made so much as a beginning of his acquaintance. Now he seemed in his element. She watched the happy faces of the girls he danced with. She watched the gliding ease of his dancing. Even big red-faced Ruth Doran seemed graceful when she had the tramp for a partner. And everyone was glad of him. Tramp or not, in that country, in that rough part of the range, a man who was a man was worth any amount of name and gentility.

Then came the first crisis. Big Joe Wynne entered the hall with Maude Willoughby. They danced. He left his partner and went smiling through the crowd, giving a word here and a hand there. No girl would ever have to be ashamed of Joe Wynne, as a husband. And was not that the chief reason for which girls married? To have a man they could be proud of and one they could trust in the making of a home?

So thought Mary Steyn, as she watched Joe.

And then, there he was, bowing in front of her, taking her out to dance.

It was a waltz. Like most very big men who know the step and the rhythm, Joe waltzed well. But she almost forgot the music and the step, for he began to talk seriously, at once.

He said: "Look here, Mary. I had your note and I stayed away. But now I want to know how long I'm to stay off the premises."

She answered:

"I don't know. As long as Speedy's with us."

"And how long will that be?"

"He wanted to go tomorrow."

"But?"

"But Father begged him to stay on for a while."

Joe almost stopped in the middle of a step, then went on haltingly.

"Your father likes him, Mary?"

"Father will sit and watch him all through an evening, as though he never saw that sort of a human being before."

Joe Wynne said: "Tell me why you warned me off the place, Mary."

"Don't command me!" she snapped.

"Don't be ugly," he returned. "I have a right to speak short and sharp. What does he mean to you?"

"He's amusing," she said.

"You like him a lot, and he's a tramp!"

"Joe," she said, "let's talk about something else."

"I have to talk about him," said he. "Mary, I love you. I mean to marry you if I can. And when you take up with a fellow like Speedy, it worries me."

"Are you proposing to me, Joe?" she asked him.

"You can call it that."

She wondered at his matter of fact manner, but he added: "You've always known that I'd ask you to marry me, sooner or later."

"You know what trouble it may let you in for?" she demanded.

"I know," he said. "I know about Winchell, and Lan-

104

caster, and Red Marvin. I know all about 'em. But I can take care of myself, I think."

She liked him better, at that moment, than she ever had liked him before, and with her usual frankness, she said so.

"There's never been a time," she said, "when you meant so much to me, Joe. But I can't say yes to you. I like you and respect you more than any man I know. But I don't love you enough to marry you."

His answer surprised her.

"Well, I expected that, too," said he. "I don't expect you to say yes at once. We'll see later on. I'm going to have another chance later on and it may turn out better. I'd like to ask you, though, if having Speedy in your house has made any difference?"

"A week ago," she said, "I would have been glad to say yes to you, Joe. But Speedy has turned everything topsy-turvy in my mind. It isn't that I like him such a lot. But he's new. He makes everything seem different. I'm like a person in a foreign country. I want to learn the language before I make up my mind about the people."

He was not angry—only gravely concerned. And just then the music stopped abruptly, and swung into a Spanish dance.

There was only one dancer, and that was Speedy. He had thrown off his coat and vest. He had wrapped a great scarlet sash around his waist, and now, as he whirled with clattering, complicated steps down the hall, the end of the sash stood stiffly out, fluttering like a flag in a strong wind, while the dancer wound himself into the length of it, and out again; never did he allow it to touch the floor.

At each spectacular maneuver, people shouted. Enthusiasm grew tense. People leaned forward and beat time, and swayed with the movements of Speedy, and lifted their feet in a foolish manner as though in sympathy with those lightning steps.

"Is that what you want, Mary," said Joe Wynne. "A professional dancer and entertainer?"

She looked up at him.

"He may be more than that," she said.

"I know that he's a good fighting man, but he's a fox, too," said Joe Wynne.

"Perhaps he is," said she.

She began to be coldly angry with Wynne.

He went on:

"Look at his face. He wouldn't be doing anything else in the world. This is heaven for Speedy!"

And, in fact, the face of the boy was flushed, and his eyes were shining. He was fairly laughing with joy as he danced.

She drew in her breath, sharply. And then she shook her head.

"You want me to be ashamed of him," she said. "Well, I like him well enough to be ashamed if he did the wrong thing. But I'm not ashamed. He's this way. He's different from the rest."

"That explains him as a hobo, too," said Wynne.

"You don't understand," said she.

"I don't want to!" answered Wynne.

"Well, Joe," she replied, "I can't be logical. There he is. You see him and hate him; I see him and like him."

"Tell me," he shot at her. "Is he the sort of a man you could marry?"

Perhaps he had overstepped the mark of even a long friendship, but now she looked up slowly and met the eyes of Joe Wynne fairly and squarely.

"Well," she answered, to herself as well as to him, "I don't know. I don't know anything about him, or what I would do."

She saw Wynne turn pale.

"I thought so," he said. "You know about me, but you don't know about him—dancing in his shirt sleeves to please —well, let it go."

"Yes," she said, "we'd better let it go. There's something else to think about, now!"

She nodded towards the door.

"By the Lord," muttered Wynne, "that's too much! He's showing his face again. Something has to be done about it!"

For, in the doorway, stood a man whose face, indeed, did not seem meant for public showing. It was a downward face, long and lean, and yet with profound wrinkles in it that flowed from the eyes and past the mouth, like the wrinkles in the face of a bloodhound. The nose was broken. Half of one ear had been bitten, or shot, or cut away and left a ragged stub. He had lips which showed no red; his eyebrows were so blond that they appeared scalped. And his eyes, like clouded agate, had no color more than a mist. He was tall, very lean, with abnormally narrow shoulders and abnormally long arms and equally long fingers.

That was Six-card Wilson, "Six" for short. And wherever he appeared, trouble was sure to follow.

–21–

THE NEXT MOMENT, Speedy was dancing with Mary. And the first thing he said to her was:

"Who's that beauty who just came in, the fellow with the half ear?"

"Six-card Wilson, the gambler, thug, gunman and general all around crook!" said she.

She felt an electric shock go through him.

"That's Six-card?" said he.

"Yes, that's the man."

"People seem to like him pretty well, then. There's the second nicest girl in the room dancing with him."

"She'll dance with anybody who's exciting. Something may be done about Six tonight."

"Your big friend Joe Wynne may do it," said he.

"Don't sneer at Joe," said she.

"I'm not sneering at him," answered the boy. "I was just thinking what a fine out he'd have with Six, as you call him."

And he laughed.

He was dancing slowly, like silk. To dance with him was to float downstream. Never before had she known what motion could be.

She said: "Will you keep away from Joe Wynne this evening?"

He answered her: "It's the one thing in the world that I won't do!"

And the anger in her swelled and made her exclaim: "Then I hope that he hurts you!"

"No more than he can hurt a mist in the wind," said the boy, contemptuously.

"You're as sure of yourself as—a murder in the dark!" said she.

And, after saying that, she asked him to take her back to her chair.

He obeyed at once. He stood beside her, smiling, calm, letting no one suspect that there was anything wrong between them.

"D'you want me to leave you for a while?" said he.

"I do," said the girl.

"Thanks," said he, and turned immediately away, as the dance ended.

Why should he have thanked her, she wondered, except to impertinently make out that he was as glad to be away from her as she could be to have him go?

Rage grew hotly in her.

As for Speedy, he went out of the room into the hall where there were many pegs along the walls for the hats and coats of the schoolchildren. On this night, every peg was crowded with three or four hats and coats, one heaped on top of the other.

Through that room went Speedy, and on the outer doorstep he stood, balancing on the sill, while he made and lighted a cigarette.

"Hot, in there," said a husky, whispering voice.

He turned his head a little. A small chill went down his spine before he answered. And there he felt, as much as saw, "Six" Wilson.

Such a sensation went through the boy as he never had known before since once, as a child, he had won a bet by sleeping in a supposedly haunted house.

And, for the first time in his mature life, he could say that he was really afraid of another man.

Yet this was the man whom he should know better. This was the man whom he really had come to find. As for the second fellow who knew the secret of the girl's fortune, Rudy Stern hardly counted. He was no more than a child in a grownup's game.

This was the keystone of the arch. Wrongly handled, the arch might fall, but it would crush all beneath it.

"Yeah," Speedy found himself saying, "it's hot in there, all right."

"Let's go outside and have a smoke, you and me."

"Sure," said Speedy.

And he sauntered down the steps at the side of the tall man.

They stood in the black shade of a group of young pine trees. Another dance had begun. Music, the rushing of feet, the clanging of voices poured out about them, but rather dimly, the sound diffusing like the light from the open doorway, in the greatness of the night.

Six Wilson was making his smoke, then lighting it, and snapping the match away with a flick of his fingers. Half of the arc which it traced was red-streaked; and then it went out.

Said Six: "I ain't introduced myself, kid."

"The world introduces you, Six," said the boy, "and that's a shame."

"Why is it a shame?" asked Six, without emotion.

"Because," said Speedy, "a name's as good as a stone to stumble over, I've noticed."

"You ever stumble that way?" asked the big man.

"Yeah, and bruised my shins, too."

"If that's all you hurt, you're lucky," said Six. "All those suckers in there, they'd like to take a crack at me."

He laughed.

His laughter, like his voice, was no more than a whisper, a raucous whisper, with no sign of vocal cords in it.

Was he a vain, egotistical fool, and no more—except for being an expert crook and gunman?

The boy waited. Two-thirds of his fear already had departed from him.

"Maybe one of them will stand up and take a crack at you," said Speedy.

"Maybe one. Not two," said the thug. "Joe Wynne, he might go to heaven that way. There ain't nobody else made that big."

Speedy said nothing.

"Thinking about yourself?" asked the big man.

"Yes."

"Thinking that maybe *you* might take a crack at me?"

"Maybe."

"Not yet," said Six. "You ain't got over the chill of my face and my voice, yet. It always paralyzes the boys, the first gunsight of me, so to speak."

He laughed again.

Swiftly Speedy revised his opinion. This man was much more than an egotistical fool. Far, far more!

"What's the big idea between you and me?" asked Speedy.

"I thought that we might get acquainted," said Six.

"All right. We're acquainted," said Speedy.

"My line," said Six, "is cards. After that, a little safe-cracking, and after that I got a few side lines. What's your line, kid?"

"My line," said the boy, "is chatter."

"Yeah, chatter for what? Green goods?"

"I'm not particular. I deal a hand, now and then, myself. Trust my hands more than I do my eyes, just like you, Six."

The ghostly laughter of the big man whispered again at the ear of the boy.

"That's pretty good, at that," he declared.

"All right," murmured Speedy. "Besides, I have a few side lines of my own. I've used a jimmy, and I've blown a safe. I can cook well enough to make soup, too, in a pinch. My soup has given a lot of people indigestion."

"I'll bet it has," said Six. "You sound to me like a good kid."

"Good?"

"Yeah, useful."

"I'm useful to myself," said Speedy.

"Never travel double?"

"Never."

"Might make a new habit."

"I don't make new habits."

"You're young. You can learn."

"Can I?"

"Yeah, if you got the right kind of a teacher."

"Like you?"

"Yeah, like me."

"Break the seal, Six," said the boy. "Let's see what the letter's about."

"Good news."

"Money, eh?"

"Big!"

"I like it big," said Speedy. "Go right ahead."

"It's got a tag on it."

"There always is."

"A tag and an even break."

"For you?"

"Yeah, for me."

"Go on, Six. You whistle a pretty good tune. What's the tag?"

"You marry."

"Do I?"

"Yeah, you marry."

The idea was clear enough, now.

"Money?" asked the boy.

"Yeah, a heap."

"What kind of a face?"

"A beauty."

"Why don't you marry it yourself, Six?"

"Because I've got my name wrote on my map. And my map is all wrote all over my name. God never made two faces like mine. He never was so real careless as to do that. He done me for an object lesson, just to make other people feel thankful."

And he laughed again.

He would laugh at death and damnation in the same way, the boy knew.

"What's the direction of the lady?" asked the boy.

"You want her name? You want all my cards on the table?"

"Sure I do."

"And then do you play with me?"

"If I like her, I might."

"If you don't, Speedy, it'll be hell on you."

"I've been in hell before. I'd rather be there than with most women that I've met."

"This is different. This is the kid inside—Mary Steyn, is what I mean!"

Of course, Speedy was prepared for the name, and still it sent a shiver through him to hear her mentioned by that whispering voice. It was as though something unclean had touched her.

"Without me," said the big man, "you're poorer after marrying her than you were before. With me, I tie you and the kid to a flock of the long green. About nine million bones."

"And you get half."

"Fifty per cent is all I get. You and her can live on the rest."

"I've got to think," said Speedy.

–22–

THE REASON THAT THE BOY had to think was because the picture as the crook painted it for him stretched clearly and plainly to the eye as far as the mind could reach.

There would be no difficulty, once Six Wilson was on his side. For Six would take care of Rudy Stern and any other objectors who happened to have more knowledge than was convenient. As for an estate of nine millions, it readily cut into halves each of which was amply big enough to make all concerned happy as kings.

"You could get her," Six Wilson was saying in the same grisly whisper. "You could get her easily enough. No trouble about that. I seen her turning up her nose and getting into a tiff with you a minute ago. She don't often do that. She don't lose her temper. And if she gets mad at you, she'll marry you. That's the way that it always works. I never knew a woman in the world that come anywheres near gettin' real mad at me. Not the way I mean now. But you got an inside track with that girl."

Still the youngster did not answer. Still his thoughts were spinning in a swift circle.

Even Pierson, perhaps, would not be offended. He would get his commission, just the same, for the handling of the big estate as it passed to the heir.

And still the boy could not bring himself to the point of acceding. He had dealt with rough men before this, and

men whose hands were far from clean. But never w̶̶̶
a ghoul as Six-card Wilson.

"Mind you," Six was saying, at this point, "if you marry her without getting my tip, it won't do you any good. You'll never collect the boodle. All you'll have on your hands will be a flock of trouble. She's actin' tame, now, but when she kicks over the traces, she smashes things up!"

"Six," said the boy, "it's a big compliment that you're paying me. Why haven't you offered the same thing to other fellows who were interested in Mary Steyn?"

"Because I tried 'em out," said Six Wilson, "and none of them was the right stuff. The sort of a deal that this is, it's gotta be with a man that's able to take care of himself— and that'll keep his word of honor when he's given it once. And you're that kind, I reckon."

"Am I?"

"You are. You'll say yes or no, and you'll mean it."

"I say 'no,' then," said the boy.

"You say no, do you?"

"Yes."

"Then God help your unlucky soul, kid," said Six-card.

"It puts you against me, does it?"

"It puts me against you," said Six, "till you get out of this part of the country. Move off of this range, son, and you'll be healthy, wealthy, and wise. Stay on this range, and worse'n smallpox is likely to take hold on you."

"You'll plug me, eh, the way you plugged three more of Mary's friends?"

"I ain't the only one that's shepherding Mary Steyn," said Six Wilson. "And I ain't the only one to do the shooting. Fact is, shooting is a thing that I hate to do, till I'm drove to it. Don't you go and drive me, son! Gimme a chance to play square with you. Gimme a good chance to help you to a fine slice of loot. You'll find me the best partner in the world, and the worst kind of a burr under the saddle blanket if you say 'no.' "

"I've said it before, and I stick to it," said Speedy.

"You don't like my style?" suggested the big man, his whisper hissing more softly than ever.

"Can't give you reasons," said Speedy. "I play this game my own way. That's all."

"Well, good for you," said Six Wilson.

ne added: "Watch your step. Walk
way. Because there's gunna be a lot of
ahead of you."

me this," said the boy. "I play a lone hand against
. Do you play a lone hand against me?"

"You're damn right I don't," said Six, "I play with a
stacked deck, and a few extras up my sleeve. Now, whacha
think about that?"

And he laughed again.

Breaking off that laughter, he said: "You fool, here I've
gone and put everything face up on the table in front of you,
and you turn your back on it. You got no brains. I'm glad
that you didn't agree to make the split. Now, mind you, I
leave you be till tomorrow. But tomorrow has gotta see you
on the out trail!"

And he walked rapidly away through the darkness, until
the silhouette of his moving figure was blotted out behind
the corner of the building.

Then Speedy made a new cigarette, and as he scratched
a match to light it, realized that perhaps he was a fool to
hold a light by which another might shoot safely and accurately out of the blanketing darkness.

He saw that danger and difficulty had increased for him
on every side.

In one direction he seemed fairly secure—and that was
towards the Steyns. On the other hand, Joe Wynne and Six
Wilson were heartily against him, and both of them were
names to conjure with.

He went back into the schoolhouse, where the dance was
less cheerfully in swing than it had been before, and a small
cluster of men, with gloomy, resolved faces, had formed
around Joe Wynne in one corner of the room.

Speedy managed to disengage Mary Steyn from a tangle,
and she said at once: "Let's get out into the open for a
moment."

He took her straight outside, and she began to walk rapidly up and down under the pine trees. Then she said:

"D'you know what?"

"Well?"

"They're going to make a pass at Six Wilson, tonight.
Joe Wynne and the rest!"

"That's pretty brave," said he.

114

"Are you sneering?" she asked him.

"Look, Mary," said he. "Don't walk around with a chip on your shoulder all of the time. What's the use of that?"

She disregarded the remark.

"Why don't you go in there and help them?" she asked.

"Because they need guns to handle Six," said he.

"Well, you can help them use the guns," she insisted.

"I never mix in gun plays; I never packed a gun in my life," said Speedy.

At this, he heard her gasp, and then her angry, controlled laughter reached him.

"What a fool you think I am, Speedy," said she. "Do you expect me to believe you?"

"Yes, I do."

She laughed again.

"I'm not a half-wit," she assured him.

"You make me out what?" said he.

"Oh, you know what you are," answered the girl, her anger increasing with the passage of every moment. "You never handled a Colt in your life, I suppose?"

"No," said he.

"That's because you prefer a Smith and Wesson, then," she suggested.

He overlooked her irony.

"You think I'm a killer, Mary, don't you? You're wrong. I never put a man in hospital in my life."

She had been pacing up and down beside him all of this time, but now she turned about and stamped.

"We can't get on together," she declared. "I thought that you and I could be frank with one another, at least!"

"We ought to be able to be frank," said he. "But you've tried to read my mind, and you're all wrong about me."

She broke off their talk with another gasp, of a different sort.

"Look!" said she.

The ground on which they stood rose a little above the level of that on which the schoolhouse was placed, and they could look over the edge of the steps, through the two doors and down the middle of the dance floor, with a slightly spreading vista. Into that vista now stepped five men with leveled guns. And in front of them was Six Wilson.

He had raised his great hands above his narrow shoulders, and his ugly face never turned from the place where Joe Wynne stood.

The full flood of the light from the lamp that illumined the room seemed gathering upon the fine brown face of the big man, now. It was the pride of the dance committee that they had managed to get hold of one great lamp with a huge, circular burner, and swinging this from the ceiling of the schoolhouse, they flooded the entire room with light. Speedy could see the glittering pendant at the bottom of this lamp gently oscillating back and forth from where he stood. But nothing else was important inside the place, except the faces of Joe Wynne and of the criminal who had ventured so rashly into the hands of the men who stood for law and order.

And still there was a half sneer upon the face of Six Wilson.

All the place was filled with silence, until Wynne said in a voice that was easily audible to the two listeners outside: "You thought we were a lot of sheep, Wilson, but we're a little better than you expected. We've got you, Wilson, and we're going to put you where you'll keep for a while!"

"Good for you, Joe!" whispered the girl. "Oh, Joe Wynne, you're a man!"

"Yeah. He's a regular hero," commented Speedy, indifferently.

"He's a lion, and you know it," said the girl. "And he's caught Six."

"He and four to back him," said the boy. "They've tagged Six, but don't think that they've caught him yet. The game isn't over, if my guess is worth a rap."

They could see that Wilson made no attempt to answer the words of Joe Wynne. And then they heard Joe Wynne giving orders—two men to fall behind the captive, one to stand on each side of him.

"And don't move those hands of yours, Six Wilson!" he directed, sharply.

The hands were not what Six moved. Instead, he dove straight at the knees of Wynne and the man next to him.

Wynne fired; with what result could not be judged, but he and another went down, rolling with Wilson on the floor. Then another shot boomed heavily, through the screeching of the women and the shouting of the men—and the schoolhouse was blotted with darkness.

—23—

OUT OF THE BLACK DOOR of the building, a monstrously tall form emerged, bounded to the ground and raced straight at the two.

"Catch him, Speedy!" whispered the girl, through her teeth.

She made no move to run from the danger. And then Six Wilson was upset by sheer bad luck, for his toe caught under a projecting root and he rolled heavily to the ground, crashing into the bushes near the feet of Speedy. One groan from him, and he lay still. The dull night light glimmered upon the revolver which he still clutched loosely. He lay limp, and the weapon was offered freely, as it were, at the feet of the tramp.

Speedy stooped and picked it up, and a whole column of men charged down from the schoolhouse, roaring through the doorway like water through a dam.

"Here he is!" someone yelled, driving straight at Speedy and the girl, then realizing that Speedy did not fulfill the dimensions of the tall bandit, he yelled: "Where'd Wilson go?"

Mary Steyn strove to give the proper answer.

But Speedy had glided behind her, and now, from the rear, he clapped a hand over her lips, while he shouted, loudly: "That way! That way! Around that corner of the school. Hurry like the devil!"

"You yellow hound, why don't you hurry yourself?" shouted the angry questioner. "This way, boys!"

But others, seeing the dim gesture in the distance, already had turned and were running on the false trail.

Up rose, with a stagger and a lurch, big Six Wilson.

"Kid, you're white," he gasped.

And then he bounded straight for the line of tethered horses. Even in his haste, he did not forget to pick and choose. A big shimmering gray was his choice, and leaping into the saddle, he jerked the big horse around with force enough to stagger it. Then off he shot into the night.

The girl bit hard upon the hand of Speedy, but he endured the pain without flinching.

For that matter, there was no need that she should cry out. Others had heard the galloping of the horse, others had seen the vanishing outlaw, and nearly every man at the schoolhouse, young enough for such work, had flung himself on horseback for the pursuit.

Then Speedy unhanded the girl.

She turned upon him, dead silent with fury.

"That's it!" she exclaimed. "That's what you are, at last! You're one of Six Wilson's gang! I'd rather—I'd rather stay at the side of a leper. Speedy, get out of my sight. You poison the air for me!"

"I'm taking you home, first," said he.

"I'll die, first," said she.

"Maybe you will," said he. "But I'm taking you home."

"A Wilson gangster!" she breathed. "Faugh!"

"Mary," he said to her, "you gave me your word that you'd go to this dance with me and go home with me after it. And you'll keep your word if I have to take you by the elbows and throw you on a horse."

He heard her panting, and moaning with helpless rage.

Then she said: "I've given you my promise. Oh, I'm a fool, I'm a fool! But we start now, and we go fast."

"We'll start now," he admitted, "but we'll follow my own pace. Come along!"

The dance was breaking up, but slowly. Someone inside the schoolhouse had found some smaller lamps and candles which were lighted, and by that light the women huddled together, and an excited cackling rose, and flowed away uselessly into the night.

So, unobserved, Speedy and the girl found their horses, mounted and took the return trail.

They rode ten minutes in black silence. Then he began to

whistle and kept up the cheerful music for another ten minutes at least.

Then, at last, she said "Speedy, I ought to ask you if you've got any explanation to offer!"

"No," said he.

And he began to whistle again, a tune which was hatefully familiar to her.

> "Julia,
>   You are peculiar;
>   Julia,
>   You are queer—"

Her blood rose; and it ran hot indeed.

And another mile drifted behind them. He rode in a leisurely fashion. She wanted to eat up the distance quickly, at the full racing speed of her horse. But Speedy dallied along. He paid no heed to her. He kept on the even tenor of his way, and his whistling rose into the night air as sweetly as the song of a bird.

She hated him with a passionate intensity. She hated him as she never before had loathed any living creature.

The horrible face of Six Wilson arose in her mind; and she placed it on the shoulders of the gallant, lithe figure that rode beside her.

Finally, in a choked voice, she said: "D'you mind going on a little faster. I'm not very well. I want to get home."

"You may not be very well, Mary," said he, "but you're a lot better than I am. You know, I never rode this far in my life, before. Sitting down won't be my idea of a good time, for a month."

And he laughed with the utmost cheerfulness as he spoke. She stared at him, feeling suddenly helpless. There was no measuring rod by which she could estimate and judge him. He was a monster quite outside of her ken.

And now a gentle, warm wind came up the valley and brought a sweetness of very distant pines about them. They must have been many miles away, but the scent was unmistakable in the air.

"Speedy," she suddenly exploded, "after all I *don't* believe it! I'll go counter to my own eyes and ears!"

"Will you?" said he.

119

"Yes!" she cried.

"About what?" he asked her, gently.

She was angered again.

"You know perfectly well," said she. "About Six Wilson and his horrible crew. I don't believe that you're one of them!"

"I didn't say that I was," said he.

"Tell me definitely that you're not!"

"You wouldn't believe me," said he. "I'm a gunman and a killer and a member of Six Wilson's gang. Why, Mary, you're the wildest guesser in the world. I'm a regular lamb, that's what I am!"

She was almost as furious as ever, because of his air of indifference to her opinion. But she had a great desire to laugh.

"Tell me, please, Speedy," said she, "why you didn't let the boys get their hands on that wolf!"

"I'll tell you why," said he. "I don't like a fox very well. It's a sneak and it's a thief, and it's a murderer, too. But when the hounds are running after it, my sympathies are all with the fox!"

"Wilson is the worst man in the world!" she told him.

"He's a bad one," admitted the boy, "but he'd just made a mighty good play. That shooting out the lamp—that dive for the floor—oh, I liked the look of that!"

There was a ring in his voice.

"You admired him?" she asked, coldly.

"Didn't you?" he asked her.

"Ask me if I'd admire the writhings of a boa constrictor!"

"All right, Mary," said he. "You don't like the looks of Six Wilson, and he's not pretty, at that. But he's got a useful pair of hands, and he's got a useful brain in that ugly head of his. I thought he was a goner; and yet I guessed that he would make a last play, of some sort. I wonder how that stone-headed fellow, that Joe Wynne you like so well, managed to miss a pointblank shot like that?"

"Joe? He was taken by surprise," said the girl.

And she was glad that the night covered the heat that she felt in her face.

"Does he seem such a glorious man to you now?" he asked her.

"I wish that you'd leave Joe alone," said she. "We were talking about you and Six Wilson."

"I couldn't throw that fox to the dogs, not when he lay at my feet, done in by a bad break in the luck after he'd won his way out," said he. "By the way, here's a keepsake for you. Here's Six Wilson's gun."

He passed it to her and she, after a moment, took it, and fingered the notches which had been cut into the stock of the revolver. She shuddered, and yet she was pleased. It was a prize of war and Speedy had won it fairly enough.

"If you wanted him to get away, why did you take his gun?" she asked.

"I wanted him to get away, but not through the door of murder," said the boy.

And suddenly she was silenced again.

Then they came to the house. The moon was up, whitening the old shack, giving it a little grace, ennobling the hills which were its setting.

They put up the horses, stripping the saddles from the sweating backs of the animals. Then they stood by the corral fence and watched them drink, plunging in their heads almost as high as their eyes.

As they stood there, he said to her: "Mary, if I should disappear one of these days—it's not because I'm sliding out; it's because I may be called on business. Understand?"

She looked at him, and saw that he was grave.

"You're afraid of something!" she said.

"Not at all. But there's business in the air."

She said nothing, as they walked back to the house, but at the door he said goodnight, and told her that he was going to stay outside for a walk alone; to watch the moon, he said.

And she, looking at him rather wistfully, put out a hand and touched his arm.

"Speedy," she told him, "I'm through hating you—for tonight!"

"I'm glad of that," said Speedy.

"Do something for me," she begged him.

"Of course I will."

"Be careful, and be good to yourself."

121

HE WATCHED THE DOOR close after her, and then, turning away, he stood as if irresolute, snapping his fingers together, his head bowed in thought.

For he was in a profound quandary.

It was true that he had befriended Six Wilson, on this night, but Wilson was not a man to be turned from an important object by such an act of kindness.

Now that the bandit had revealed something of his mind to a stranger, the stranger had become a grievance and a danger because he had not fitted himself into the scheme that was in Wilson's mind.

What would Wilson do?

Well, men who have shed blood very often, are likely to turn again to the same method of solving their difficulties. It is a keen knife and severs easily many tough knots.

Now the position was too easy for Six. He was a hunting wolf, and the boy was a quarry that remained in a fixed place. Whenever he pleased, the giant could swoop down on the house of old Steyn with some of his gangsters—and the life of Speedy would be blotted out.

So, revolving the matter deliberately in his mind, the boy saw that there was only one thing remaining for him to do— cut himself adrift from the Steyn house and hunt the hunter until he had disposed of Six Wilson forever.

Now that he had reached a conviction, he started briskly towards the barn. Old Steyn would not grudge him the loan of a horse unasked, he was sure. And a horse he must have to pick up the swift trail of the bandit.

As he passed the corner of the house, he saw a shadow stir behind it—guessed, rather than saw it from the corner of his eye, and his side leap was as swift as the spring of a startled cat. But already there was a hiss at his ear and the falling of a slender shadow. Then his arms were jerked tight against his sides by the pressure of the lariat pulled home. The force of it flung him to the ground.

He did not cry out. There was no one near to bring him help except an old man of seventy, and Mary Steyn herself.

So he lay grimly, and then pushed himself to a sitting posture. Three men stood by him, over him.

"Get up!" growled one, in a subdued voice.

He rose.

"Three of us for a job like *this!*" said one voice. "What the devil is the matter with the old man to send out three men for one boy's work?"

"Right about face and march!" snapped another.

Speedy turned obediently about and marched.

He was guided over the rim of the hill to a place where four horses stood, with reins thrown—big, strong-looking animals, standing over plenty of ground.

"Get on that horse, kid," came the order.

"Boss," said Speedy, "if you don't mind, I'll walk. I'm already a little on the raw side!"

A rumble of laughter greeted this remark.

"Don't seem to be such a bad kid," said one. "Hop on that hoss, boy, and stand in the stirrups, if you want to. But we ain't got three men's time to waste on you."

Speedy mounted without further argument, and, as soon as he was in the saddle, a bandanna was tied around his eyes.

"It's no use, boys," said he. "I'm new to all of these mountains. I won't remember the trail, no matter where you take me. Around the corner is lost for me."

"Shut yer face," he was advised. "You got too much lip, kid."

And presently the horse was trotting under him—a long trot, eased by the silken play of supple fetlock joints. Speedy knew that he had high-priced quality between his knees, now!

Hard rocks rang under the iron-shod hoofs of the animals. Then they scuffed through sand; then they were climbing, climbing, climbing.

After a time, one of his guides said: "Kid, know where we're takin' you?"

"Sure," said the boy, "to a soft bed and a long sleep."

Someone chuckled at this.

"What makes you think it'll be a soft bed?"

"Any bed will be soft for me tonight," said Speedy.

They chuckled again.

"Fresh, ain't he?" was one remark.

"Like paint," said another. "Deacon, does he know why we grabbed him?"

"Kid, you know why we grabbed you?" asked the Deacon.

"Sure," said the boy. "Because I'm a Van Astorbilt in disguise."

They laughed again.

"You're gonna get some of that paint took off of you, kid," said the gruff-voiced Deacon. "But you're makin' a pretty fair start. I like to see 'em start high. They got that much further to fall!"

A few moments later, the horses halted. Someone sang out: "Hello, strangers!"

"Strangers yourself, you wall-eyed, mutton-headed figure four," said the genial Deacon. "Come in here and take these hosses."

"I can't take 'em, Deacon. I'm on the job out here."

"All right, stay there. I hope you catch a hunderd degrees of moon-frost, you damn pumpkin-head. Strangers, he says. Strangers, eh! The blind bat, he ain't got the sense of a one-eyed toad. Come on, boy."

A few steps later on, the horses halted again, and this time the boy was told to dismount. He slid gladly to the ground, and stretched himself.

"This way," said the Deacon.

Speedy was led forward. His shoulders rubbed either side of a doorway, and he sensed through the bandanna the shining of a not over-strong light.

"Here he is," said the Deacon. "I dunno why you sent three for this layout. Any pup could of done it as well alone."

Then he added: "Shall I peel this?"

"Yeah, peel it off him," said the expected whisper of big Six Wilson.

The bandanna was jerked forcibly from the head of the boy, and he found himself blinking at a lantern, behind which sat Six Wilson, in the act of attacking a great slab of fried meat. A pint cup of coffee steamed beside his plate, and and a huge wedge of cornbread was also at hand.

He was staring out of his clouded, unhuman eyes at the boy.

"They got you easy, did they?" asked he.

"Yeah. They got me," said Speedy. "Any objections if I smoke?"

"Cool and easy right from the start," observed the Deacon.

"Shut up," said Six to the Deacon. "Who told you to shoot off your face, eh? You got him easy, did you?"

The boy was rolling a cigarette. He lighted it as the other said: "Yeah. Just done a stand behind the house, and the fool of a kid walked right in on us, and we doused a rope over him. That was all. He was so scared that when he lay on the ground he didn't even bawl for help!"

He laughed at the memory.

A broad, red man was the Deacon, with immense and beetling brows, and a great hook of a nose. The corners of his mouth twisted upwards when he smiled. He was not handsome, even in the presence of Six Wilson.

"Too scared to bawl out, was he?" asked Six.

"Yeah. I'm telling you."

"You're a fool," said Six. "Is he scared now?"

"He don't know who you are," said the Deacon, "or he'd be on his knees, I'm tellin' you."

"You got sawdust for brains," said Six Wilson. "This kid knows more about me than you do."

"Yeah?" said the Deacon, dubiously.

"You're all ivory," said the chief. "You oughta be sawed up and sold in chunks for billiard balls. You ain't got no live blood in your bean. That's one of the troubles with you. This is the slickest kid in the country. Fan him."

"I fanned him right off the bat. Whacha think I am?"

"Then gimme the gun that you got off of him."

"I didn't get no gun."

"You lie," said Six, "you beef-faced son of trouble, you lie! Gimme that gun you took off to him!"

"I tell you, I didn't take no gun off of him."

"I tell you again, you lie like a rat!"

"You talk, Six. One of these days, you're gonna shoot off your face too much."

"You'll tame me down—you'll quiet me, will you?" whispered the uncanny voice of the chief.

"I tell you, I didn't find no gun on him!" roared the Deacon.

"Didn't he get no gun off you?" asked Six, pointing his horny finger at the boy.

"No," said Speedy.

"Why didn't you say so before we got into a fight about it?" demanded Six.

"I don't care when you start eating on one another," said Speedy. "You're nothing out of my pantry, either of you."

"No?" murmured Six, with a gleam coming into his dull, whitish eyes.

"No," said the boy, shrugging his shoulders.

"Gimme five minutes alone with him and I'll learn him some manners!" suggested the Deacon.

"Aw, shut up, shut up! How many times I gotta tell you to shut up?" asked Six Wilson.

Then he said in his gasping voice, like the sound that a fish sometimes makes, as it struggles on the shore: "Whatcha do with my gun, kid?"

"Hey, did he have your gun? Where'd he get your gun?" asked the Deacon.

Six Wilson carved off a quarter of a pound of beef and stowed it all in his face by dint of some pushing. Then, his eyes bulging with the effort, he slowly masticated the immense mouthful. His head moved up and down as he worked. And his stare fixed with a painfully thoughtful intensity upon the face of the Deacon.

The latter waited, a little uneasily, until the chief had swallowed a portion of his mouthful.

Then said Six Wilson: "He got it by takin' it out of my hand. Now whacha think of this kid that didn't need three of you to take and hog-tie? You're crazy with luck, that's all. The only reason that I sent you three down, was because I expected him to chaw you up. And I wouldn't of missed you none. You only had a pile of luck, damn you!"

– 25 –

Speedy had time to look around him, and what he saw was a half ruined shack. The stars peeked through a great rent in the roof. The stove leaned upon rusted and decaying legs, two props of wood helping to support it, and the very flooring was eaten away by time in two large gaps. A single lantern gave the smoky light to the face and the meal of the chief.

"I hear you talk," the Deacon was saying. "Talk don't buy nothin'. I mean, you sent me after the kid; I wished that I'd gone alone!"

"You, kid," said Six Wilson, "whacha do with my gun?"

"Gave it away for a keepsake," said he.

"Gave it—away?" shouted Six.

He half rose from his chair. It was strange to see the grotesque creature moved in this fashion. Sweat actually formed upon his forehead.

"You didn't know," said he, "that that was the fastest and straightest shootin' gat that ever was packed by a man, did you?"

The boy shrugged his shoulders.

"You didn't tell me, Six," said he.

Six Wilson stowed another great carving of meat in his mouth and masticated it with difficulty. Soon the desire to speak came over him and he gave signs of his impatience by glaring at the boy and drumming rapidly upon the table with his bony fingers.

At last partial speech was possible, and it came in a thick, dim roar.

"You been and made a fool of yourself. Know that?" he shouted.

The boy shrugged his shoulders again.

"What's all this lead to?" he asked.

Six Wilson glared at him again, with invincible dislike.

Then he said to the Deacon: "What happened, you lucky hound?"

"Aw, just what I said," answered the Deacon. "Just went down there and cached ourselves behind the house and waited for this here tiger, that you'd been tellin' us about. He was talkin' to Mary Steyn in front of the house."

"Was he?"

"Yeah, he was."

"What say?"

"I dunno."

"Take the cotton wool out of your brain and remember!" boomed Six Wilson.

"Well," said the Deacon, "the kid didn't say much. Something about if he disappeared, she was to think that he'd gone on a business trip."

He roared with laughter.

Even Six Wilson smiled, saying: "Yeah, he went on a business trip, all right."

"He sure done that," said Deacon, and they roared in unison.

"What else did she say to him?" said Six.

"Why, she went inside, and the last thing she says is he's to do something for her, and he says he will, and she says, be careful, and be good to himself."

"Is that what she said?" asked Six Wilson, scowling intently on the speaker.

"Take it or leave it. That's what she said."

"She ain't the kind to soft-soap nobody," declared Six Wilson, in deep doubt.

"Take it or leave it," answered the Deacon again, "I heard her say it, with a throb in her voice, too."

"Go on and get out of here," said Wilson. "Get out of here, then. I gotta talk to the kid."

"Where do I chow?"

"You got the whole range to eat in," answered the brutal leader. "Don't bother me. I'm busy."

The Deacon, grumbling loudly, left the shack.

And then, for a time, Six Wilson went on with his meal, watching the boy at times, and at times glancing away in the profundity of his speculation.

Speedy, in the meantime, had found a stool which he sat upon, uneasily.

But he composed his face and strove to show no doubt or trouble.

The meal of Six Wilson did not occupy a great space in time, to be sure. But the moments dragged, rather naturally, for the boy.

At last, Wilson poured himself his third cup of coffee, and wiped his greasy mouth on the back of his hand. He began to roll a smoke and gather his darkest frown.

"Kid!" said he.

The boy answered nothing.

"Kid," said Wilson, "we gotta talk."

Still Speedy said nothing.

"Dumb?" asked Wilson, his voice lifting to the question.

"Waiting to hear what you'll talk about," said Speedy.

"You couldn't guess, eh?"

"No. I don't care to guess."

"Ain't interested, eh?"

"Look," said the boy, making a gesture. "You've got me. You can slam me with a club or a knife or a gun. All right. That's that. I'm not worrying. The world will get on without me, pretty well, and I'll have to get along without the world. That's all."

He even smiled, and the other regarded him over the rim of the cup as he swallowed down his last, scalding portion of coffee. Then he pushed the cup away, with a rattle, and said:

"You make it simpler than it is, son," said the tall man. "This what I'm talkin' to you about is the difference between heaven and hell."

The boy considered him for a moment.

"You hear me?" roared Six Wilson, suddenly.

"I'll tell you a story," said Speedy.

Wilson nodded and grinned.

"I wanta hear you talk some," he agreed.

He crossed his legs and settled back.

"Make that story damned good, and pronto," said he.

"I'll make it good," said the other. "Open the flap of your ears, will you?"

"They're open."

"How long can a man live without food or water, in hot weather?"

"Four days," said the other, with much certainty.

He even made a wry face. "I could tell you a story about five days on the desert," said he.

"This story is about a boxcar. A refrigerator car that was locked down, and left on a siding, a thousand miles from nothing, with me inside of it."

"You got me interested from the start," remarked the chief.

"You know Arizona in August?"

"Yeah, I know; hell in December, too. Go on."

"It was a brand new car. I guess that was why it had been sidetracked in the middle of nowhere."

"I know," said the bandit. "Got no brains, on railroads. Just meanness."

"That's right," agreed the boy. "Well, there I was inside of the car, and I had along with me one pocket knife. Small blades, but good steel."

"You cut your way through, eh?"

"I cut for five days and five nights," said the boy. "It was slow work. I got dizzy. The knife was always slipping in the blood that ran out of my hands."

"A thing that I've noticed a lot of times," said Six. "The way blood's slippery."

"It's slippery. all right," said Speedy. "Finally, I flopped."

"Went out, eh?"

"Yes. I broke the last blade of the knife, and that made me pretty tired."

"You waked up, though."

"You see me sitting here," said the boy. "I woke up and looked at the work that I'd done. It was easy to see, because it was painted red all around. Only the bottom of the grooves was white where the last cutting had been done. I had no knife, but it seemed to me that those grooves were pretty deep, so I backed up across the width of the car and let drive and hit it with my shoulder—and fell right out into the daylight."

"And found water, eh?"

"I told you that siding was the middle of nowhere. I started hoofing down the track. I was pretty dizzy. It was August, in Arizona."

Six Wilson licked his lips.

"I'm gunna have another whack of that coffee," said he, and was instantly as good as his word.

"Go on," said Six.

"After a while," said the boy, "a train came along. That was the end of the fifth day. I stood in the middle of the track and waved my hands. But the train kept on coming. I saw the engineer leaning out the window and laughing at me. I wasn't very trim in my dressing, just then."

He nodded at the memory.

"Go on!" said Six Wilson.

"Well," said the boy, "when I saw he was coming right on through me, I first thought that I would let the train finish me off, because that way would be so much quicker. But then I decided that I had one good reason for wanting to live."

"To find that engineer, eh?"

"He was a *big* hound," said the boy, "and he laughed till his ears wiggled. So I side-stepped and saw the train go roaring by me, filling my eyes with dust and cinders. Then I humped along down the track. It was ten miles to water."

"Did you ever meet up with that engineer?" asked the other.

"It's a small world," commented Speedy. "I met him in Denver, on the street. I tapped him on the shoulder and asked him if he remembered me. And the surprising thing was that he did, Six, though I was all dressed up at the moment."

"What did you do to him?" asked Six, grinning like a man thirsty for cold drink.

"That crook was fond of cards," said the boy. "That's what I did to him."

"Busted him?"

"I busted everything about him and put him on the bum. He got a gun and came for me, but I had all the luck. That sounds like boasting, though."

"It's all right with me," said Six Wilson. "But what's the point of this little story?"

"I thought you were talking about hell," said Speedy.

Suddenly the other leaned forward and nodded.

"All right," he said. "If I was bluffing, you've called my bluff. Whatever happens between you and me will be fast."

HE WAS IN NO HURRY to continue, however. At last he said: "You done me a good turn at the schoolhouse, son."

Speedy watched him, and waited.

"But?" suggested Speedy.

The other grinned.

"I kinda like you, kid," said he. "You're hard-boiled. That's what you are. I like 'em hard-boiled. You been around. That's where you been."

Still Speedy waited, and this time without comment of any kind.

"What I was gunna say," continued the other, "is this. You and me together could get on like nothing at all."

Speedy nodded.

"But agin one another, we couldn't get on at all!"

The boy watched him carefully. Finally he said: "Why not, big boy? It's a fairly big world. I'm not crowding your show, so far as I know."

Six Wilson shrugged his shoulders.

"Listen, kid," said he. "You're crowding Mary Steyn, ain't you?"

"She doesn't care a rap about me."

"She asks you to be careful of yourself."

"I won't argue, if you take that line."

"Speedy," said Six Wilson, "you're a bright kid. You're one of the slickest and the smoothest that ever happened. I never met up with nobody that I could take a real fast likin' to quicker than I could to you. Know what I mean?"

"Thanks," said the boy. "You certainly are the little flatterer, Six. You make me blush!"

Six Wilson laughed with a genuine enjoyment.

"Maybe you think that you'd get along better without me

than you would with me," said he. "But you're wrong. I'll tell you how wrong you are."

"Go on and tell me," said the boy. "I've got to listen."

"Keep your first seat," said Wilson. "Don't get five inches nearer to that door, or I'll shoot the brains out of your head, son!"

He laid a revolver on the table as he spoke; but he had not raised his voice.

However, Speedy took his first seat. He knew business when he heard it.

"The kid is soft on you," declared Six Wilson. "She likes you. She tells you to go and be good to yourself. That's what she tells you. She don't never talk to the boys like that. I've heard her, and I've heard reports of her. You've socked her in the right spot. She likes you."

Speedy listened once more without reply. He saw that argument was not invited.

"She'll marry you," said the tall man, nodding with conviction. "And the man that she marries has gotta throw in with me; or else she'll marry him dead!"

He cleared his throat; his husky, whispering, horrible voice went on:

"You dunno, what time I've put in on that case. It took me a whole year of my own money and time to work up the case. When I learned that it was all about, I couldn't go ahead and collect. No, I had to sit still and wait. Three years I waited. Waited for the right man to come along. The man that she'd hook up with. And he never come. Or, if he come, he wasn't the kind that I could work with. He was a slippery sneak, or something. He wasn't the right kind."

"You wanted an honest man, like me," suggested the boy, ironically.

"You're a tough kid," said the other, "but you'd keep your promises. That's what's held you back from your fortune, more'n once. You been too clean in the pinches. Ain't I right?"

Speedy shrugged his shoulders.

"It's the trouble with a lot of good yeggs," said Six Wilson. "It's the trouble with Snapper Dan McGuire, come to that. I ain't got a better man than Snapper Dan. But he's got too much conscience. He lets the under dog up, too many times. Can't make money like that."

133

"No," agreed Speedy.

"If you gave me your word that you'd split with me, I could trust your promise."

He added: "Ain't I right? No, you don't have to answer that. I know. I can tell a man by what's in his face and his eye. He don't have to talk to me. Now, kid, the girl will marry you; she's the key to nine million; if I let you go free, you marry her, but you don't split with me. Not unless I get the promise out of you. I've got you in my hands now, Mr. Fish. And you don't jump back into the sea. No, not till you've given me your promise that you split the coin with me."

Speedy sighed.

"So you see," said Six Wilson, "you might as well knuckle under. It's a bargain for you. Without me, she ain't worth a nickel. With me, she's worth nine million. I lead you both right by the hand to it. Understand?"

The boy nodded.

"Suppose I say no?" said he.

"You ain't such a fool," said Six Wilson. "But if you should be, you're a dead man, kid!"

"I'll take tonight to think it over," said the boy.

"Is that the way?" whispered Six Wilson. "You're too good to do business with me, are you?"

"I didn't say that."

"You meant it, though! You want a night to think it over? You lie! You want a night to slide out of this!"

He deliberately picked up the revolver and sighted down the barrel. There was no mercy in his relentless eyes.

"Now you talk, Mr. Turkey," said he. "You talk, or you be damned."

"Don't be a fool," said the boy, calmly, looking back at the round, black muzzle of the gun. "You don't throw away four and a half millions like this."

"Don't I?" snarled the other. "I give you five seconds to see if I don't."

"I take tonight to think it over," answered Speedy. "I said that I'd need tonight to think it over, and I'll have tonight. If you don't like that deal, you can be damned, for all I care—and shoot when you're ready, Wilson!"

Slowly, he saw the gun lower.

"You're a tricky young snake," said the other. "I oughta

put a slug into you now. But I got a kind of a weakening, just this minute, thinkin' of how you turned that pack of hounds back there at the Nixon school, when they had the taste of me, and was all ready to lap me up like warm milk. I kind of weaken for a minute, but I know that I'm a fool. I ought to take and slam you now. No good'll come out of waiting. Because no matter what you say, you've made up your mind already. But I'm gunna take the chance. Might be you need a sleep under your belt. There's many a man that's a hero after supper that's weak in the knees before breakfast."

He laughed in his soundless way, as he suggested this.

Then, putting two fingers between his lips, he emitted a shrill, ear-cutting whistle.

The Deacon strode through the doorway a moment later.

"Call Snapper Dan," said the chief.

"Yeah; all right."

"You and him has got work together; tonight," said Six Wilson in continuation.

"Him and me? Not him and me!" said the Deacon. "I'll work with anybody else, but I won't work with him."

"You won't?"

"I've told you that before. Him and me, we don't get along. The little runt thinks he's a better man than me. I'm gunna murder him, one of these days. I'm gunna take him apart and see what's wrong with his insides!"

"You beef-faced fool!" said the chief, "call in Snapper Dan!"

The latter still hesitated, but only for a moment. He was crimson with excitement, when he turned to the door and bellowed:

"Snapper! Hey! Come here, runt!"

"That's a good start for the pair of you tonight," said Six Wilson, "but that's the way I want it."

Rapid footfalls came. And then a small man, with a face as lean as a knife and eyes small and black as beads came into the room. He wore the high heels of the dandy, the high heels of the small man who wishes to appear taller than nature made him.

"Who called me runt?" he asked, staring fiercely at the Deacon.

The lip of the big man curled with angry disdain.

"The chief wants you," said he, shortly.

"Who called me runt?" insisted Snapper Dan.

"Shut up!" said the gasping voice of Six Wilson.

Snapper Dan was silent, but his lips moved with inaudible threats as he continued to stare at the Deacon.

"Listen," said Six Wilson. "The pair of you listen, and listen hard, too. You hear me?"

They faced towards him at last.

"The two of you," said the chief, "are gunna spend the night in the shack, here. I'm gunna sleep out. They been too close on my heels, lately. They've offered too big a reward, too. I'll trust you boys when I got my eyes on you, the rest of the time, from now on, I'm sleeping out. Tonight, you move your rolls in here. And you're gunna have company. The company you'll have is the kid, here!"

He pointed at the boy. Neither of them favored Speedy with a glance. Their attention was reserved for one another, still glaring wickedly.

"You'll keep each other awake," said Six Wilson, "and the first fellow to sleep, the other one has my permission to slam him. Slam him hard, and no comeback!"

He laughed and rubbed his hands.

"You'll hear some pretty sweet conversation between these two!" he concluded to the boy. "You two get your things in here!"

They departed at once, and while they were gone, Six Wilson personally tied Speedy hand and foot. It was a good job—not quite enough to paralyze all circulation, and yet enough to make the ropes bite deeply. He tied the ropes with heavy knots. In the meantime, the other two returned, and Wilson went on:

"If the kid so much as takes one roll towards the door, shoot him. If he does anything else funny, salt him away with lead. If he's dead in the morning, when I come in, I ain't gunna call it murder; that's all I gotta say. Mind you, he's slick, mean and worse'n a snake for danger, I tell you. Believe me that I'm right!"

– 27 –

AT THE DOOR, before leaving, Six Wilson turned towards the boy, and said: "Tonight, you think. Or it's your last night! You savvy?"

And he strode off into the darkness, carrying blankets.

There was no regret in Speedy as he watched the chief go. He had known bad men, in his life, but never one who in one evening could return so much evil for good as Six Wilson had done. Humanity was not in the fellow, nor decency, nor any trace of human kindness.

The two who had been chosen as guards now were left alone with Speedy, and regarded one another silently, for some time.

Then the Deacon said: "Go on and roll in and sleep. I'd rather sit out the watch all by myself than have your sneakin' birdeyes open and watchin' me."

"Deacon," said the other, his voice trembling with passion, "there's only one way to do this—with your mouth shut!"

And then he set deliberately about making down his blankets. The Deacon, after a snarling moment, followed his example. The Snapper, finishing first, put on a pot of coffee. And the Deacon, without asking if there were coffee enough in the pot for two, picked up a rusty pan and began to prepare coffee for himself. No words were heard until the Deacon, crossing the floor in some haste, pretended to find Speedy in the way. Brutally, with the full force of his thick leg, he kicked the limp body out of the way. Speedy was rolled over on his face. He thought, at first, that his hip had been broken by the impact, but gradually the numbness turned into a spreading pain. He rolled over on his back again and was still, smiling a little at the ceiling. Cold hell was in his heart.

The Deacon sat down on a stool at the table with his coffee. The Snapper sat down in the chair, in an opposite corner.

"Snapper," said the boy, "you're Snapper Dan McGuire, aren't you?"

There was a moment of silence.

Then: "What's that to you?" demanded the Snapper.

"I just wondered," said Speedy, half closing his eyes and shaking his head. "I'd heard a lot about you. I didn't think —"

He paused.

"You heard about me, eh? Where'd you hear about me?" asked the Snapper, suspiciously.

"Where? Oh, everywhere! I guess every cop in the land knows about Snapper Dan McGuire."

"He's pulling your leg, Dan," said the Deacon.

"Shut your face," advised the Snapper. "I ain't talkin' to you. I ain't wantin' to talk to you."

The Deacon growled like a sullen dog. Said the Snapper:

"Where you been, to hear about me kid?"

"Montreal," said the boy, "was the first place, I think. I met a fellow called Side-wheel Dugan."

"Hey, you knew Side-wheel, did you?"

"Yes, and a rat he was, but he admired you a lot."

He had struck at random on the name of Dugan, simply because the latter had been over most of the country. It was luck that Snapper really knew of him.

"Yeah, he was a rat," said the Snapper. "But he was kind of funny. I mean to listen to the way he had of talking."

"Yeah, he was funny," said the boy. "That's what surprised me—I mean, after hearing what he said for you."

"What surprised you, kid?"

"Why, he said that you never took a sidestep for the sake of dodging any big thug; nor for the sake of kicking anybody in the face when he was down."

"I don't dodge no big thug," said the other. "If they're big, I whittle 'em down to my own size. And who'd I ever kick in the face when he was down?"

"You kicked me," said the boy.

"That's a lie," said the Snapper. "The Deacon did that."

"It's just the same," said the boy. "You stood by and let the big hound do it—the big, blow-hard!"

138

The Deacon swayed to his feet.

"You *do* get it in the face, this time," said he.

Speedy laughed.

"Go on. Let him do it, Snapper," said he. "I'll live through it, and I'll tell the boys the truth about you!"

"Hold up, Deacon," said the Snapper.

"He's pulling your leg," said the Deacon.

"Maybe he is."

"You—the Snapper—the gentleman!" sneered Speedy. "The dead-shot Dick, the finest man in the world with a knife! I see the truth about you, now."

"Do you?" asked the Snapper, dangerously.

"Yeah, I see it. You're just a cheap yegg, like that pile of red beef, there!"

"I'm gunna kill him!" choked the Deacon, and strode forward.

The Snapper laid the muzzle of a Colt gently in the pit of the Deacon's stomach.

"Back up, sweetheart," said he.

The big man recoiled.

"You jackass," said he, "are you gunna swaller that soft soap?"

"I'm gunna skin him alive," said the Snapper, "but I'm gunna do it for my own self."

"Go on, then," said the Deacon. "I don't mind watchin' you."

The Snapper, at this, resheathed his gun, and turned a cruel, birdlike face towards the captive.

"By the Lord," exclaimed the boy, "it *is* true, and you're not afraid of 'em, no matter how big they come."

"Who said I was afraid?" asked the Snapper.

"Why," said the boy, "what I always heard was that you were a runt, but that you had the biggest heart in the world. But when I saw the Deacon—I thought that he could open his mouth and swallow you. But I've just seen him back up. He turned green, too, when he did it!"

"You lie!" said the Deacon.

The Snapper laughed with great enjoyment.

"Did he turn green?" he asked of the boy, with the highest good nature.

"I saw him," said Speedy.

"You lie!" shouted the Deacon.

"Oh, that's all rignt," said the boy, "but I know what I saw. He's afraid of you, Snapper. I saw his hand jump for his gun, and then come away again. The big yellow-livered tramp!"

"Did he make a move for his gun?" asked the Snapper.

And he laughed again, leering at the Deacon.

"Why, I'm gunna eat you, kid!" said the Deacon. "I'm gunna pulverize you, and then swaller the fragments!"

He started towards the boy again.

"Hold up, leave him be," said the Snapper, with an imperial air. "He kind of interests me, the way that he sort of talks."

"Who are you," asked the Deacon, "to tell me to hold up?"

"I'll tell you who he is!" broke in the boy.

"Shut yer mouth!" shouted the Deacon. "I'm talkin' to you, Snapper. Whacha mean by tellin' me to hold up?"

The Snapper toyed, not with a gun, but with the long handle of a knife that protruded above his belt.

"You tell him, kid, if you got any idea," he said.

"I'll tell him," said Speedy, "because I know. He told you to hold up because he's a better man than you are, Deacon, and in your sneaking heart you know it!"

"By God!" breathed the Deacon.

And his face swelled, and was splotched with purple. He stood swaying a moment, his hands extended, the fingers stiff, prepared for taking hold of some living thing and throttling and tearing it.

"I ain't hearing straight," said Deacon. "I'm crazy in the head."

"You're not crazy," said the boy. "You're only a big four-flusher, and now I'm seeing your bluff called!"

"Snapper," gasped the big man, "fill your hand!"

And, at the same time, he snatched at his own Colt.

Perhaps passion made his big fingers stumble. An any rate, he was easily and distinctly beaten to the draw. Cleanly and clearly was he beaten by the flashing hand of the Snapper.

The first bullet of the little man hit the Deacon in the middle of his body and doubled him up so quickly that the second, aimed for the head, smashed into the wall, instead.

But, though he was dying on his feet, the Deacon, for

140

all of his brutality was a brave man, and determined to live long enough to kill his enemy.

Before a third shot could fly from the Snapper's weapon, the little man was hit, and the weight of the shot knocked him flat.

The Deacon laughed. A red gush of blood cut that laughter short, and he began to sink to his knees, a dreadful sight.

Speedy, in the meantime, had not lost an instant.

One second had not been occupied by that gunplay. The next second, rolling across the floor, the boy had put his teeth in the haft of the Snapper's knife, and still holding it firmly gripped, he drove the point into the floor. That made a secure, firmly held edge, and one brush of the rope against it gave Speedy free hands.

He was reaching for the ropes that held his feet when he saw the big Deacon, now on his knees, his crimsoned face frightfully contorted, one hand gripping his death-wound, lift his revolver and cover the escaping captive.

Understanding was in the face of the dying man; well he knew that his destruction flowed from the talk of the boy, and he meant to pay him in full. But he was blind with the coming of the long night. The gun shook crazily in his hand, and the bullet that he fired was wide of his mark, as Speedy leaped up.

He saw the Deacon pitching forward, like a slowly leaning tower, on his face, and as he went, the boy snatched the gun which lay beside the Snapper.

The little man stirred and groaned at the same time.

Now came a rushing footfall.

"Who's here? What the devil's loose?" gasped the whispering voice of Six Wilson, thrusting the door open and rushing into the room.

"Yours truly," said the boy, and gave Six the heel of the Snapper's heavy gun full between the eyes.

He pushed the toppling body out of his way, and raced on into the open.

28

HE WAS NOT ALONE, as he sprinted out of the shack, with the voice of Six Wilson gasping behind him.

He saw forms running, and the gleam of weapons in their hands, but all very dimly, for a cloud had gathered over the stars and the moon, and the night was thick.

He saw horses, too, and for them he made, wondering why people did not cut in to intercept him. Instead, they all made for the house. A pleasant scene they would find there, something that would make them riper than ever for murder. Well, perhaps necessity had widened his eyes.

As he came closer, he saw the horses fling up their heads from grazing, but they did not run away; they were all hobbled short.

Nearby was a great heap of tackle. He grabbed a bridle that lay on top; there seemed no time for anything else. And then he selected the tallest horse of the lot, one so black that it was more perfectly lost in the night than any of the rest. It closed its teeth hard against the bit. He remembered having seen people put their thumbs inside the mouth of a refractory horse in order to make it yawn for the bit. He tried this with no success.

He had seen others take a cruel turn on the upper lip for the same object. This he tried now, and instantly the black horse admitted the bit.

It was high time, to be sure.

Behind him, from the house, he heard an outbreak of many voices. And, above them, the whining, barking cry of Snapper Dan, yelling curses.

Well, Snapper had plenty of reasons to be irritated; the bullet that had knocked him down was one of them.

And, out of the shack, streamed many forms, one taller than the rest, running ahead of all of the others with gigantic strides. That was Six Wilson. He knew the man as well as though a spotlight had been cast upon him, for a sense of loathing reached to the boy even this far through the dark.

He sprang, therefore, on the back of the big horse. He only delayed to open his pocket knife and slash the hobbles. And the instant that its feet were free and the man on its back, the black giant started running.

One jump, and the quivering of its loins seemed to show that it was settling to its power, and feeling its stride. Another jump, and it thrust out its head and jerked the reins through the hands of Speedy to the very end of them. Lucky for him that they were well knotted! Then the big fellow began to run in such a way as Speedy had never seen, never had ridden, save in wild dreams.

It made straight for a patch of shrubbery and smashed through it. It headed on towards a wilderness of rocks.

"He's crazy mad with fear," thought the boy, and sawed with all his might at the reins.

As well pull at a mountain as strive to influence that mouth of iron and the arching neck behind it!

He considered casting himself to the ground. But the ground was covered with pointed stones that he could see. To throw himself down at that speed would be like flinging himself into the mouth of a dragon. He would be pierced or crushed to death by the fall.

And then they went through the rocks.

They reached for him like spear points, they reached for him like hands, as it seemed, but still he was brought wavering through the peril by the big charger. It was as though water flowed through the interstices, dodging actively, and yet smoothly. There were eyes and brains in the very feet of this flying monster!

Then, through the hedge of rocks, they came into the open, and sped.

He did not know where he was, where they might be bound. Only he saw before him a ragged range of mountains, and in the midst of it two lofty peaks, with a level place between them. They looked to Speedy like the outward canted ears of a donkey, and the round head between the ears. Was it a pass towards which the big horse was running?

Now, it turned sharply to the right. The white ghost of

dead cactus of great size had sufficed to make it change its course.

And still it ran as a bird might fly. Without a saddle it was easier to sit that matchless gait, like the blowing of wind, than to stick on the back of an ordinary animal, such as those Speedy had recently ridden.

And now he saw before him, and to the right, very dimly, far in the night, several forms of riders, vaguely silhouetted.

He jerked with all his might against the mouth of the big animal. It was merely to urge him faster ahead.

He looked back over his shoulder.

Others were there behind—three or four, he could not tell.

Well, it was plain that he was lost. If only the black had kept straight on, his matchless speed would have made all well, but his change of direction had enabled the others to follow the beat of hoofs and come up.

A gun cracked behind him—a thin, absurdly small sound, but not absurd was the whiz of the bullet past his ear. They could shoot well even in the dark, these men of Six Wilson!

On went the black.

And then Speedy saw the end of the world, and knew that he was dead.

He had thought that the ground merely dipped down before him, suddenly.

Now he was aware that it dipped indeed—that it was a cliff, in fact, and for the edge of that cliff plunged his horse! Nothing could stop him! Why did not Speedy fling himself, then, to the ground, and give himself broken bones, but a chance of life?

It was because he could see the face of Six Wilson, in vivid prospect, when the monster would lean over him and, perhaps, strike a match to make out the extent of his victim's sufferings. Better to leap the cliff and die swiftly and sweetly in one instant than to endure what Six Wilson might pour out for him in the way of bitterness.

He was not fifty feet from the nearing riders on his right, as he came towards the edge of the rocks.

Why did they not open fire? Because one of them was shouting lustily: "Don't shoot! That's Coal Tar! Don't shoot or the chief will pull your hides off over your heads!"

He even had time to think of that, to grin faintly at the

conception, while the stiff gale of the gallop got inside his mouth and puffed his cheeks.

Then he jerked downwards over the rim of the rock.

Down to quick death, he thought. He relaxed his whole body. His shoulders were loose, and his head rolled a little, his face tilting upwards.

So loose was he on the sweating, hot back of the horse that the first shock almost knocked him to the ground. But true it was that the black had found a footing.

How could he have found it? Never, if he had not been mountain bred, with winged feet, and the wits of a goat. Looking down, aghast, the boy saw what seemed a sheer descent—no, there were here and there dim ridges thrusting out a little; but the angle of the horse's body was such that Speedy had to wind both hands into the wisp of mane above the withers and, so braced, he held himself on with difficulty.

For as a goat goes down a flumelike crevice, bounding from side to side, its nose thrust down almost as low as its feet, its four legs bunched dexterously together to break the shocks of landing, so did the black horse go down the cliff of that great rock.

Despair turned into terror, in the heart of Speedy, and terror into wild hope of life, and that hope into a vast exultation.

"I'm riding the king of the world!" he told himself. "I'm riding the only horse in the world. Old Coal Tar! Old hero!"

And, suddenly, as water after a cataract strikes a smooth slope, and straightens, and gathers speed again, and rushes almost soundlessly along, so the big horse gathered his stride, and, flowing noiselessly, over soft ground, swept along a valley that widened, momently, to the right and to the left, as smaller ravines dropped down into it.

There was no slackening in the tremendous gallop of the big creature. He went as though he trusted the wind of his gallop to blow the rider from his back.

But fear had left the boy, so long as he was on the back of this magic thing. He merely laughed at the flight of the wind past his face. With one free hand he slapped the wet neck, and he called aloud the name of the horse, and sang it to the sweeping sky above him.

At that, to his surprise, the dead run of Coal Tar

145

changed, drew into a gallop, and finally became an easy, swinging canter.

He was breathing hard. His swelling sides, at every breath, forced out the knees of Speedy; but he ran, now, with his head turned a little, and he seemed to be studying his new rider through the darkness.

In another moment, he was as docile in the hand of Speedy as a family pony with the youngest child of the house on its back!

The same joy, the same trust flowed out of the heart of Speedy towards the gallant fellow.

And then that joy of his turned into a deeper and soberer pleasure. It was a very odd feeling, but as though a voice had spoken at his ear and told him that he was saved for some purpose different from the old course of his life.

Then he drew the black to a halt, and listened. There was no sound behind him. All the danger from Six Wilson and his band of human hornets was far to the rear. Whatever way they followed would not be down the face of that rock he could well guess.

In the meantime, this sea of mountains that surrounded the valley was a mystery to him; the very waves of the ocean could not have been more similiar one to another than were these peaks to his unaccustomed eyes.

He rode on again, at a walk, trying to think back to the most likely direction in which he could find the way to the house of Steyn, and in a moment, he caught a flickering of light far away and to his left.

He laughed with the pleasure of that sight, and turned the horse towards it at a trot, at a canter. From this point he could quickly get the proper directions. All worry dropped like a useless cloak from his shoulders.

29

IT WAS THE SORT of a house he would have expected to find, low, rather long for its height and width, a shed or two nearby, and a tangle of corral fencing. That was all.

A dog ran out and barked at the feet of the big horse; and Coal Tar went straight forward, striking with his fore-hoofs. The dog fled; Speedy laughed. And in the midst of his laughter the door of the lighted room opened and a man stood in the opening, with the glow from behind sur-rounding his face with a halo where it struck through a dense brush of hair and beard.

"Who's the devil's here?" asked the mountaineer.

"A friend in need," said Speedy, good-naturedly.

"Yeah, everybody's in need. You don't get no handouts here, bum," said the other, and started to close the door.

"Hold on," said Speedy. "I want some directions. I don't want a handout."

The other threw the door wide again.

"You want what?" he asked.

"Directions," said Speedy, and dismounted.

"Directions to what?" asked the man of the mountains.

"Directions to get out of this valley," said Speedy.

"He's lost his way, Pete," said a woman's snarling voice.

"He wants directions, Annie," repeated Pete, helplessly.

"He's lost his way, that's all," said she.

"He's gone and lost his way?" said Pete. "How could anybody lose his way, I wanta know, up here? This ain't a desert or the ocean, is it?"

Said Speedy: "I want to find out the shortest way to get to—"

"Hold on. Are you lost?" asked Pete.

"Yes. I'm lost."

"How come you're lost?" said Pete. "Ain't that Mount

Tozer, and ain't that old Baldy, and ain't that Twister Mountain, yonder?"

"I suppose that those are the names," said the boy. "But I couldn't know that. I never saw them before."

"He never seen them before, he says," remarked Pete, over his shoulder.

"I don't know north from south," said Speedy.

"Can't you look at the stars and tell?" asked Pete.

"The stars are covered up behind those clouds," said the boy.

"Well," said Pete, "you're right, for once. Where you wanta go?"

"I want to find the house of a friend of mine."

"What in hell does that help me to know where he lives?" demanded Pete.

"I wanted to tell you his name. He's Arthur Steyn. Do you know him?"

"Steyn? Yeah, I seen Steyn once."

"You don't know where he lives?"

"Well, maybe I don't, but I could find out, if I wanted to."

He said it sullenly. He seemed aggrieved because a name had been mentioned to whose house he did not know the way.

"If he can pay his way, he can stay for the night," said the voice of Annie.

"Yeah, you could stay for the night," said Pete, nodding his head into darkness and swaying it up into the light again. "If you can pay, we'll put you up."

This was not the mountain hospitality to which the boy was growing accustomed. It was not the same breed of which he had heard so many tales.

"I don't want to spend the night," said the boy.

Far indeed was he from that wish, with such pursuers as the Wilson gang somewhere on his trail.

"But," he added, "if you can find out where I can find the right trail, I'll pay you well for that. I have to be moving on."

"Well," said Pete, "you oughta know that you can't buy what a man ain't got to sell."

And he was starting to close the door again when the woman called out:

148

"Wait a minute, Pete. We got that old map of the county. If he's got a brain in his head, he'll know some place near the Steyn house."

"I can find my way back from the Nixon schoolhouse," said Speedy.

"Well, the schoolhouse would be on the map," said Pete. "Come on in then. Wait a minute. It's a tolerable lot of trouble, to start to readin' a map at this here time of night. It'll cost you fifty cents, about, to find out where the Nixon schoolhouse is."

"Well, that's all right," said the boy.

He tied the reins of the horse to the hitching rack, as he spoke, and then started for the door.

Pete had come out a step or two.

"Darn my socks," said he, "there ain't no saddle on that hoss!"

"I was a little rushed, when I started on this trip," said Speedy, smiling.

"Hey, Annie," said Pete, "doggone me if there's a saddle on his hoss."

"You don't say!" cried the woman, her voice going up the scale.

"It's a whoppin' biggish hoss, though," said Pete. "Well, come on in."

The boy stepped through the door into a hovel. Behind one partition, he heard cattle munching hay; behind the other, chickens stirred and complained sleepily on their perches, then were quiet again. And in the one occupied room there was a bare, earthen floor, a stove in a corner, two bunks built one above the other. And that was all. Yes, a homemade broom here, worn clothes hanging from pegs, a board across a pair of sawbucks by way of a table, a gun, a fishing rod. Little else. Some greasy tin dishes littered the table.

And in a chair beside the table sat a hag bent with age, but her arm, bare to the elbow, was sinewy with strength, nevertheless. From under a gray mat of hair, perennially bright and youthful eyes looked up at the stranger.

"Come in and rest your feet," said she.

Speedy stood by the table and made himself smile at that face, deformed by long hatred of all the world.

"I don't need to sit down," said he. "I simply want a

149

look at that map of yours, and then I'll go. There's the fifty cents."

She picked up the coin which he put on the table, frowned at it, spun it in the air, and rang it on the wood.

"Yeah. Maybe that's all right," said she. And she thrust the money into a pocket of her man's coat. It had been brown once. It was chiefly gray-green, now.

"You gone and got yourself all sweated up, ridin' a hoss without a saddle," said she. "Don't you know no better'n that?"

"I had to make a quick start," said the boy.

"I call it kind of disgustin'," said Annie.

And her upper lip curled with distaste, as she looked him over.

"You ain't from these parts, I reckon," said she.

"No," said Speedy.

"I reckoned as how you wasn't," she answered, with a disapproving shake of her head. "What made you start so quick that you couldn't stay for a saddle?"

"It's a long story," said Speedy.

"Well, I got time to listen," said she.

"I haven't time to tell it, though," said Speedy.

He turned impatiently towards the door, wondering what kept Pete so long, but as he waited, Pete in person strode through the door, adjusting the half suspender that held up his greasy overalls and frowning with a very magisterial air. The frown was directed towards the boy.

"Where'd you get that hoss?" asked Pete.

And, as he spoke, he gave a point to his question by drawing out an incredible length of revolver from beneath his ragged coat.

"Where'd you get him?" he demanded.

Speedy was stumped.

And then it seemed to him that there was only one thing for him to do—tell the truth. A theft of a horse, in this region of the world was, as he well know, an offense as terrible as murder. More grimly punished because more despised, in fact. But a theft from an outlaw was not a theft at all.

"That's Six-card Wilson's horse—or one of his horses," said he.

"Hey!" broke in Annie. "One of Six's hosses? Which one?"

"Not no less'n Coal Tar!" said the man of the house, grimly.

"Coal Tar!" she cried.

She turned on the boy and pointed with her dirt-blackened hand.

"I reckon that you was in a considerable of a hurry when you got on that hoss, you sneakin' thief, you! Fifty cents, eh? Turn out his pockets, Pete. A thief like him, that steals from Six Wilson—what're we gunna do? Let him get away with nothin'? I hope to tell that he ain't gunna get away with nothin'."

"You want me to turn out his pockets?" asked Pete.

"Yeah, ain't I just told you to? D'you know better than me? You fuzzy-headed fool, you!"

Pete ran his thumb under the strap of his suspender and smiled with the superiority of his idea.

"You got a good head on your shoulders, Annie," said he. "You was bright even when you was a girl. Too damn bright, you mighty well know, or we'd be rollin' in money, instead of leadin' not much more'n a dog's life, up here at the end of time. You got a good head on your shoulders, but this time you're wrong."

"You go and tell me why," said Annie, "and stop talkin' about what's done and ended, will you?"

"I'll tell you why," said Pete. "This here—he's gone and stole Wilson's hoss, ain't he?"

"Yes, he has."

"How can a man steal from a thief?" broke in Speedy. "Wilson wanted to murder me—"

"Shut yer face or I'll bash in yer teeth with the butt of the gun," directed Pete. "He wanted to murder you, did he? You hear that, Annie? Six wanted to murder him. Well, then, would Six be kind of pleased or not pleased, if he was to come along down this trail and find his man held here good and safe in our house?"

"I was thinkin' that," said she.

"And if Six got here and found that this here thief hadn't been touched, and that everything about him was just the way we picked him up—I mean, if all of that was pointed out to him, would he be pleased, I ask you, or would he rather find the bird picked?"

"It's true," said the woman. "You got an idea for once in your life. Go out on the hill and swing the lantern, and give the signal ten times over, if you have to, till you get an answer from up the pass."

–30–

A THOUSAND IMPULSES flashed through the brain of Speedy. He remembered, well enough, the heavy gun he had stolen from Snapper Dan as the later lay on the floor of Wilson's hut. He might draw that, but the easy and confident way in which Pete handled his own weapon showed that he was a master of it.

Plainly that was a part of the world where one needed a knowledge of guns of all kinds, and of revolvers in particular.

"I'm to go out on the hill, am I?" said Pete. "And let this bird fly out of the coop while I'm gone? You're a fool, Annie. You go out and swing the lantern yourself!"

"I'll see you rot, first," said Annie. "Ain't I got rheumatism or something clean across my back, and you want me to go and stand out there in the night air, do you."

Pete did not debate the point of her rheumatism. He simply said: "Well, how we gunna make sure of this here thief, will you tell me that?"

"Reach me that there shotgun," said the hag.

He side-stepped, keeping a strict eye on Speedy, and handed her the heavy, old-fashioned weapon.

"Is it loaded?" said she.

"Yeah. It's loaded."

"With buckshot?"

"Whacha think? With birdseed?"

"Gimme no more of your flip back talk," said Annie.

She laid the shotgun across the table, pointing the barrels at the breast of the boy. And she curled a capable fore-finger around both of the triggers.

"Now go out and swing that lantern, like I was tellin' you to do," said Annie.

"You'll keep care of him?" asked Pete, dubiously.

"Say," said she, "if you was standin' there in his socks, would you think that I was keepin' care of you?"

Pete suddenly laughed.

"Doggone me, you're a card still, Annie. That's what you are. You're a card."

He picked a lantern from a peg on the wall, and pushed up the chimney with a screech of rusted iron against iron. In the meantime, he fixed his scowl upon the old woman.

"If he so much as blinks an eye, blow a hole through the middle of him," said Pete. "I dunno but it's the best way, anyhow. You take Six, he'd be mighty likely to be pleased. It'd show that we was friends of his. A slick and easy life we'd live around here for a while, if Six was a friend of ours."

"There ain't gunna be no killin' unless there's gotta be," said Annie. "He might be safe dead, but we might be safe choked, too, for that matter. You go and do what I told you to do, and if he so much as winks, I'll settle his hash for him. I'll turn him into hash, by jiminy jump-up!"

Pete, lighting the lantern, presently went to the door, and there paused to look doubtfully back upon the scene. But then he smiled, reassured.

"Yeah," said he, "if I was in his socks, I'd feel took care of, all right."

And he went out, his laughter booming heavily and trailing behind him as he walked away.

Speedy stood frozen in place, meeting the hard, steady eye of the woman. He would rather have faced any two men in the world. The Deacon and the Snapper, hard as they were, were nothing, compared with her.

In the meantime, her companion had reached his hill, apparently, and it could not be far away, for presently, across the darkness outside of the door, the boy saw the pale glimmer of light, traveling in three waves—then darkness again. It was clear that the first signal had been sent, calling Wilson and his gang that way.

He could curse his fate; he could grind his teeth and

damn his folly for coming to this house. But that would not help him.

It was useless, as he had learned in many a predicament, long before, to stand still while his hair lifted and gooseflesh formed on his body. The cold of the Arctic does not reach the heart so quickly as the icy touch of fear.

And he looked about him, desperately, forcing himself to be cool.

"No," said the woman, "there ain't no hole in the roof for you to jump through, and if you did, I'd shoot you on the wing. I ain't no common woman, boy. I can handle a gun. I'm telling you that. Because it'll be safer for you to wait for Six Wilson than to try to play any monkeyshines around here with me!"

He nodded at her. He even managed a ghost of a smile.

"I feel taken care of," he told her.

And she actually grinned back at him; but her finger remained locked around the triggers of the big gun.

"You're taken care of, all right," said she.

"Who's your musician?" he asked, seeing a guitar that hung from a nail on the wall.

"Him? He's gone," said she. "He's gone, and he ain't comin' back."

He stepped to the guitar.

"Stand fast!" said she.

He moved his hand slowly, so that she could not mistake the gesture.

"I'm not reaching for a gun," said he, and took the guitar off the nail.

"Leave that be!" she commanded, angrily.

"I won't hurt it," said Speedy. "Guitars are second nature, for me. Friend of yours have this?"

"He was my boy," said Annie. "Ay, and there was a boy for you. He wasn't no sneakin' hoss thief! Not him! There was one that could jump over a hoss, and rip the innards out of a whole town. When my boy Bill, he got started, he was a hurricane, I tell you. And then he'd come home, and he'd set there in that chair, and he'd lean back his head, and twang that old guitar, and he'd sing me *Annie Laurie* like it would make the tears come into the eyes of a mule to hear him!"

Speedy sat down in the chair.

154

"Mind what you're doin'!" said she. "And hang that guitar back on the nail. I been and tuned it every day of my life since he died."

"Died?" said Speedy, sympathetically.

"He gone and had a flock of bad luck," said Annie. "He gone and laid out a good plant, and everything was all right and he stood to clean out about a half a million, maybe. But there was a crooked swine of a clerk in that bank that he'd bought, and that hound, he doublecrossed my poor Bill. He goes into that bank, and he lays out his duds, and he starts to work runnin' the soap mold around the door of the safe, and right then and there they up and tell him to hoist his hands."

"Hard luck," said the boy.

He swept the strings, softly; it was amazingly true that they were perfectly in tune.

"My Bill, he wouldn't go and hoist his hands," said Annie. *"He* wasn't the kind that no woman could keep standin' still, no matter whether she had a gun on him, or not. He'd of gone roarin' through the roof, he would. He was that kind of a boy, I tell you."

Speedy nodded.

He swept the strings louder, and still louder.

"And he reached for his guns," said she, "and they took and heaved lead into him, and he died fighting like a man had oughta die, God bless him. One of 'em he killed right out, and paid the score, and two of 'em, he put 'em into the hospital, and somebody else could pay the bill. And that was the end of—"

Her voice died away. Speedy, singing softly into the very train of her voice, began *Annie Laurie,* as he had sung it many a time before. But never had he sung it as he did now. He had sung it for amusement, or on request; now he sang for his life—not too loudly, not loudly enough, he prayed to let the sound of his voice reach to that man on the hill near the house, whose repeated signals were still flashing dimly over the ground beyond the door of the house.

He sang with his head back, his eyes half closed. Only through the lashes of his half-closed eyes did he study the face of Annie, and see her harden and shake her head, and sneer with disapproval. But in a moment, that disapproval was gone.

155

The song, in fact, was sinking to that moment when the teller would lay him down and die for bonnie Annie Laurie, and if ever Speedy threw melting pathos into his tones, he sent them now.

Ay, and for the best of all reasons—for he heard, far down the valley, the rapid beating of the hoofs of horses.

He did not have to be a prophet to tell that they were the horses of Six Wilson's gangsmen, coming as fast as a gallop would bring them!

The chorus came again; he struck the strings more loudly, his voice flowed out more tenderly than ever.

And suddenly the harsh voice of Annie broke in upon him, as she said:

"You worthless, hoss-stealin' rascal, I see through you and your soft-soap tricks. But—get the devil out of here!" And, tilting the muzzles of the gun towards the ceiling, she pulled the triggers, one after the other.

Speedy saw the table, the gun, the holder of it, also, jarred by the shocks of the roaring explosions. But he only saw these things from the tail of his eye as he leaped through the doorway.

The guitar, unfortunately, fell from his hand as he sprang and smashed upon the floor.

But here he was in the open, with the fresh wind of hope and the night striking his face.

Off to the side, he saw big Pete running, the lantern swinging crazily in his hand, shouting as he strode: "Hey, Annie! What you gone and done, you fool?"

Speedy had unknotted the reins, by that time, his fingers stumbling with haste, and now he flung himself on the back of the tall horse.

And, at that moment, he heard old Annie screeching: "Help! Help! Hey, Pete! He's give me the slip—he's busted the guitar—oh, damn his heart black and blue!"

But Coal Tar was already under weigh, and sliding like a wind down the valley.

SPEEDY RODE FAR through the night.

The matchless stride of Coal Tar, eventually, dropped the rattle of hoofs behind him into silence.

He struck difficult trails. Even Coal Tar, at last, grew weary and began to stumble, and the boy got off and walked, toiling, it seemed, ever upwards.

The night ended. The mountains grew black. Finally, in the east and then all around the horizon stretched a thin band of pale light. The morning was definitely there. The color began; pink, and purple on the highlands, and rose, and gold. And finally the sun pushed up a rim.

Between a pool and a rock, he found a shepherd's hut, and paused there. His weary black horse stood still behind him. Weary was Speedy, also, and wavering a little even as he stood still, but his voice was hoarse, stern and abrupt, as he called the shepherd to him.

An old man, he came with stumbling steps, supported by a long knotted staff. He might have been a shepherd out of twenty centuries before, judged by his shapeless rags.

"Where's Nixon?" asked the boy. "I want to find the house of Arthur Steyn!"

The old man turned slowly, like a weather vane in a veering wind, and pointed.

"Right down there," he said. "There's Nixon lyin' under your eyes."

Speedy, dimly, strained his tired vision towards the point, and through the pass in the heart of which he stood, he saw the slope step down, from hill to hill, and the valley widen, until the windows of a little town blinked with red-gold light, far away.

"Nixon?" he said. "Is that Nixon?"

"That's Nixon, as sure as I'm Sam Rogers!" said the shepherd.

And Speedy, with a wave of the hand, by way of greeting and farewell, walked on.

He went on for an endless time. The sun rose hot and high above him. He began to sweat and stumble. At last he lay down in the shade of a rock. Coal Tar made a brief pretense of cropping at the sun-dried grass, and then he lay down in turn, like a dog, and hooked his head around, gave his tail one vain, last flourish at the flies, and went to sleep.

Speedy watched him with a tired grin.

Then he slept, also.

He wakened with the sun in his face, burning him, stinging his nose like an acid.

Coal Tar was already standing, busily eating this time, and his neck arched as of old. He raised his head when his dizzy master stood up, and it seemed to the boy that a new light came into his eyes.

Then Speedy mounted, and rode on.

It was such a short distance, that he wondered how he had given way to weariness, in this manner. In half an hour, he was before the door of the house of Arthur Steyn, and there he dismounted.

Half a dozen horses stood before the door of the house. He thought he recognized the great black horse of Joe Wynne among the rest, but he was not quite sure. He only knew that the place seemed a harbor of infinite refuge to him, just then.

He came to the door, and as he approached, he heard the calm, old, but unwavering voice of Steyn saying: "Of course it was the work of our friend Six Wilson. And I think that the time has come when we have to band together to put an end to him. He has done other murders, my friends. But this time he has taken away a man out of my house, like a tiger taking a child out of an Indian village. I am prepared to ride out by myself and do what I can to stop this man-killer. I have called you together because I think that you are the best fighting men in the district. I talked it over with my girl, and we agreed on you.

"Now, then, I want to hear what one of you is unwilling to ride with me against Six-card Wilson?"

Speedy stepped into the doorway, and he saw at the long

table in the dining room, old Steyn, Joe Wynne, Rudy Stern, and four others. He did not know the other four, but they looked like men, one and all.

"Hello, Mr. Steyn," said he.

It was as though he had dropped a bomb among them. They started up, with exclamations. The six men of the range rushed up about him. They even, with their charge, dragged him closer to the door, as though they needed the additional light by which to view him.

But Arthur Steyn ran to an inner door and called, loudly: "Mary! Oh, Mary! Believe it or not, Speedy has come back safe and sound."

Then one of the men cried: "By the Eternal, Joe, there's Coal Tar back again!"

And all the six poured out through the door, bearing Speedy along with them.

Big Joe Wynne stalked up to the head of the black horse.

"That's Coal Tar, all right," said he.

"You can thank Speedy for that," said Rudy Stern, looking, however, without pleasure upon the boy.

"I'll thank Speedy," said Wynne, "for finding the right horse for himself."

He turned on the boy, smiling a little.

"Where'd you get that horse, son?" said he.

"Am I a horse thief because I have him?" asked Speedy, wearily.

Wynne shook his head.

"That's the best horse I ever bred," said he. "I know him like a book. I knew him even better before Six Wilson stole him. Did you get him from Six?"

"I got him from Six," said Speedy.

"Mind telling me how?" asked Rudy Stern. "Because I reckon that we all of us know that Six would rather lose a couple of eyes than that hoss!"

"Well," said Speedy, reminiscently, "there was a sort of a mixup. The Deacon and the Snapper—you know 'em?"

"Know 'em?" they chorused. "Better'n sin!"

"They had me tied up," said the boy carefully, "but they got into an argument, and the argument led to guns, and when they shot each other up, I borrowed the Snapper's knife, and cut myself loose, and skinned out. This Coal Tar looked bigger than the rest, so I borrowed him from Six

Wilson, to help me on my way. That's about all there is to it."

He spoke slowly—so great were the gaps in the narrative which he had slipped over.

"Tied up," said Rudy Stern, "and the Snapper and the Deacon guarding you—and they fight—and you—oh, I see, just a little quiet, ordinary adventure for you, Speedy. Is that all?"

He laughed, in an oddly sharp, high voice.

Said Joe Wynne: "You like that horse, Speedy?"

"Like him?" answered the boy. "Ask me if I like my life! I'd be dead, except for him!"

He went to Coal Tar, and rubbed his nose, and the big stallion nuzzled against the breast of his last rider.

"Look at that," muttered one of the men. "And yet I remember Joe spending three weeks to make him wear a saddle ten minutes at a time."

"Six Wilson tamed him, I suppose," said Speedy. "He ran straight enough for me—and too fast for the rest of Wilson's nags."

Old Arthur Steyn came down the steps and touched his shoulder.

"Speedy," said he, "we've decided to go after Six Wilson, and stay after him until we've washed this section of the range clean of him. Do you ride with us?"

"No," answered Speedy, surprisingly. "I don't ride with you."

"You don't?" echoed the old man.

"I don't have to," said the boy. "Wherever I am, he'll come to find me. And I'm pretty tired of riding!"

He laughed a little.

"I'm tired of everything except a bunk and a blanket," he finished. "I'm going to turn in."

"He wants to turn in," said Arthur Steyn, wagging his head as though he had made a discovery of the profoundest importance.

"The kid is fagged," said Rudy Stern, in a similiar tone.

Speedy, with knees that bent uncertainly, found his way into the big room, found a bunk and a crumpled blanket on it, and flung himself down. He made only a feeble gesture at drawing the blanket over him.

Then, to his surprise, he found that other hands had arranged it, carefully.

"The kid's fagged out, and no wonder," said a hushed voice.

"I've got to see Mary," said Speedy, his eyes still closed.

"I'm here," she answered, instantly.

He looked up at her, amazed.

"You here?" he asked, stupidly.

She smiled a little, staring down at him.

"Send the rest away," said he.

She merely waved her hand. He saw only her face, but he heard the retreating footsteps.

"What is it?" she asked. "We're alone, now."

"This is a pinch," said the boy, in a tired voice. "In a pinch, the truth is worth more than a barrel full of lies, eh?"

"Worth a lot more," said she.

She pulled up a chair and sat close to him.

"What's that perfume you're wearing?" he asked, his eyes closing in spite of himself.

"Lavender," said she.

"I hate perfumes," said he.

She said: "Well, I'll drop the lavender, then. You wanted to say something?"

"Yes. I wanted to say something. I'm going to slide out. I'd like to get Six Wilson. But I've got to slide out. He's got a crazy idea. He thinks that you're fond of me. He thinks that you'll marry me. Don't laugh. I'm too tired to listen to laughing."

"I'm not laughing," she answered, quietly.

"He'd rather marry the two of us, than have that happen," said the boy.

"Why?" she asked.

"I can't tell you why. It's a long story. It's a crazy story. You wouldn't believe it. Only, I wanted to tell you, I'm going to breeze along. Understand?"

"I understand," said she.

He opened his eyes and frowned at her.

Steadily he stared up at her face.

"Look here, Mary," said he.

"I'm looking at you, Speedy," she answered.

"Look at my idea, not at me," said the boy.

"Well?" said she.

"You're getting serious," said Speedy. "Don't be serious. Hear me?"

"I hear you," said she.

He went on, painfully:

"You think that I'm all right. Because I've done a few little things around here that look spectacular. You're wrong. I'm not all right. You hit me off the first time that you laid eyes on me. I'm only a tramp. I'm good for nothing. I'm telling you that because I'm pinched for time, and to save you finding it out for yourself. I'm only a tramp."

She waited a moment, then she said: "You don't think Six Wilson was right, then?"

He answered, half groaning: "Yeah, I think he's right. Every girl's half a fool. She'll step out and marry any loafer that looks like a real man to her. But I'm just the way I look to the naked eye. Don't you make any mistake about that. All I care about in the world is an easy time, and nothing to worry about. A grand husband I'd make. A grand provider for kids, for one thing."

She said, after a moment: "You mean it, Speedy? You don't care about anything else in the world?"

"Nothing else," said he. "I had to tell you the truth. I'm tired—of everything. Mary, you're all right. You're a grand girl. I had to let you have a look at the truth. Now I'm going to sleep."

"All right, Speedy," said she. "I guess I understand. You sleep tight, will you?"

"Thanks, Mary," said he. "That's just what I'll do."

He reached out his hand, half blindly, and hers closed on it, and then he fell into a profound slumber.

–32–

WHEN HE WAKENED, it was late in the afternoon.

He knew the time by the dead heat of the air, and by the drowsy buzzing of the flies, as it seemed to him.

Then he sat up, and wiped the beads of sweat from his forehead. The blanket had been too hot and too long upon him. His body, where it had crossed, was wet through the shirt. Now a wave of wind entered the room through the open door. It did not cool him; it simply burned the moisture of the perspiration dry in one gesture, as it were.

Through the doorway, he saw several broad shoulders, several wide sombreros above them. The heads nodded up and down, and hands rose, bearing cards. They were playing poker out there in the shadow of the house, where more air stirred. Perhaps all six of them were playing poker.

"Feeling better, son?" asked the voice of Arthur Steyn.

Speedy looked sharply aside, and saw that the old man had been sitting like a stone, unobserved.

"I'm a lot better," said Speedy. "But this is a pretty hot place."

"Yes, it's hot," answered Steyn. "Want a drink?"

"A whole well of water," said Speedy, "and a couple of roast beeves."

"Mary's been cooking for hours," said Steyn. "She has a whole table ready to load for you. Let's go into the kitchen. It's a lot cooler out there, in spite of the heat from the stove."

That was true. By a freak of the wind, that end of the house was cooler.

Speedy stood for a moment to appreciate the draught. Then he went outside and pumped a granite basin full of water. He washed his face and hands. Then he shaved. The back of his neck was a little raw and chafed against the flannel collar of his shirt. But he felt fresher and hungrier, every moment. Then he went inside and stood by the door.

The table was literally loaded, and Mary leaned against a chair, red-faced from cookery, her sleeves rolled up to her elbows. She was not the perfect picture of a housewife. Her face was not innocent of perspiration; two or three wisps of hair stuck flat against her forehead, darkened and glistening from the wet. But Speedy looked at her as the jockey looks at a fine horse.

"You could run for my money, Mary," said he. "You're wonderful. Every time I see you, you're more wonderful."

"That's all right," said she. "You don't have to pay before you eat. Sit down and get to work."

He said: "Who's with me? Any of the boys?"

"They've eaten. I'll keep you company," answered Arthur Steyn.

And he sat at the head of the table and passed dishes, and pretended to eat.

Mary went outside, singing, carrying a saddle and a bridle.

Then her father said: "Speedy, you've surprised me."

"Have I?" said Speedy. "You mean that play about Coal Tar and Wilson. I had a lot of luck, that's all."

"I'm not speaking of Wilson," answered Arthur Steyn. "He's far from my mind, just now."

"What's in it?" asked the boy, his mouth full of hot cornbread.

"You are," said Steyn, thoughtfully. "I thought you were a cunning rascal—a worthless thief of time. I find that you're an honest man. All my thoughts about you were wrong!"

Speedy stared in a real astonishment.

"Look here, Mr. Steyn," said he, "right from the first you killed the fatted calf for me."

Steyn smiled.

"You know, Speedy," said he, "that a shrewd man generally tries to play a simple part."

It was Speedy's turn to smile, though for different reasons.

"I see," said he. "Tell me what you thought I was after?"

"There's only one thing I possess that's worth having," said Steyn. "Not my wretched strip of land. I'm the only one in the world who could love these naked hills, I suppose. I thought you wanted Mary."

"You did?" murmured Speedy.

He looked at Steyn with an awe unusual in his hardy soul.

"Yes," said Steyn. "I was sure of it, until you talked to her before you went to sleep."

"Oh, yes, she told you about that, did she?" said the boy.

"She did not have to tell me," said Steyn. "I heard it."

"Hello!" said Speedy. "I didn't know that you were in the room."

"No, I was eavesdropping from the outside. The walls of my house are conveniently thin, Speedy!"

"Ah?" said Speedy.

He stopped eating. He smiled in a friendly way of understanding at the other.

"You listened in," nodded Speedy.

"I've heard nearly every word you've said to my girl," answered Steyn.

Speedy blinked.

"The first—" he began, and then paused.

"The first night?" said Steyn. "Oh, yes. I had my ear pressed against the door, because I thought that you might talk a little more freely when I was out of the room."

Speedy openly gasped.

"Yes," went on Steyn, smoothly, "pride and honor don't exist for me, where the welfare of my girl is concerned."

"That stops me!" breathed the boy. "But the next day when she accused me in front of you, you seemed to think that she was all wrong and that I—"

Steyn nodded.

"You see, Speedy," said he, "when I listened through the flimsy door to you, the night before, I suddenly realized that I was a very old and dull man, and that you were a very young and clever one. I saw that nothing but diplomacy would help me, then."

"So you let me drive her out of the house?" said Speedy, incredulously.

"You drove her out because you expected her to come back, I think," said Steyn.

Suddenly Speedy smiled.

"That's right," said he. "I was only giving her rope enough to hang herself."

And he added: "I thought I was as deep as clouded glass and I was as thin as a windowpane, all the while!"

"I thought that I saw your motive," said Steyn, as cautiously as a professor. "Of course, I could not be sure, but I was at least certain that I would be helpless against your youth, your activity, your adroitness, as long as I openly opposed you. So I held my hand and played the part of the fool."

The boy was silent, only murmuring, after a time: "You found me a pretty black rascal, Mr. Steyn."

"The blackest I ever have known," answered Steyn, in his gentle voice, still. "Much blacker than a man-killer like the great Six Wilson. For he only kills with bullets, and you, I thought, with lies. But now, in a moment, I am disarmed. You have put your cards on the table, and told my girl the truth. I thank God and you, Speedy, for doing that! It was a good, shrewd blow at her pride, I daresay, but she'll recover from that. She has agreed with me that you're not like other men, you see!"

He laughed a little.

But there was no laughter in Speedy. He was thinking that never in his life had he known the wisdom of such a man as this.

Then he said: "And now, Mr. Steyn, by telling me frankly what you think, you feel that you've tied my hands for good and all?"

It was the turn of old Steyn to stare for a moment, and then he answered in his gentle way: "Yes, my boy. That was what I hoped. I think that you'll never marry Mary, now."

Speedy bowed his head a little.

She seemed, at that moment, the most gloriously glowing vision that had ever entered his mind.

But old Steyn was saying: "By the way, while you slept, a man was out here to see you, but we sent him back to Nixon because you were asleep, and partly because, although he looked a gentleman, he might have been one of Six Wilson's hired men."

"Who was he?" asked the boy.

"He called himself John Pierson; he seemed rather anxious to talk with you."

"John Pierson!"

"You know him?"

"Yes, I know him. In Nixon now, you say?"

"Yes. In Nixon."

"I've got to start now," said Speedy.

"And returning when?" asked Steyn, gradually rising from the table.

"Never!" said the tramp.

—33—

WHEN HE WENT OUTSIDE of the house, he was saying to old Steyn: "Will you sell me a broncho, Mr. Steyn? I want a lift into Nixon."

Big Joe Wynne stood up, at the same moment that Mary Steyn rode her dancing mare around the corner of the house.

"You think that I was joking, Speedy," said he. "But I wasn't. Coal Tar is your horse, if you'll have him."

The upper lip of Speedy curled a little.

He stepped close to Wynne, and said softly: "There's only one thing I'll take—or exchange—with you, Wynne!"

And the big man, frowning, made no answer, and did not repeat his proffer.

The rest, very delicately, referred to it with not a word. Perhaps they could guess at what had passed between the pair in that brief moment.

Old Steyn, without a word, went to the barn and brought back a strongly built pinto.

"This horse will take you to Nixon. If you want him farther than that, you can pay me fifty dollars. If you change to the railroad from Nixon, give the horse to the hotel keeper. He'll send Pinto back by the first rider that comes out this trail."

Speedy waved his hand.

He had gone to the girl, moved by a freak of fancy.

"Mary," said he, "you've started making a collection of guns, and here's another for you. Take this!"

And he pulled out the long-barreled revolver that he had picked out of the hand of the fallen Snapper.

She received the gun with a studious frown, turned it in her hand, and then rubbed her finger over certain obvious notches that had been either cut or filed into the handle.

"Whose gun?" said she.

And then she gasped, for turning the weapon a little, she saw a name scratched, and the shallow furrow of the scratch was filled with the glint of silver, spelling: "The Snapper"!

"The Snapper!" said she.

They crowded suddenly about her, all of those men, fairly panting with curiosity.

And heard Rudy Stern saying: "He shot up the Snapper and the Deacon all in one party. God knows how! But here's the proof of it. The two of 'em all at once!"

"I tell you," said the boy, "I didn't do it. I didn't shoot up the pair of 'em."

"Sure you didn't," said Ruby Stern, soothingly. "You wouldn't do a thing like that. You're a little doggone shorn lamb, is what you are, and you dunno how to take care of yourself, with all the big rough men of the world around you. Ain't that the fact, kid?"

They all laughed, at this remark. Only Speedy was silent, and Joe Wynne.

He was not free from them even when he had mounted his horse and waved farewell.

But Mary Steyn sent her little mare up beside his pinto and leaning a bit from the saddle, she said: "You think that you're riding out of this, but you'll ride back again, Speedy, take my word for it!"

Then, as he rode off, he saw that four of the six riders had followed him at a short distance; Rudy Stern and big Joe Wynne were among them.

It was not hard to guess the reason why. They had heard what he had reported to Steyn. The great Six Wilson would follow him as that bandit would follow no other bait into a trap. Therefore, they rode behind him, in part as a guard of honor, let us say, and in part hoping to find a pelt and a bounty worth having.

Something over ten thousand dollars was being offered at this time for the arrest or the capture of Six Wilson, dead or alive.

But Speedy made up his mind that he would act as though he were alone, and after the first glance to the rear, he paid not the slightest attention to the others during the entire eight miles to Nixon, and not one of them offered to ride up beside him.

He went to the hotel in Nixon, his horse stepping deep in the liquid white of the dust down the way. And, when he had tethered the pinto and made his way into the lobby, he did not even have a chance to ask for his man. Big John Pierson rose from a corner and strode up to him.

He stood a moment before the tramp, scanning him from head to foot, and then he smiled a little as he shook hands with the boy.

"You've burned the tip of your nose, Speedy," said he.

"To a crisp," said Speedy. "But that's all right!"

"That's all right, if you feel it that way," said Pierson. "Come over here and sit down. No, we'd better go up to my room."

He led the way up creaking stairs to a corner room. The shades were down, but the burning heat had seeped through them until the room was oven-hot.

So they threw off their coats.

"Drinking?" asked Pierson.

"Not with you," said Speedy.

"Not friendly, eh?" asked Pierson, unabashed.

"No, but I need to have my wits about me."

Pierson smiled.

"We'll have some ginger ale and ice," said he.

And he was as good as his word.

They sat sipping at the sticky, oversweet, artificial mess, poking at the ice with spoons, deeply and gloomily discontented with such a beverage, and Pierson said:

"How do things go?"

"Things have finished," said the boy.

"Finished?" answered Pierson, unconvinced.

"Yes, finished. I'm through."

"That brute of a Wilson turned the trick, eh?" said Pierson, almost sympathetically, although he sighed as he spoke.

"No, not Wilson. I've been in his hands and out again."

"What! In his hands—and out, did you say?"

"It's not Wilson," said the boy. "It's another thing. It's Steyn—and the girl."

"What about them?" snapped Pierson.

"They're too white. I couldn't go on with 'em."

"You liked 'em, eh?"

"Yes, I did."

"Liked 'em too well to introduce 'em to nine or ten million dollars. Is that the idea?"

In this light, Speedy had never viewed the problem. He could only shake his head, stubbornly.

"I was doing a rotten thing," he insisted. "I wouldn't mind, ordinarily. But I told you before—women are not my line!"

"Oh," said Pierson, "you couldn't get along with Mary Steyn, eh? Well, I don't suppose that I'm surprised. I told you beforehand that she's a hard one to handle."

Speedy stirred in his chair and looked uneasily at the blinded window next to him.

"She's too white," he managed to say. "She's one of the white women of this world, man!"

"So," said the other, "you wouldn't clutter up her fine life with several millions of dollars. Is that it?"

Speedy stared gloomily at the lawyer.

Then he broke out: "Why don't you come clean with her? Why don't you go straight to her and tell her what's what?"

Pierson shook his head.

"No woman under thirty," said he, with sage conviction, "can be trusted. I know that. I haven't been a lawyer for that many years, almost, without learning a little something about women, my lad!"

Speedy watched him with a growing dislike.

"What fetched you down here?" he asked.

"Not enough reports from you," said Pierson. "I had to be on the spot, anyway. It's too important. I couldn't leave as big a fish as this to some other fellow's single net."

"Well, I'm through with the game," said Speedy.

"I'm not surprised," said Pierson. "I was only making a cast in the dark, when I picked you out. I knew that you were too young and too inexperienced for the job."

Speedy stirred again in his chair.

Then he stood up.

"I'll be getting along," said he.

Suddenly Pierson leaned back and laughed.

"Sit down, Speedy," said he.

The boy shook his head.

"I'll be moving," he answered, grimly.

"Why, because you're beaten?" asked Pierson.

"Yes," said Speedy, after a moment of thought.

"No," said the other, "but because the game was too easy for you! Isn't that true?"

"What game?" demanded Speedy. "What are you talking about, Pierson?"

"She was tamed to your hand, and came at the call. Am I wrong, Speedy?"

The boy frowned blackly.

"Certainly not," said he.

"Very well," went on Pierson. "What's your next move? New York?"

"My next move? I keep that to myself," said Speedy.

"Don't trust me, Speedy?"

The tramp made a sudden and impatient gesture.

"All right," said he. "I'll tell you, and I'll tell you because I'm going to tell the whole world. I'm going to spend a little time being gotten, myself, or else getting Six Wilson!"

The lawyer whistled, and slowly raised his head, like one peering at a distant, gradually looming object.

"That's it, is it?"

"Yes."

"Six Wilson got under your skin?"

"He did. And I'm going to scratch him out."

"Well," said Pierson, "that's the best job that you could do for me. I'd like to ask for a small promise."

"I make no more promises blind to you," said the boy, sullenly.

"It's only this. Spend two or three days with me, because when he knows that I'm here, Six Wilson is going to want to break me open and see what makes me tick. Will you do that?"

Speedy suddenly grinned.

"I might do that," said he. "I'd sort of like to look on and see what he finds!"

—34—

HERE, THE DOOR of the room next to theirs opened and shut with a slam and through the paper-thin wall sounded a hearty voice which said:

"Now that we're up here, Sheriff May, I can tell you my name. That thing that I wrote on the hotel register doesn't mean a cipher. I'm Frank Rivera."

"That don't mean a cipher to me, neither," said the blunt voice of Sheriff May.

It meant something to the two who were eavesdropping from the adjoining chamber, however. For they sat up stiffly erect, and looked meaningly at one another. Lawyer Pierson raised a finger to his lips; but he did not need to give the caution, for the boy sat as still as a stone.

"I'm going to make it mean something to you," Frank Rivera was saying. "I'm going to make it mean a thousand dollars hard cash to you."

"What's your game, son?" asked the sheriff, dryly. "Craps?"

"No," said Frank Rivera. "My game is straight. As straight as a string."

"Gunna give me a thousand dollars for luck?" asked the sheriff.

"I'm going to tell you a strange story," said Frank Rivera.

"I'll bet it's strange," said the impolite sheriff, and yawned largely.

"That's all right," answered Rivera, who had the voice of a booster and an optimist. "I'll wake you up before long. I wanta introduce you, Mr. Sheriff, to a southern land by the Rio Grande and the estate of Rivera, the great estate of Rivera."

"With the banana cactus and the beefsteak trees growin' everywhere?" suggested the sheriff.

"Yeah, more or less," said Rivera.

"Thanks," said the sheriff. "But I'm not buying big estates. It ain't my day of the week for that."

"Will you shut up and listen?" asked Rivera, though his tone was still mild and genial. "Or do you kick a thousand dollars in the face every week, on this day?"

"I've seen a thousand dollars pass me in the street," said the sheriff, "but I never had his hand in mine."

"Shall I tell the yarn?"

"I can't stop you, son," said the sheriff. "It's too hot to move a lot, this time of day. You might ice that breeze through the window, if you don't mind."

"I'm gunna make you forget the climate," said Frank Rivera. "Open your eyes, brother, and look!"

"Beautiful as a dream," yawned the sheriff. "Go on, kid."

"Hill and valley as far as the eye walks," said Frank Rivera, "and God Almighty pullin' the grass up by the roots, it grows so doggone fast. Cattle everywhere. You could tether a calf with a ten foot rope anywhere it was dropped, and without moving outside of the circle, that calf would find so much to eat that it'd grow up and die of fatty degeneration of the heart."

"I believe every word you say," said the sheriff, solemnly. "I'm a Christian, I am. And here's my other ear."

Frank Rivera laughed. It was a contagious chuckle.

He went on: "What's on top of the ground ain't all. Underneath there's a lot of good paying ore."

"Sure," said the sheriff. "You wanta give me a thousand dollars in shares of one of those mines you're gunna uncover, eh?"

"Oh, shut up and listen, will you," said the mild Frank Rivera. "I tell you, some of the coverings has been lifted already. Nothing big found. Just a couple of strikes in pay dirt. Nothing much. Just forty-fifty thousand a year, with old-fashioned methods used. A little thing like that wouldn't make much difference to your way of living, I guess?"

"I could pick my teeth with it," said the sheriff. "Go on."

"There's a little private line to join up with the main railroad. That private line hums, what with beef and hides and tallow and whatnot. I ain't been talking about the sheep. They don't count, hardly. You wouldn't bother with fifteen-

173

twenty thousand sheep, just brushed in around the edges of the picture to make the hills stand out."

"Wouldn't you bother?" said the sheriff. "I can do everything with mutton except eat it. Go on, son. Are you tied to this picture by anything more'n a name?"

"Wait a minute. You ain't seen the heart of the thing, yet. You put a coupla hills in the middle of that paradise, and plant those hills with big cottonwoods, oaks and whatnot, and fill up the hollow with a fine lake, and make the grass green around all year long, and lay out some fine paths wanderin' about high, wide, and handsome, and put blood-hosses into the pastures, and blood bulls into the corrals, and build up ten-twelve big barns, and then you set down and sketch out a house that's laid out not in feet but in acres, and you begin to get near the main thing."

"No trouble at all to lay out the acres," said the sheriff. "I'm just putting the gold gilt on the chandeliers and the uniforms on the footboys. Now get down to the main thing."

"The main thing is an old man that's eighty plus. He's got eighty years in both eyes, and can't see farther than the end of his nose. He's got five hairs on his head and only one idea in it."

"And what's the idea?"

"That the long lost heir is coming back."

The sheriff yawned.

"You're not the heir, then?" said he.

"No, I'm not. Not in his mind."

"Who is, then?"

"Somebody that's dead as the hills."

"Is he batty, the old boy Rivera?"

"Kind of—on that subject. You wanta hear the story?"

"I wanta hear how you and me and a thousand dollars long and green fit into the yarn."

"I'm gunna tell you, brother. I'm only a third or fourth cousin, or something like that. But I wear the right name by means of leaving off the last half of my name. John Rivers White, I used to be, but White's a hard color to keep where the Chinee laundries ain't so common, and Rivers is harder to say that Rivera, anyway."

"So that's how you got to be a Rivera, eh?"

"That's the way," said Frank Rivera, laughing again, with his amazing and frank good nature.

He went on: "Now all I have is the name, and a lot of good intentions. It ain't that I'm interested in the inheritance. Oh, not at all. But I got a natural affection for the old man, and I can't help showing it every day in every way to make the world bigger and better, if you know what I mean."

"Oh, I know what you mean, all right," said the sheriff. "The old man swallers the guff and puts you into his will."

"He would, if he could make sure that the 'vanished heir' ain't left any trace behind him, but old Rivera still has that dream, so I start out to run it down for him.

"You see, in the old days, Rivera has a son, big as a horse, clean as a whistle and wild as mustard. The old man worships him, and wants to make him king of Mexico or president of North America, or something like that. He would take the backbone out of the Rocky Mountains to make a comb for that kid's hair. He would pour the Mississippi into a bucket to give his hoss a drink, if you know what I mean."

"I gather the idea."

"And then the kid goes off and finds him a little school teacher with no more gold mines in her purse than there is titles onto her name. She says yes to the kid, and his old man says no. But her yes was all that the kid wanted to hear. So he picks up the girl and rides forty miles, and marries her, and keeps right on traveling till he hits California. That California was full of hope and real estate, in those days, and the kid mortgages his four hind teeth and slices off a thousand acres of dobe nearest the rock and a thousand acres more of hope nearest the heart, and he sets down and makes him a home."

"Go on," said the sheriff. "But put in the spurs. Did he catch malaria?"

"No, malaria caught him. He raised ten sacks to the acre; but the mosquitoes beat him to the market. He ups and dies, about five days or so, after his wife gives the world a girl baby and turns up her own toes. He buries his wife today, and the neighbors order a coffin for him, tomorrow. They bury him free of charge, and the bank waits till the first collection day and puts that little old ranch back in its trousers pockets."

"Yeah, banks has got thousand-acre pockets, all right,"

observed the sheriff. "I recollect when—but go on with your yarn."

"I go out on the trail of that kid," said Rivera. "Alive, she owns old man Rivera and his cash on hand, and all his futures. I gotta find her. Then I find out that the neighbors had let an Injun woman on the next reservation adopt that white baby, until a Colonel Townsend comes along and decides to raise her white. But she brings everybody bad luck. The Injuns get smallpox, and the colonel gets a busted neck from his favorite ridin' hoss. And when he passes on, the kid passes to a Townsend cousin. But them second-hand Townsends don't know a Rivera from a hole in the ground, and they main manhandle that kid, and one day, when she's nine years old, she picks up and hauls her train, and heads south and west. I follow her trail. Nine-year-old girls don't walk across the Sierras without havin' even the grizzly bears set up and pay attention. I spot her trail. She gets out of the land of hope and real estate and hits the desert, and the last I hear, she's goin' with a limp, and yaller with malaria, and kind of miserable all around. You know what happens to weak kids in this kind of district, with alkali water, and alkali dust? Well, she's dead and gone. There ain't any trace of her, anywhere. That's a good ten, eleven years ago. Things shift pretty fast, around here. For all I know, some old miner or prospector might of took her in, and dug the kid's grave. But that grave is what I wanta find, and dig up the bones, and take them back to old man Rivera. By the time I got them bones properly buried in the village churchyard, and a nice white monument raised, old Rivera will be ready to turn up his toes, bein' long overdue, and if he don't get writer's cramp, I expect to cash in when his will is made. Now, old son, you see where you make a thousand dollars. You find that grave for me, and I pay it in cash. So's you can hear it talk for itself, here's the face of that coin, and this is how it whispers!"

35

THE SHERIFF was more than doubtful.

As he pointed out, the range was full of elements of moving population, all of whom might be willing to take in a sick child, but few of whom could be found, ten years later, and made to give an account of her end.

There were drifting Mexicans, who came north in summer for the roundups; there were Indians—plenty of them, in those days—who enjoyed nothing more than a chance to pick up a white waif and absorb it into the lazy comfort of redskinned ways; there were the prospectors, the squatters, adventurers of all kinds who came into the great land and shrank away from the face of it again, like water from the back of a well-oiled slicker.

However, a thousand dollars made the chance worth looking into. He would do what he could, and after making a few inquiries, he would give whatever answer he had picked up.

With that, Sheriff May stepped out, and Mr. Frank Rivera went along with him, his step short and quick and hurried beside the long and jingling stride of the Southwesterner.

It left Pierson and the boy to stare at one another, Pierson in grim dismay, and the boy smiling.

"There goes your future up the chimney," said young Speedy. "There you are, chief. You go home and get to work in your office. And I'll find the shortest trail to the railroad, and my happy home in the blind baggage."

"You think so?" said Pierson, his forehead gleaming with sweat. "Well, I've had my hand in this deal too far to snatch it out at the last moment. I'm going to try something else."

"Go out and give the good news to the girl, direct," said Speedy. "That's what I'd do, if I were you. You'll have a grateful father and daughter handing you the whole business of the estate, anyway."

"Bah! Just trimmings, trimmings!" said the lawyer. "And I want something off the joint. I'm not through, my lad. But, Speedy, I want you to sleep in this room. There's an extra bed for you. I need you, I think. I might need you a lot worse than I dream, even. For if I'm right, Big Six will have wind of me, and he may start in this direction."

"I'll be back," said the boy. "I'll be back for dinner time. And then we'll talk about Six Wilson, and the rest of the ghosts."

He went out and down to the lobby, where he spoke to the room clerk.

"Who's the gent in 217?"

"Why?" asked the clerk.

"I was trying to talk to Mr. Pierson in 218, and all that we could hear was the thinking that went on on the other side of the wall."

"We're not soundproof," said the clerk, grinning. "This 217, he's a booster, or a real estate dealer, I guess. He talks like he wanted votes. Wait a minute. Here's his name. Franklin P. Franklin. That's a funny moniker, ain't it?"

"Yeah. That's a funny moniker," agreed the boy. "Funny looking, too."

"Yeah. He's kind of round and red. If he started rolling, he wouldn't stop before he found the bottom. He's in there with the sheriff—right through that door. It's the bar on the far side, if you ain't found the shortest way to the oats."

Speedy went into the barroom.

He saw Joe Wynne, first of all, and Rudy Stern, drinking together at one end of the bar. Closer at hand were the sheriff and the man from the Rio Grande.

As the voice of Mr. Rivera had sounded, so did he look —small, fat, erect, with his chin carried tucked in, and a continual smile that made fat waves rise before his eyes. He looked like a man who smiled before breakfast and snored all night. He had one hand in a trousers pocket, jingling coins, while he talked to the sheriff.

Sheriff May, a moment later, left the saloon, and Speedy stepped up beside the other.

"Hello, stranger," said he. "I'm introducing myself."

"You're good news," said Rivera, with his ready grin. "What do you cost a copy?"

"Ice water," said the boy.

"That's cheap," said Rivera. "What headlines you carryin', partner?"

"Something that you'll wanta know, Mr. Franklin Franklin. That sounds like a firm name."

"It only needs an 'and' tucked in the center," said Rivera. "My mother was expecting twins, so she named me twice. That's all."

Speedy grinned.

"I wanted to tell you," said he, "something about this hotel."

"Go right on," said Rivera. "Is it free news?"

"Yes. It's a private printing of an extra. The beds in this hotel are too soft."

"Are they?" said the other. "Yes, for a mule that sleeps standing. I punched my bed upstairs and sprained my wrist."

Speedy shook his head.

"That bed's dangerously soft," said he.

"Is it?"

"Yes."

"You said 'dangerously?' "

"Yes, I said that."

"Look," said Rivera, "the more you talk, the more I see that I met you a long time ago and that we've got a lot of old memories to talk over."

"I guess we have," said Speedy.

"You try first," said Franklin P. Franklin. "I see a lot of memories coming up in your eyes, I think."

"No," said Speedy. "The way it is with me, I'm farsighted."

"You see the future, eh?"

"Yes. Especially I see tonight."

"What do you see, brother?"

Speedy paused. He was, to be sure, shooting somewhat in the dark, but, after all, the plump little man seemed to have little malice or meanness in him. He was simply one who wanted to take the easiest opportunities that life could afford to him. An attitude with which Speedy had the profoundest sympathy.

"I see you lying on your back, snoring," said he.

179

"I knew we were old friends," said Rivera. "You've been in hearing distance of me, anyway. I've been the champion of Montana. I've had more boots throwed at me at night than any man in the world. Go on. You see me snoring on my back."

"And in the morning I see you still lying there, without the snore."

"I always lie a while and wiggle my toes," said Franklin P. Franklin.

"You're not wiggling your toes," said the boy, "the way I see you. Your toes are as stiff as a board."

Rivera rose on his toes, and shuddered, as though he had been hit under the chin.

Then he swallowed, and the smile was gone from his face. He looked pouchy with softness, all at once.

"Well, brother?" said he.

"I've said my piece," said Speedy.

He turned. The other caught his arm.

"What's inside the idea?" he asked.

"All I know," said Speedy, "is that Nixon is bad for you, perhaps. About one chance in three, it's bad for you tonight. Two chances out of three, it's bad for you tomorrow. Three chances out of three, you're ready for planting the day after."

The little plump man, his eye darkening, thrust out his jaw.

"You think you can four-flush with me, brother?" he asked.

Speedy sighed.

"I've said too much," said he. "Mind you, it's not my party. I have no hand on either side, except that I think I know the hound who might want to eat you. And he wants to eat me, too."

"Eat me? Eat me?" said the fat man. "I never was in this dump before in my life."

"It'll likely be your last visit, anyway," said Speedy. "I'll tell you what you do. If you spend the night in this hotel, keep your window locked and your door barred. That keeps the snakes out."

Franklin P. Franklin lost his angry air.

"What's your name?" he asked.

"The boys call me Speedy."

"Are you the one they're all talking about?"

"I might have sneaked into the papers," said Speedy, "but I was never in the advertising section."

"You're Speedy," said Rivera, pointing a tubby, quivering forefinger. "And if you're Speedy, you're white."

"Thanks," said the tramp.

"Then, for God's sake tell me what you mean by all this guff!"

"I'm not telling you any more, because I don't know anything," said Speedy. "I'm guessing, and that's all."

The other blinked, and groaned while his eyes were still fast shut.

"Look here," said he, "will you go one step further?"

"If I can."

"Will you tell me what it looks like—the man or the snake that might walk into my room tonight and poison me?"

"I haven't time," said Speedy, "and I'm bad at describing, anyway. Any other these fellows can give you a good idea of him though. Just mention the name of Six-card Wilson, and they'll do the rest for you."

"Six—Wilson?" gasped the fat man.

He grasped the edge of the bar. His face was sick and white.

"I never seen him—I never crossed him!" said he.

"I don't suppose you have," said the boy, in answer, "but he doesn't need much to attract his attention. I've nothing more to say. I may be all wrong about my guess. But I had to tell you what was in my mind."

Speedy turned away, but he heard the other murmur, slowly, softly, to himself: "Where's the sheriff? Where'll I find him? Where'll I find him quick? God help me for comin' to this end of the world!"

36

Franklin P. Franklin could no longer find the sheriff. May had ridden briskly out of town.

He went to the manager of the hotel and said: "Friend, I'm in danger of my life!"

"You're what?" asked the manager, who was suffering from stomach trouble.

"Life!" said the fat man.

"You look like you enjoyed your meals pretty good," said the manager.

"I've been warned."

"About what?"

"That the outlaw, the man killer, Six Wilson, is after my scalp."

"You look out, then," said the cruel hotel man. "Because he mostly gets scalps that he's after."

"I tell you," said Franklin P. Franklin, "I been warned, and by a man that had oughta know!"

"Who?"

"Speedy!"

At this, the manager forgot his ill humor. He put back his head and laughed.

"Did Speedy tell you that?"

"I'm saying that he told me that!"

The manager laughed again.

"Speedy, he's a joker," said he. "He's a great kid, but he's a joker."

"A joker?"

"Sure. Don't you know anything. He's a scream. He's a regular entertainer."

"He entertained me, all right," said Rivera, his face growing hot at the suspicion that he had been done.

After all, it was a country of practical jokes, and at this

moment, Speedy might be telling around the town the jest he had played upon the stranger.

All through the supper hour, Speedy remained in the mind of Rivera, as an object of wrath. One day, he would find a way of entertaining the entertainer, and to good purpose, God willing!

Entertainer indeed!

He worried through his supper, divising expedients, none of which quite fitted the mark, and then he went upstairs to his room, when he had finished looking through some old newspapers that were in the lobby rack.

He was well enough contented with himself and his cigar, when he entered the room, but once in it, his state of mind altered. It seemed to him that the open window yawned at him like the mouth of a cannon. It seemed to him that footsteps were stealing up the hall towards his room.

He jerked the door open, and peered out.

He almost fainted, when he saw, in the hallway, the silhouette of a big man, but, in another moment, he noted that the face was one he had already seen in the barroom. Joe Wynne, that man was named, as he recalled, now.

Joe Wynne turned in at a door just across the hall, giving in silence a keen glance at the fat man before he turned the key in the lock of his door.

Then Franklin P. Franklin retreated into his room.

The face of Speedy no longer appeared, in his imagination, stretched by a widely mocking grin. Instead, it was serious and frowning, and the quiet gravity of the warning voice re-echoed again in the ears of the fat man.

He took his window and drew it down, and turned the two latches.

He drew the shade, and then drew the curtain.

He removed the writing pad from the top of the table and turned the table upside down under the window. That might impede a clever crook who was able, soundless, to enter the room in the middle of the night.

Then he went to the door. He locked it.

There was a bolt inside the door, slender, but better than nothing. It would make a noise, at least, if forced.

That bolt he shot home.

There were two chairs in the room, and these, side by

side, he adroitly braced against the door, putting their backs under the strong, solid handle.

After that, he stood for a moment, looking about him.

Fear that had made him cold had nevertheless made him sweat. So he mopped his forehead. It would be hot and close, sleeping in that room.

And the wreaths of smoke from his cigar slowly curled upwards, dimming the ceiling with blue-brown fog.

Regretfully, he stamped out his cigar on a saucer on the washstand.

It was better to go without a smoke than to stifle himself as in a coffin with his own smoke. Darkly, bitterly, he wished that the morning were already there!

He got off his clothes, and stood for a moment, thought-fully rubbing his swollen stomach, regretting his stale cigar—regretting also the easy target that he made with his prosperous figure.

Someone had said: "A man shot between the neck and the hips—he's done for. Give him a shot of dope to make him die easy.

"That's all you can do, about."

He shuddered. He felt that his own flesh was very deli-cate, and sensitive.

There was one more preparation that he could make. From his suitcase he took a short-nosed revolver. It was no good for distances, but it threw a forty-four caliber slug hard enough to knock down a man. And he knew that gun. He had used it for years, and he was a good hand with it. Only, he never yet had practiced at a human target. Lucky devils who had early chances at a mark that might shoot back!

He hoped that he would not get deer fever, so to speak.

Then he lay down.

He decided that he would sleep a little, and then rouse himself. Because it was not likely that any attempt would be made before the witching hour of midnight.

Ghosts rise, then—but his ghost might be laid forever!

Then. as he reached for the lamp to turn down the wick, he decided that it was too dangerous to venture to sleep. He might not waken, except when the bullet crashed through his brain. Or might it not be as the deadly knife edge slashed across his throat, and lift him voiceless, his life gushing, to kick one moment in agony, like a headless chicken—and then to die, twisted in the bedclothes as though in red mud!

He felt his throat. It was soft—terribly soft, he thought. Then he braced himself up in bed with pillows.

Well, it was not the first time he had sat up all night. Only, there had been company, on the other occasions. In this town, this fiendish town, he did not dare to hunt for company. He could not trust what he might find.

And to sit up without smoking!

He crossed his legs under the covers, cleared his throat loudly, and shifted his position in the bed. The springs squeaked noisily under him as he did so. The noise was a comfort. In this old rattletrap of a frame building, every sound could be heard from one end of the place to another.

He picked a magazine out of his suitcase.

It began with a ghost story, progressed to a murder mystery, and ran on to a tale of gang warfare.

He threw that magazine of murders across the room, with a flutter and a crash.

Somebody in the next room beat on the wall. The wall boomed and vibrated like the tympanum of a drum.

"Hey, shut up in there and let a fellow sleep!" called an angry voice.

"Sure!" sang out the fat man.

He was comforted by the nearness of that voice, and the anger in it gave him, somehow, the assurance that an honest man was there. Pity that there were not more honest men in the world—men honest *and* brave!

He looked at his watch.

Only half an hour had passed since he came into the room!

And the long watches of the night lay all ahead!

He folded his arms upon his stomach and bent his eyes upon his thoughts, for he prided himself upon being a man of mind.

And then, though the flare of the lamp was full against his eyes, his sight grew dim.

Once he wakened with a start, and told himself that he had been almost asleep.

But he composed himself again. Somewhere in the hotel a long-drawn snore was resounding. He blessed the homely sound!

Now, and he was unaware of it, the lamp began to smoke. And time passed.

The window stirred slightly. A latch, without visible touch, stirred, also, and then, with a slight creak, quite turned from the catch. The second latch was operated with even less sound.

Then the sash of the window began to rise.

That was not an easy operation. But it went on by degrees and degrees. Inch by inch it rose, softly, softly.

Once, the sleeper stirred with a groan, and grasped at his throat with hot hands. And, after that, for five or ten minutes the sash of the window did not stir.

At last the operation began once more.

Finally, when it was half up, a sinewy leg slipped over the sill, cautiously, noiselessly, found and avoided one of the legs of the overturned table, and reached the floor.

Then the curtain parted, with the faintest of whispers, and the face of Speedy looked into the room.

He slipped across the floor without making a sound, and looked for a moment down into the face of the sleeper. He saw the tight, agonized expression, saw the revolver tremble in the grasp of the fat man.

Then he slipped into the corner, and crouched there in the deep shadow behind the chair over which Franklin P. Franklin had thrown his clothes when he undressed.

It took some skill to bunch his body into so small a space, but he managed it to his own satisfaction, and remained there for a long time, gradually flexing muscle after muscle to keep them from cramping.

And then, at length, he heard what he expected—a sound at the window, no louder than the scratching of a cat's paw as it walks on a naked floor.

37

SPEEDY DID NOT MOVE. Instead, he crouched a little closer into the meager shadow that covered him, but not with his eyes, with hearing only he marked the progress of the second intruder.

He heard the stealthy turning of the catches on the window, which he had been careful to close behind him, and he heard, next, the gradual process by which the window was raised. Next, there was the most delicate of whispers such as might be made, say, by the friction of cloth, very gently rubbed against wood.

The second man, then, was stepping over the windowsill!

Speedy, in his corner, smiled a little, but his lips pressed hard together, like those of a boxer about to deliver a blow.

And then he heard the faintest of creakings. Someone was crossing the floor.

Little by little, Speedy arose. And he saw, as his eyes came over the edge of the clothes on the chair's back, the form of a tall man leaning just over the bed of the sleeper, a great, gaunt body, oddly narrow in the shoulders, and with vast, dangling arms. For a trade mark to identify this midnight prowler, there was the red, ragged remnant of an ear, visible over one shoulder.

His purpose did not seem entirely sinister, however.

First, he leaned close over the sleeper, and as his shadow crossed the face of Franklin P. Franklin, the fat man groaned in his dreams and struck blindly, as though at a mosquito.

At this, Six Wilson slowly re-erected himself, and then, with a gaping grin, moved towards the door.

He moved swiftly, easily, with long steps, and yet the floor, flimsy as it was, did not complain under his weight.

Even cat-footed Speedy wondered as he watched.

Arrived at the door, the big fellow moved the bolt gradually, noiselessly back, and next he turned the lock.

Speedy was crossing the floor in turn, crouching low, hands spread out, as though a cat should partially rise to his hind legs only, while stalking.

The door opened, now, and before he stepped into the hall, Six Wilson drew a revolver, and gripped it twice, flexing his fingers carefully about the handles.

It was plain that he was using the room of Franklin P. Franklin not as a scene for a crime, as the boy had feared, but as an entrance to a more desired place—such a place, for instance, as the chamber where Speedy was supposed to be lying, soundly asleep—where in fact John Pierson was now in deep dreams.

Now, with one long stride, pitching his body low and turning so that his muscled shoulder would be the forward edge of his leap, like the head of a club, he drove straight at the tall man.

He made no sound, even in springing, but perhaps a shadow flew before him, and Six-card turned about, from the waist upwards, not shifting his feet.

It was the worst position he could have been in, to receive a shock. The right hand of Speedy caught the gun; it exploded to send a bullet through the floor. And the shoulder of the boy, at the same time, crashed against the hip of Six-card.

He seemed to break in two, like a slender stick. Then, dropping the gun so that he might use his hands more freely, he grappled with Speedy as he fell.

He reached for the throat of the boy, and only found the head of Speedy, stiffly bent down.

He took that head by the flying hair and, with the power of a gorilla, jerked it up and back.

The spine of Speedy almost snapped, under the shock. Clouds of red sparks flew upwards in his brain. And amazement seized him. There was everything about Six Wilson to suggest the incarnate devil, but there was nothing to point to almost superhuman strength. But his muscles seemed to be those of an ape, not those of a human creature.

Yet, though his head was flung back, and the other hand

of the thug raised to deliver a stunning blow, the wits and the arms of the boy kept working.

When in doubt, says the prize-ring maxim, work in close and hit as fast as your hands will work. When stung, charge!

Out of the air, half blindly, Speedy caught a thumb and forefinger of the elevated hand. He caught them, and jerked them back with a quick, twisting pressure.

Franklin P. Franklin, at that moment, wakened from a nightmare in dreams to one in reality. He began to scream for help, and shoot at the struggling monsters by the door. But the bullets flew wildly from his trembling hand.

And, through and over that noise, Speedy felt rather than heard a bone snap.

He had a one-handed man against him, to all intents and purposes, from that moment.

No, now big Six-card jerked the elbow of his free arm around and the blow glanced off the forehead of Speedy.

He felt his knees buckle, and darkness washed across his eyes. But through that darkness he saw the convulsed face of Six Wilson, his lips grinned back from yellow fangs, like a beast about to bite into the throat, and search for the life, and the sight cleared his brain.

His hands had not been idle, and now they found what they wanted. His right hand, working up behind the shoulder of Wilson, now dipped over and to the front, the arm of the boy straining to its uttermost length, until his hand gripped hard around the lean, hard point of Wilson's chin.

He had a leverage, then, that multipled his strength of hand by ten. Even so, it was not easy to bend back the head of Six. It yielded, but only an inch at a time, fighting stubbornly. And, in the meantime, Six Wilson beat with his broken hand into the face of his tormentor.

He was like a great horse, attacked by a wildcat, torn, succumbing, and he struggled valiantly against his fall.

They had risen to their feet, the legs of Wilson lifting the double weight of the entangled bodies. There he stood looking more gigantic than ever, the clinging weight of Speedy appearing less than the body of a child.

If the hand of Wilson had been whole, in two efforts he could have beaten the boy senseless. But, as it was, even from his iron lips groans were wrung as he strove to use the hand as a club.

189

And, in the meantime, his other arm was tied close to his body by the encircling grip of Speedy, while the lifting shoulder of the tramp worked hard and high into the armpit of the big man, and that small hand seemed to increase and increase its pressure.

And the neck muscles of Six-card, overstrained, wavered, shuddered violently, gave away. Back went his head with a jerk; his mouth came open with a horrible gasping moan. And, close to his breast, he heard the snarl of Speedy, like a fighting animal.

Fat Franklin P. Franklin had rushed towards the door, still screaming, and at the door, he encountered men, big men. One was Joe Wynne; the other was Rudy Stern. But even they could not brush aside the hysterical clawing of the fat man as he strove to get out into the hall, away from the fight. In the instant they were delayed, over the shoulders of Rivera they saw big Six Wilson stagger backward, clawing at the air to get his balance. And they saw his head strained down and down by a remorseless pressure. They saw his whole body arching backwards—and then, like a tower, he crashed.

The weight of the boy was above him. And the force of the doubled body landed fairly upon his head.

He shuddered once, and lay still.

While Speedy, rising, staggered a little, and then he picked up the revolver which the big man, in the fury of the attack, had cast away from him.

"Hello, boys," he said to Wynne and Rudy Stern, as the pair pushed into the room. "Six-card seems to have mixed up the room numbers a little, and you see that he's gone to sleep in the wrong place."

After that, he abandoned the chamber and went to his own room.

The screeching voice of Franklin P. Franklin, in the meantime, was trailing and streaming down the stairs like a comet. And the whole hotel was wakening.

Not many seconds had passed since Speedy first flung himself at the big body of the bandit. But doors were opening, voices were shouting everywhere.

Then he opened the door of his room—to be covered by a revolver held in the hand of John Pierson.

The lawyer, half dressed, with a grim fighting face, glared

down the barrel towards the intruder, and it was a long moment before he realized his mistake.

While Speedy said: "Don't be a fool, Pierson."

He crossed with slow, short steps to his own bed and let himself gradually down on it. Then he lay flat on his back. One arm hung over the edge towards the floor.

And every muscle, every tendon through his arms and shoulders seemed strained out of place—pulled thin.

Pierson stood over him, picked up the limp arm, and laid it across his body.

"Speedy, lad," said he, with surprising emotion in his voice, "you've been shot! Where's the hurt?"

"Not shot," muttered Speedy, keeping his eyes tightly shut, while the sparks still flew upwards in his brain. "Only a little tired. Too much noise in this damned hotel. Can't get any sleep."

"Not shot?" said Pierson, nevertheless fumbling anxiously about the breast of the boy, fearful of touching hot blood with his fingers. "What's happened?"

"Oh, nothing," said Speedy. "They're all standing on their heads because Six Wilson is in the next room, there, spread out flat with a bump on the back of his head. You better go and see what they do with him."

"Six Wilson!" breathed the lawyer.

"Six had a bad break," said the boy. "Break in the fingers of his right hand, as a matter of fact. Except for that—well, you go and see what they do with him, will you? If they put him in the jail, see that they keep two fellows guarding him night and day. He's a snake, and he can get out through the fingers of most people, I take it."

He added, as Pierson rushed from the room: "Poor Six! His gun hand, too!"

38

PIERSON CAME BACK in half an hour. He was jubilant. Everything was easy, now, he said. The great Six Wilson was securely lodged in the jail, and four men had been detailed to keep guard over him in pairs, keeping sailor shifts.

"He'll get out, just the same," said the boy.

"He'll hang," said Pierson. "They're thirsty and hungry to hang him!"

"They're thirsty and hungry," said Speedy. "But he's not meant to die from a rope around the neck. He's not that kind, I tell you! He'll turn up his toes on horseback, filling the air with more lead than language, right up to the end."

Pierson sat down beside the table and stared at the boy, who remained limp, and with his eyes closed, on the bed.

"Are you sick, Speedy?" he said.

"I'm trying to think," said Speedy, "and that's what makes me feel a little sick."

"You'd better not go outside without a bodyguard," said the lawyer.

"Why not? Do they want my scalp, too?"

Said Pierson: "Every man in Nixon wants to shake hands with you and pound you on the back. You know the way they are. And they'd like to clip a few souvenirs off you, too, if they have a chance. They'll pull you to shreds, Speedy, if they can!"

"That's good," said Speedy. "Nixon and all the people in it can be damned, as far as I'm concerned. They're not what bothers me."

"I know," suggested the other. "It's because of the rest of Wilson's gang; you think that they'll get on your trail and never leave it till they've polished you off. But I wonder— tell me if it's true that you shot a fellow called the Deacon to death and dropped another celebrated thug named the Snapper in one evening's entertainment?"

"I talked them to death, that was all," said the boy. "I hate gun fights. I told you that I never shot a bullet out of a gun in my life, and I don't intend starting now. It's not the Six Wilson gang that worries me most, just now."

"Go on," said the lawyer. "Tell me if you can."

"It's because something's gone wrong with me and I don't know what to do about it."

"What's gone wrong?"

"Something inside of me; something that I never had before."

"How does it feel?" asked Pierson, anxiously.

"Kind of giddy, Pierson, and a hollow feeling in the pit of the stomach."

"Indigestion," said Pierson. "I know. You've been under too much of a nerve strain."

"I'd call it conscience," said the boy. "It's new to me, but I'd call it conscience."

"You would?"

"Yes. I never had it wrong with me before. But I'd call it conscience, all right. The trouble is that I'm worrying about doing the right thing."

"Don't be foolish," said Pierson. "I'll keep you inside the law in this business, my lad."

"What I'm talking about has nothing to do with the law of the land. It's my law for myself that I'm thinking about."

"Go on, Speedy, and tell me all about it."

The boy opened his eyes and looked up at the ceiling.

"It's the old man that poisons everything," said he.

"What old man?"

"Old Rivera."

"What has he to do with your conscience, Speedy?"

"Ever since I heard that fat-faced fool in the next room talking about the old boy, I've had a picture of him."

"Well, what sort of a picture?"

"Of an old boy on a front veranda, leaning on a cane and looking down the drive with eyes that he can't see out of. A blind old boy waiting for something to turn up."

"Hello," said Pierson. "Is that troubling you?"

"Yes, that's troubling me."

"I'll cut that trouble out of your mind, well enough," said

Pierson. "That old Rivera was the meanest piker that ever rode a horse, when he was a youngster, they say. And he drove his own son away with his meanness."

Speedy shook his head.

"That was twenty years ago," said he. "He's had twenty years to think things over. He's had twenty years to wait. God pity him! I can't get him out of my mind, Pierson."

The lawyer frowned.

"What can you do about it?" he asked.

"Come clean," said Speedy. "You broached the deal to me. Now I suggest that the pair of us come clean."

"A few millions," said the lawyer, "means nothing to you?"

"Oh, hell, Pierson," said the boy, sighing out the words, "you know what money is. It's all right in a daydream. But when you have it once, it doesn't make the sky any bluer or beefsteak any tenderer. You know that?"

Pierson leaned suddenly forward in his chair.

"Do I know that?" he asked, slowly.

And his answer went no farther. He was lost in frowning thought.

"I don't like the job, any more," said the boy. "I told you that I'd go through with it. I want you to let me off the promise and give me a chance to do the white thing."

"What's the white thing?"

The lawyer was talking nervously, his lips and his fingers twitching.

"The white thing," said Speedy, his eyes closed once more, "is to get hold of the girl, and tell her everything straight, and then take her on the jump for the Rivera place. How far is that?"

"Five hundred miles. That's all!"

"We can do that in ten days. If it's that far, we'd better make an early start. You may shake your head and curl the lip at the Wilson boys, but I've nearly been their meat and I'd rather have somebody else digest me. Pierson, have a look at that idea, will you?"

John Pierson sat silent for ten long minutes.

Then he swore, not once, but many times. He jumped up from his chair and went to the window, before which he stood with his arms akimbo. Still he swore, from time to time.

"Tough, isn't it?" said the boy. "I've been spending that easy money all the way from Cincinnati to Paris. I've traveled in special cars and raised champagne boils on the end of my nose. I've killed foxes in the galloping counties and smoked a cigar under the chin whiskers of the Sphinx. But it's no good!"

Said Pierson, gloomily: "I've been buying real estate. I've founded a big family fortune. I've been nursing it and building it bigger and stronger in my daydreams, lately. But you're right. It's no good. It's a thing that would make my wife and girl despise me, if they knew the ins and outs."

"Regular Bible talk, Pierson," said the boy.

"Shut up, Speedy," said the other. "You annoy me, when you speak like that. I'm going to chuck the whole business, though."

"And help to put it right?" said the boy.

"How can I help?"

"There's a tidy little job on hand," said Speedy. "Five hundred miles on horseback looks to me like five hundred miles through hell. I'll be worn through to the bone. I'm going to carry air cushions, and carve a hole in the center of my saddle. I'm so sore, Pierson, that I'd hate to ride a rockinghorse on the front veranda; but I've got five hundred miles before me. And I need you, and at least one more. You'll help to make the escort."

"Escort be damned," said Pierson. "I'm going back to my business. I've had enough of this infernal conscience business! Two weeks of riding, when I have cases—"

The slender hand of Speedy rose in the air.

"Think it over, Pierson," said he. "You like hunting. And on this ride, trouble is going to come hunting down the trail of whoever tries to get that girl to her grandfather. There'll be shooting. And I'm no hand with a gun. You know that. I'm just going along to give moral support, if you know what I mean."

He stared up at the ceiling, and the lawyer grinned, sourly.

"You'd even tempt the devil to take a change of air, Speedy," said he.

"You're sold, then," said the boy. "Now, I want to lie here and taste this conscience of mine until I'll know the sour tang of it the next time it gets high in my throat. I want to know what it is, in time to run the other way from it. You send for Mary Steyn and Arthur Steyn. And send for Joe Wynne, too, the big, blue-eyed puncher with the two big guns and the thoroughbred nature. I'll stand here without tying until you arrive again."

Pierson, for a moment, idled up and down the room, trying to find something to say, but he found nothing.

At last, he went out without further speech, and found his way, scowling, down into the lobby. A hum of voices rose from many throats to greet him.

The hotel proprietor rushed to him, sweating, beaming. "How's the kid?" said he.

"Sound as can be," said Pierson. "You can't put a hole in that armor plate."

The proprietor rubbed his hands together; then he laughed with joy.

"We want him down here," said he. "We want to look at him again and see the sort of skin that handles fire without gloves. The whole town is happy, Mr. Pierson, except Mr. Franklin P. Franklin, and he's in the bar trying to get drunk, but he's still so scared that the liquor won't work on him. If you—"

"I want to get hold of a fellow named Wynne," said Pierson. "Speedy wants to see him."

"Wynne's right outside the door, as big as life. He'll go right up, and—"

"And I want to send a message to Mr. Arthur Steyn and his daughter to tell them to come to town at once—"

"They're already in town," said the proprietor.

"Good!" sighed Pierson, his face falling in spite of himself. "Try to collect the whole lot of them, will you? And tell them that Speedy and I are waiting upstairs in hopes of seeing them."

The proprietor agreed, and Pierson took a weary way up the stairs again. Glancing once out the window, when he reached the room, he could hear hoofs beating, and see fresh clouds of dust rising. Other punchers were coming fast to Nixon to see the latest hero of the hour!

And there, on the bed behind him, lay the hero in person —sound asleep, and snoring lightly!

39

SLEEP LEFT SPEEDY only when big Joe Wynne came into the room and stood stiffly, like a soldier at attention, near the door. His eye was straight as ever, but his color was far from high.

"I hear that you want to see me, Speedy," said he.

Speedy slowly rolled to his feet, yawned, and eyed the other up and down. Then he deliberately walked across the room. When he was close to Wynne he thrust out his chin.

"You don't look so doggone big to me," said he.

"I'm big enough, son," said Joe Wynne, with a gleam in his eye.

"Some day we'll see about that," said Speedy.

Most impolitely, he turned on his heel and walked to the window. It was Pierson, a somewhat amused spectator of this scene, who offered a chair to the guest.

"I want to know what Speedy wants to see me about," said Wynne, steadily.

"God knows that I don't want to see you," said Speedy, without turning. "All I want to do is to hit you on a corner of your beautiful Greek chin. That's all I want to do. But I've got to talk nice to you about something else. Shut up and sit down, and let me get my wind, will you?"

"You'll understand before long," said Pierson, and got Joe Wynne, reluctantly, to take a chair.

Almost immediately, there was a knock at the door, and Steyn and Mary came in.

She smiled at Wynne, shook hands with Pierson when Speedy introduced her, and then said to the tramp:

"What have you been doing, Speedy? Making yourself famous, or just having a good time?"

"Oh, you know," said he, "trouble always comes to him who waits."

"Of course it does," said she, "if it knows the room number so that he can wait in the right spot."

"Sit down, Mary; sit down, Mr. Steyn," said the boy. "I've got a speech coming over me. I need elbow room when I make a speech."

They sat down, all except Pierson, who fidgeted in a corner of the room.

"Hadn't I better explain the thing in detail, Speedy?" said he.

But the boy dominated the room easily.

He answered: "You'd make it too long. The main point is that this is a blue moment for four of the five of us. It's a happy moment for Mary Steyn, yonder."

"Go right on, Speedy," said Steyn. "This isn't one of your jokes, I hope?"

"I wish that it were," said the boy. "But I'll soon rub off all the smiles except from Mary's face. Mr. Steyn, you're going to lose her. Wynne, you and Pierson and I are going to ride five hundred miles with trouble behind us all the way, in order to plant her in the middle of umpteen thousand acres of grass and cows and about nine or ten million bucks."

Wynne sat up higher in his chair. The girl narrowed her eyes and searched the face of Speedy.

"I'll go back and explain a little," said the boy. "Mr. Steyn, about ten-eleven years ago, you picked up in the hills a ragged, nine-year-old brat, on the thin side, and yellow in the eyes from malaria."

"I found Mary in somewhat that way," said Steyn. "Speedy, do you mean it when you say that I'm to lose her?"

"You can't lose her," said Speedy. "She's not the kind to forget anyone she cares a rap about. And she cares a lot of raps about you. Only, you'll be seeing her in Paris models, from now on. And a little while from now you'll be standing on the promenade deck of the Ritz Hotel, steering for bigger and better drinks. Mary when you found her, had hoofed it all the way from California. She's been kicked around a good bit by some hounds, who had her from Colonel Whatnot, who took her from an Indian squaw, who adopted her when her mother died and also her father, who left home in Texas because *his* father disapproved of the

198

marriage. Does that clear the decks somewhat? The point is that for twenty years grandpa has been sitting on the edge of the Rio Grande, forgetting his bank account and letting his cows multiply regardless, because he wants his darling granddaughter. He's eighty plus, two-thirds blind and hungry to die; but he's hungrier still to give his estate to something nearer home than charity."

Old Steyn stood up and drew in his breath. Then he sat down again, slowly, without a word. The girl came and stood behind him. Her hands rested on his shoulders. Her big, doubting eyes studied the face of Speedy.

"Now, then," said Speedy, "we ride into Six Wilson, who learns about the bank account that's waiting for Mary, and rides off every prospective husband that might not give him a split when the good news breaks. That places Six for you in the game. Enter a hobo, Speedy. He gets wind of the quarry, decides that he wants to be a married man, and comes down the wind to pick up Mary. But she's too hard for him," he said, looking her fairly in the eye, "and so he throws up the sponge and comes to Nixon, where Mr. Pierson persuades him that the best thing is to go straight and tell Mary the whole story."

"Hold on, Speedy," said Pierson, growing very red. "You don't need to save my face, like this. I'll take all the punishment that comes my way."

"Besides Six," went on the boy, waving aside Pierson's protest, "Rudy Stern is also on deck. He doesn't know whether to try to be a power behind the throne or to write himself down as a suitor for the nine millions. Pierson here, has worked out the whole thing from the legal end; so he's in on the know. And there's also another in town who knows the story. He's a little fat pig with a happy eye and more names than you can shake a stick at. So, Mary Rivera, that brings the yarn down to the present. And the future is this: You pack a grip. You get your toughest horse. A pair of 'em, I suppose. And you and Pierson and I start for the Rio Grande."

He turned on Joe Wynne.

"This is where you come in, Joe," said he. "You're the only one of us who's played absolutely straight from the start. I owe you a sock on the chin, but I have to admit for the present that you're the only white man on the range. You make number three in the escort, with a pair of your best nags, and half a dozen guns guaranteed to shoot straight. Because there's no doubt in my mind that trouble is going to run on our heels. Too many people know that the fat's in the fire the minute that we ride south."

"There's the law, Speedy," said Steyn, "that can give shelter and assure—"

"There are a lot of fourth and fifth cousins," said Speedy, breaking in abruptly, "who know that old Rivera has already made a will and put them down for something better than hope. And if you wait for the law to work, the law will find a dead old man down there by the Rio Grande, a will to be contested and everything tied in a muddle for ten years to come. Mary Rivera will turn into an old maid waiting for hard cash, and the only people to profit will be the lawyers. My way is the only way. Pierson will come. Wynne, will you?"

Joe Wynne stood up and held out his hand, silently. Speedy looked at it, and then up to the blue, honest eyes of the big rancher.

"Not till we're all square," said Speedy.

He raised his hand.

"If there's no more business to come before this meeting," said he, "we're dismissed. I need some sleep before we start."

"There's this much business," said Joe Wynne, who had remained staring at the boy ever since the last rebuff he had received. "I have eight horses that are doing nothing, and one of them is your horse, anyway. You refused him once, but this time you'll have to take Coal Tar."

"Business is business," agreed the boy. "I'll take the nag for the trip, Joe, and a lot of thanks to you—afterwards—well, afterwards can take care of itself."

And he looked hungrily at the fine, strong jaw of the larger man.

Joe Wynne left at once. Mary and Steyn were to return to his house, and there she would pack up. And Speedy and Pierson went down to the head of the stairs, and saw the two go down arm in arm, old Steyn leaning a little against the girl, his head down.

As they disappeared: "He's close to crying," said Speedy, with a sneer which was not what it seemed. "No more chance to spend money on her, and he'll probably have to accept a necktie that he doesn't want every Christmas and birthday. That's the way women are. A man works for 'em all his life, nearly, and right at the end, he starts in sorrowing because they're not on hand to be cried over, anymore, and more worked over, too, and—"

"Be quiet, Speedy," said Pierson, and for once the boy obeyed him.

They were only halfway down the hall, however, when frantic footsteps rushed up the stairs and pursued them.

It was Franklin P. Franklin, who threw himself upon Speedy.

"Keep him off! Keep him off!" he gasped. "You're the only man that can keep him from murdering me!"

"Keep who?" demanded Pierson, helping to push the fat man away.

The white face of Mr. Franklin-Rivera was shaking like soft pudding.

"Six Wilson!" he screamed.

"He's loose already, then," said Speedy, with a resigned nod.

"Loose?" cried Pierson.

And, as though to dismally echo his words, they heard from outside the hotel a confused roar of voices, and a beating of hoofs.

"Yes, he's loose! Six masked men raided the jail, and covered the guards. There's two men shot, and one of 'em likely to die—and Six Wilson—he's gone—he ain't there! He's coming to finish his job and murder me! For God's sake, protect me, Mr. Speedy."

Speedy did not sneer. He merely held up one finger and said: "Listen!"

Franklin P. Franklin was as still as a child at school.

And Speedy said: "You're as safe as a clam in its shell in the bottom of the sea. Six Wilson wants my scalp, and not yours. He was only turning your room into a corridor that led to mine, last night. Now, you go to bed and rest your nerves, and you'll wake up to find that Speedy, and Six, and the whole bad business, have started south!"

40

FAR OUT on the desert, the greasewood flowed like thin smoke in the hollows where water gathered, for a few brief days, in the spring of the year, and then soaked down and down, many yards, the earnest roots of greasewood and mesquite following it. And there was a blur of vegetation covering the ground. In the distance it held out some hope, being a fairly solid dusty green. But the ground over which the four rode was only sparsely set about with grisly forms of cactus, horribly defended, every one, with thorns.

They rode in single file, because the horses went better in this fashion, although the third and fourth man might be bothered, a good deal, by the rising of the alkaline dust. And the sun that beset them was bitterly hot. There had been a severe dust storm, the day before, though it had passed, the air was filled with indescribably fine dust which did not serve, apparently, to ward off any of the rays of the sun, but which blanketed the horizon in a dull and purplish mist.

But under the blast of the sun, which dried the sweat in streaks of salt as soon as it sprang, the horses went on at a good, free-stepping walk. Perhaps they were a little jaded by the work which already lay behind them, but this could not appear in their gait; not for nothing had Joe Wynne bred them for blood and looks, together, and tested his string with the hardest of endurance trials. Now that they were tried, they would not be found wanting.

Joe Wynne himself rode at the head of the line, just now, a magnificent figure of a man, looking nobler and bigger than ever, now that he had the whole setting of the desert around him.

A jack rabbit, long, lean-legged, fast as the flash of a

whiplash, jumped from behind a cactus and sped away. Joe Wynne snatched out a revolver and opened fire. Four times the muzzle of his gun jerked up, four times the spray of sand which the bullet kicked up made the rabbit sky-hop high into the air and to the side. Four times, it bleated like a sheep, small and far.

Then Mary Steyn, hurrying her horse up, pulled down the gun-hand of her friend.

"He's run his gauntlet, Joe," said she. "Let him go, poor devil!"

"Four misses—in a row," said Joe Wynne, "and three this morning."

"Every one of those misses would have killed a man," said John Pierson.

He was red-faced from the extreme heat. It was true that he loved the wilderness and wilderness life, but his choice was the grand, green quiet of the mountains—not that wide-stretched furnace floor.

"Yes," commented Speedy, who was last of the four. "If men were rabbits and ran, seven men would have flopped today, because of you, Joe. You're getting better and better! Pierson, show him some real shooting, will you?"

"Leave Joe alone," commanded the girl.

Wynne put up his revolver, flushing a little, but very little. He was growing accustomed to the badgering which he received from the tramp.

"That's only Speedy," said he. "I don't mind Speedy."

She smiled kindly on him, for a reward. And, since Pierson stopped his horse now to tighten a cinch, and Speedy paused with him, the leading pair were soon out of earshot of their followers.

"Look here," said Joe Wynne, turning half about in the saddle. "I'd like to get a line on something. I ought not to speak about it. But I've got to. It's stuck in my throat."

"What?" said she. "There's nothing in the world that you can't ask me about."

"Then let me have it straight. I never can make out. Sometimes you go all day and never speak to him. Sometimes you rag and wrangle with one another for an hour at a stretch. How much do you like Speedy?"

She met his glance frankly.

And he hastened to put in: "It's not that I'm trying to

push him out of the way. I'm not ambitious about you, Mary. I know that you're out of my horizon. But Speedy's brighter than I am. He's not out of *any* horizon that he cares to step into."

And she said: "I wish that you hadn't asked me. Not that I mind telling you; but it's a thing that makes me a little unhappy to think about. All I know is that I'm a lot more interested in Speedy than he is in me."

The big man stared.

"All right," said he. "But he's top man, isn't he?"

"He's top man with me," said she, firmly. "And then— if you don't mind being second—I think about Joe Wynne."

He grew very hot in the face.

"My God, Mary," he said, "I'm a happy man to hear that! If a horse is in the race it may win—if the leaders fall down!"

She said: "We won't speak about it again, Joe, will we?"

"Never a word," said he.

"There's another thing. Have you tried, really, to make friends with Speedy?"

"Yes," said he. "I've tried. But I might as well try to get close to a winged horse. He hates me. Not because he thinks I'm such a bad lot. Otherwise he never would have asked me to come along on this trip. But it's because I manhandled him, that unlucky day. He'll have to pay me off for that with a broken bone before he feels right about me."

"Oh, Joe," said the girl, "what sort of a man is he? How can anyone make him out?"

"Nobody can," said Wynne. "He's the straightest fellow in the world, and the crookedest. He has the slipperiest tongue that ever talked; and his promise is a rock of Gibraltar. He's a fighting devil; and he never wore a gun. He'd move mountains to help a friend that he really likes—and he never worked for a dollar in his life!"

She sighed as she thought these things over.

"It's all true," said she. "But whatever he wants to do, he does. He's brought us halfway to the Rio Grande, already, and not a thing has happened."

"Has he done the bringing?" asked Wynne, smiling a little.

"Oh," she answered, "I mean that you all have been wonderful about it. But what keeps enemies at a distance is

Speedy. People are afraid of him, once they've seen his teeth!"

"Yes," nodded Wynne, seriously, "he's riding here without a gun, and yet thugs like the Wilsons would be more afraid of him than of all the rest of us put together."

Then the other two came up, the voice of Speedy rising and ringing over the accompaniment that he struck from his guitar. That useless weight and burden added to the expedition!

A more ungraceful horseman never was seen in the Southwest.

He rode to the side, like a Greek muleteer, one stirrup dangling unoccupied, and only the stirrup leather of the other filled, while one foot swung free and bumped against the ribs of Coal Tar. It was an indignity that would have made the big stallion bolt like a streak if any other rider had offered it; but he had learned to endure much from this womanishly helpless, maddeningly reckless rider.

A horse is apt to be like a girl; as long as it is interested it is docile, and Coal Tar would never come to understand this whimsical master.

"Are you singing because you're happy, or because you want to be?" asked Pierson, at last.

"I'm singing," said Speedy, "to make both ends of me forget the middle. Pierson, I haven't got enough skin left to go around me. I walked all day yesterday, and I'd walk again today, but I took the skin off my feet yesterday; and now I'd have to walk on my hands. Pierson, I'd give a thousand dollars for a bread and milk poultice. I'm willing to go to bed and lie on my face for six months. If ever I buy a house, I'll burn all the hard-bottomed chairs in it for the sake of *Auld Lang Syne*."

They were entering a narrow valley, ragged with rocks that cropped up on both sides, and the trail wound unevenly through the middle.

The sudden voice of big Joe Wynne blasted against their ears:

"Ride! Ride like the devil! They're at us! They're at us! Mary, go first!"

The whole valley was ringing, at the same moment. From the rocks along the upper ledges, on the right side of the canyon, the marksmen were placed, in total safety. Ay, and right up the valley itself, behind the four riders, came a swarm of horsemen—four, five, six! They shot as they galloped, letting their horses find their own ways among the rocks.

Speedy was last, as the four got under way.

But he was last for only a second, in that miserable trap.

John Pierson suddenly swayed, lost his stirrups, and lurched to the ground.

Speedy, jerking hard back and shouting to the stallion, leaned down and grasped at the shoulder of the fallen man.

But the lawyer turned a set, blood-stained face towards the tramp.

"I'm only the first cash payment on account," said he. "I don't mind. Ride on, you fool! Get Mary through! Ride like the devil, while I trip up a few of 'em!"

As he spoke, he picked up the rifle that had fallen to the trail beside him, and instantly he was pumping lead at the riders from down the gulch.

And Speedy rode on!

He felt a wrench as though his heart was torn out of his breast. But he knew, in a blinding moment of revelation, that he would have wanted the lawyer to play the same role if he, Speedy, had gone down.

On raced his horse. The gulch vanished behind them, and looking back, he heard the rattling of the rifles far away, where John Pierson must be dying for the sake of the three who remained.

There was no pursuit. And Speedy came up with those who galloped ahead. The immense strides of Coal Tar devoured the distance between.

The girl, as he came up, turned and looked a horrified question at him, and he answered, coldly: "Pierson went down. I thought he'd serve to keep the teeth of the pack busy for a while, so I left him lying there, and came along."

He stared hard at her, and with amazement and bewilderment, he saw that she half believed that he had meant what he said!

—41—

THEY WENT ON SOUTH for three more days, unhindered, but they were three dark days for Speedy. He never sang so much, so gaily, or so well, seated more like a Greek muleteer than ever in his saddle, but all the while he was black in his heart, for he was sure that both the girl and Joe Wynne blamed him bitterly for having "deserted" John Pierson.

That was the way they would have put it. They drew together more and more. He fell into the habit of lingering a good ways out of earshot to the rear, and he had a sense that when he came up, they talked less, and changed the subject of their conversation, often.

So he smiled and sang all the more, because that was his nature, but the blackness seeped through and through him, like a poison.

And their horses went well. They could see the hills behind which was their goal; in two days they would be there.

So, on the evening of the third day after the fall of John Pierson, just before the sun set, when they were casting about for a proper place to make the camp, riders swept up out of a shallow draw whose existence they had not even suspected, and came at them in a long line.

The earth was paved with russet and gold from the evening light, and the shadows of the riders fell far before them. Swiftly they came with their guns, and in the center was the unmistakable and grotesque outline of Six Wilson, his narrow shoulders, his sombrero was wider than his shoulders. His right hand hung from his neck in a sling, but he managed his horse with knees and heels, only, like an Indian, and kept the left free for a revolver.

So they came, not yelling to strike terror into the enemy,

and raise their own courage, but silently, like people who know their work, each man relying confidently on himself. They seemed to be racing to beat one another.

Speedy saw the girl whip her rifle from its long holster as their horses broke into a sweeping gallop. And then he heard a great, strange shout, that hardly seemed to come from a human throat, and on his right he saw Joe Wynne turn and charge straight at the Wilson gang.

He rode straight in the saddle, the brim of his sombrero curling back from his noble face in the wind of the gallop, and a revolver smoked in either hand. This Speedy saw, and beheld the line of the Wilsonites part in the center, and sway to this side and to that, heard the ringing of their guns, and saw them close around the big man like wolves around an elk.

And that was all.

Waves of swelling ground arose and shut away all view of the melee; he was riding at the side of the girl, now, the guitar giving out a little jingling at every stride, as though the fingers of a ghost were dallying at the strings and striving to begin a tune, but never getting past the first opening chords.

She looked neither to the side nor back, but straight ahead, and he saw that her face was wet.

Well, they were only two days from the Rio Grande. He would be glad when the two days were over!

They galloped into twilight, into darkness. Then they found running water, where the horses drank; they filled their canteens and went on to halt in a mesquite tangle, in a hollow. The girl would have gone on, and she spoke the first time, to say so, but Speedy answered:

"They've got Joe Wynne, now, and he's enough to satisfy them, for a little while. Even the Wilsons don't get a Joe Wynne every day in their lives."

He spoke lightly, with a purpose, and then he added with a cheerful briskness:

"Pretty good thing, wasn't it, the way old Joe turned around and smashed into 'em!"

She did not answer; then he heard her sobbing, a sad and regular pulse in the darkness.

After that, he waited until he was sure that she slept; then he untwisted his blanket, slipped away, saddled, not

Coal Tar but the good bay gelding which was his lead horse, and turned straight back across the desert.

He rode for an hour, and then he found the guiding star that he wanted—a yellow ray shining along the face of the ground. He stalked it closely, left his horse and went on, on foot, stealthily. So he came close to the fire and the three men beside it. Two were faces he did not know; the third man lay some distance from the blaze, very still, his face turned up to the stars. That was big Joe Wynne.

The two were drinking coffee, bending over their tins, smoking cigarettes at the same time. Five horses were picketed nearby, grazing on the scanty grass among the rocks. Bridles, saddles, and packs lay in one confused heap.

Said one of the pair: "Bill's got the idea, Wynne."

"What is it?" asked Wynne, his voice clearly heard in spite of its quiet intonation.

A slight shudder went through the boy. It was like words from the dead.

"We're gunna make a regular rock grave for you, Wynne," said the speaker. "Here, Bill, you up and tell him."

Bill laughed.

He was a short man, with such heavy muscles around the shoulders that his arms were always carried thrusting out a little from his sides. It gave him a jaunty appearance, and now as he laughed, his elbows rose up and down and worked in and out. He looked like a bulldog. His nose and forehead retreated, as though to give his teeth a better chance to bite.

His companion was a bald-headed picture of vice, young, lean, with a crooked throat that looked as though it were broken in the center. He was always smiling.

"All right, Dan," said Bill. "I'll tell him. It's not gunna be any argument about how we finish you off, Joe. When the chief told us off for this job, he gave us a coupla hours to think it over, while he went ahead to rake in Speedy. He told us to think up the best way. Feeding you into a fire, he said would be good enough. He's kind of irritated agin you, Joe. Know that?"

"I can guess that," said the admirably calm voice of Wynne.

"He's mostly irritated because that feller Pierson crawled off into the bush, and we couldn't afford the time to go and

209

hunt him down. What the chief says is that the luck is rotten, because our guns don't kill, no more, and I says to him, I says: 'Six, you gotta remember that we was doin' all the shootin' off of horseback. That shakes a gun up, considerable.' Which he admitted that I had the rights of it. But now me and Dan, we been thinkin' it all over, and I got this idea. You might as well have dynamite for executioner, and grave-digger, and chief mourner at your funeral, old son."

He laughed again.

"I always pack some powder along with me," went on Bill. "I keep it over there in that saddlebag. Some of the boys, they call me Dynamite Bill, for that reason."

"Naw, that ain't the only reason," said Dan, chuckling.

"Maybe it ain't the only reason neither," said Bill, laughing with a conscious vanity. And he went on: "But it's a funny thing how handy old dynamite will come in, almost every trip. Sometimes they's a door that don't open none too easy, and then it's powder that makes a key to fit the lock—and there you are, inside. And sometimes the path is blocked, and then again old dynamite, he speaks one word, and that path is clear! And there has been a time when we was starvin' on the edge of good fishin' water, and dynamite, it was what killed the fish and drifted the dead of 'em onto the shore, and we ate right plenty, that time. And I recollect, and so does Dan, here, a time when the folks was gettin' thicker'n mosquitoes on our trail, and I just light a short fuse and drop it down the side of the rock onto the trail in the midst of 'em, and they begun to yell, and they pull their hosses around, but the direction that they started in wasn't where they wound up, because they landed in hell, Wynne, if you know what I mean."

Laughter choked him, and he went on, after a moment: "So now, as soon as we finish this here coffee, we're gunna stretch you out there under that high rock, Wynne, and we're gunna put a coupla sticks under the hind end of that rock, and blow it over onto you. This here is a pretty well-traveled trail. Every coupla hours in the day, folks come along, and they'll look at that rock, and they'll say that there must of been an earthquake, or something, and they'll never think that little old dynamite lies on top, and big Joe Wynne, he lies under. Joe, does that sound right to you?"

"That sounds all right to me," said Joe Wynne, as calmly as ever.

"Well," said Dan, "he says that it sounds all right to him. So as long as we got his permission, why shouldn't we do the little job now—ask dynamite to do it for us, I mean! What's the use of holdin' back, when the crowd is so doggone anxious to see the job done?"

"No reason at all," said Dynamite Bill, and he rose to his feet.

Speedy rose at the same time.

He had reached the designated saddlebag by working along the ground like a snake. He had probed the inside of the bag and found what he wanted, not one stick, but three. One, however, was all that he wanted.

He made careful aim, sighting the distance to the fire, and then he threw the stick well up into the air.

It was some yards away, but Dynamite Bill saw a shadow flick across the corner of his eye, as it were, and whirled with a shout of surprise and anger, snatching out a gun.

There he saw the dim silhouette of the boy standing in the starlight, one hand raised in the completion of the gesture that had thrown the powder.

"Now what in hell d'you want, and who are you?" Bill asked.

"Speedy," said the boy.

And as he spoke, the stick descended from its long arc and struck the fire.

Speedy himself was knocked headlong, staggering, though he had been at such a distance. But when his mind and eyes cleared, he saw a queer heap of something that was neither brush nor stone near the place where the fire had been burning.

And far away, running with blind veerings, ran the tall form of Dan like a snipe flying down the wind, and as he ran, his screaming blew behind him, growing fainter and fainter with his swift strides.

IT WAS WELL BEFORE daylight when Speedy wakened the girl.

"It's time to start," he told her.

She got up without a word, and started pulling on her boots. He, beginning to saddle the horses, called over his shoulder:

"Joe is all right."

"What!" she cried.

She came running, hobbling, for one high-heeled boot was on, and the other was off.

"He's all right," said Speedy. "He's back there lying in a shady spot, with plenty of food and water, and on a trail where people come along every couple of hours in the day."

"Speedy, Speedy!" cried the girl. "How did you do it? How did you manage to get him away from them? And is he badly hurt? And what happened?"

"They put about a dozen bullets into him," said the boy. "But what do slugs through the arms and legs matter? He might have a stiff shoulder, later on; but every hero ought to have a limp, somewhere or other. He's going to be all right. He's a little weak, but he'll do fine."

"But you haven't said what happened?" insisted Mary Steyn. "You haven't said how you managed—"

"Oh," said the boy, "the Wilson gang changed its mind. They were going to murder him, of course, but they changed their mind. They were too anxious to pick you up, Mary. So we'll just hit the high spots. By the way, they told Joe Wynne, before they left, that Pierson got away from 'em, too. He did it at night, by crawling off into the brush, and he lay so low that they couldn't find him, in the time they could afford to spend searching."

He heard her crying and laughing at once; but he went on cinching up the saddles.

"God had a hand in it!" said the girl. "If there's a God, he had a hand in it. Only, Speedy, I don't believe what you say. You *drove* them away!"

"Look at the guns," said the boy. "Just as much ammunition in them now as there was last night."

She shook her head.

"Your way is magic," said she. "Not guns, but all hand and head."

She began to sing under her breath, and when they mounted, he found her eyes turned constantly towards him, but for his part, he looked straight ahead. The black and bitter poison was still in him.

So they rode into the rose of the morning, and into the brilliant, terrible sunshine.

That day ended. They climbed hills. They came, in the late evening, in sight of a deserted, ruined shack, with massive 'dobe walls, and a growth of poplars crowding together at a little distance from the place. There they halted, and looking down the long slopes, they saw the green of the fields, the rich pasture lands, dull in this faint light, and the thin and curving gleam of a river beyond.

"That's the Rio Grande," said Speedy. "We'll wait here for a while and let the horses rest a bit. Then we'll forge ahead. There's a good moon to the west, now, and we'll make our start and the first hour, or so, by the light of it."

"Is it safe to stop?" she asked him.

"It's not safe," he answered, bluntly. "Nothing's safe, I suppose. But these horses need a rest. We can build a fire in the shack. You make some coffee, and I'll hobble the horses."

He did as he had said, and the coffee was steaming when he came in. They drank some of the night-black, bitter stuff before eating, for they were both weary to death. And, while they were sipping, they heard the first sound of the approach. It was only the popping of a single dead branch. But suddenly they looked up at one another, agape, and each studied the horror of the other in the red firelight, like a thin wash of blood over the face.

Then he said: "I think this is about the finish, Mary."

She got up and gripped a rifle.

"Suppose that we make a break," said she.

"On foot?" said Speedy.

He merely smiled. Then he trod out the fire, kicking dirt over the embers.

Outside, there was a murmur of voices, and one saying, clearly: "There's Coal Tar. The chief'll be glad to see the old devil again! Hey, you inside—Speedy! Speedy! Come out and take your medicine, you sneaking coyote, you poison-faced hound! Come out here and take what's comin' to you!"

He actually made a step towards the door; the girl clung to him with both hands, shuddering, but strong with frenzy.

"If you go out—if you let them murder you—I'll kill myself, Speedy!" said she. "I won't let them take me!"

"They don't want you," said the boy. "What could they do with you? It's me that they want—but I won't go out yet, for a little while. Take your hands off me and stay back in the corner. This is my job."

She shrank from him, and heard him call: "Hello—is Handsome out there?"

"Handsome who?" called the answer.

Speedy paused, saying rather loudly to the girl, "You keep your eye peeled through the slots at the back of the house, will you? And shoot at anything you see moving."

A sudden, hasty rustling answered this speech, from the rear of the house.

"I mean," went on Speedy, "handsome Six-card Wilson. Is he out there?"

A bawling voice answered: "He's here, and he wants me to tell you that he's gunna eat tramp-meat, before sunup. You've made a good play, Speedy. We're gunna remember you, too. It was a good ride and a long ride, but we nailed you in the finish. You can tell the girl that she's not gunna be hurt. She's only gunna be delayed a mite. We'll give our word for that. But you, Speedy, come out and take what's comin', or else, by God, we'll heap up wood and burn out the pair of you."

"That's a lie," said Speedy, calmly. "These walls are 'dobe, there's no roof to hold the smoke, and you can burn wood and be damned, but you'll never smoke me out. There's only one thing that will make me move."

214

"Speak it out, Speedy," said the spokesman. "What's that?"

"A fair crack at Mr. Six Wilson."

"You fool! Six has only got one hand."

"I'll tie my right hand behind me," said the boy. "I'll meet Six in the moonshine right in front of the shack. You boys can watch from the brush with your rifles, and see that there's fair play. The girl will watch from inside with her rifle, and see that there's fair play. I'll wait for Handsome, until he shows his face."

There was a murmuring of many voices; several minutes passed, and suddenly the giant stepped forward from the trees. His right arm was crossed behind his back. His left hand dangled empty.

"Speedy, don't go," pleaded Mary Steyn. "I think I'll go mad."

He said nothing. He simply struck her detaining hands away, and she, the rifle shaking in her grip, leaned half fainting in the darkness inside the doorway.

She heard the big man saying: "Now I got you in a fair open place, where there ain't any walls and no surprises to help you, and one hand will be enough to choke you with, you rat!"

Said Speedy, in answer to that ghastly whisper: "From the minute I laid eyes on you, I knew that you'd be my first kill, Six. I've been tasting the death of you all of these days. And tonight's the time."

She heard not so much the words as the voice which uttered them, and her blood congealed.

Then they closed.

The stride, the lofty height of Six, the great, poised hand, made him seem like one of those fierce birds which kill snakes, and snakelike was the weaving, darting approach of the boy. It was not human. It was simply horror past words.

They closed; they parted, they closed again. Six Wilson staggered, and a roar of excitement and dismay went up from his men; and the girl heard a man shrieking: "Six, Six, what's the matter with you? You can break the shrimp's back. What's the matter with you?"

But Speedy like a wildcat had followed in; and they whirled together. The legs of the boy seemed wound into those of the gaunt outlaw, but by his left hand he kept his best hold, and that hold was on the throat of the big man. She saw both their faces, ghastly in the moonlight; one killing, one dying.

But it was not ended, yet. Six Wilson had not come into that battle prepared to trust all to fair combat. Instead, his free hand now jerked up high, with a blade gleaming in it.

Mary Steyn screamed, but only half the scream was uttered as she saw the knife descend and the blade buried in the body of Speedy.

Then the rifle snapped up to her shoulder, and she took aim.

Twice and again the knife struck down, and twice and again her finger curled on the trigger, only to find that the body of Speedy had each time whirled in between her and the target.

She would have to try the head.

Coldly, without a quiver of her body or of her nerves, she drew the bead; but the pair collapsed to the ground before she could shoot.

A man ran out, wildly shouting, from the brush. She put a snap shot close to his ear, and he fell backwards to the ground, in his eagerness to get back to safety.

And then—she saw it with eyes that would not close— the pair were twisting on the ground, snakelike, and the throat hold of Speedy was broken. Was he dying? No, the knife was in *his* hand, now.

It drew back, and once, twice, thrice, it went home. Distinctly, on her own heart, she felt the impacts.

Then both bodies lay still.

"They've killed each other. I'm kind of sick," said a groaning voice from the shrubbery. "I'm gunna get out of here."

"And the girl?" said another.

"Only Six would of known what to do with her. Leave her be. She can bury 'em, and be damned to her."

Quickly they went, as men go from a plague spot. The treading of many hoofs died in the distance. And still Mary Steyn, like a statue, stood in the dark of the doorway, and looked at men, and life, and death, and thought such thoughts as she would never think again, in the course of her life.

And so, as she stood, she saw the slender form of Speedy arise, slowly and steadily, and heard him saying, in the calmest of voices: "I had to play 'possum till they left. Must have been hard on your nerves, Mary. But now if you'll do a little bandaging, we'll be starting along, I think."

—43—

OLD RIVERA WAS CALLED, through all the length of the river, Don Alfonso, though his eye was as blue as the next man's. But there was a dignity and a grandeur of living about him that called for a title, and this one was given to him.

Being very old, he kept the hours of a bird, asleep by dark, awake by dawn; and in the heat of the day he slept soundly, for two or three hours. So the fire of life remained in him, perhaps, but clearly burning. He was not changed from his younger self; there was simply less of him in body and in will.

But on this morning, he was having a sop of dark bread in neat wine for breakfast on his veranda. He had eaten just such a breakfast, all the days of his life, when he was at home. The morsel of bread satisfied his hunger. The wine put a warmth in his blood.

And, leaning both his hands upon the round head of his cane, when he had finished his breakfast, he looked fixedly down the avenue under the trees. That was his habit; that was the vista up which the only remaining joy of life could come to him, and down that vista went his thoughts, night and morning. So he lifted his head, a little, when he heard the grinding wheels of the buckboard on the gravel, not in hope, but in interest. Everything that approached the house always gave him that dim, small wave of expectancy, followed by the thin shadow of disappointment.

On the front seat of the wagon there was a Mexican driver, whipping the little pair of mustangs cruelly. In the rear seat of the buckboard a man and a girl were sitting, he with his coat huddled loosely about his shoulders and white bands going around and around his body. He lay back in the seat, his chin on his breast. And the girl beside him was holding one of his hands.

But it was not the youth that held the eye of old Don Alfonso. It was the girl.

As the buckboard came nearer, he rose, helping himself up with a strong push of his hands against the head of the cane. Then he walked to the edge of the steps, and finally halfway down them, staring.

She seemed to pay no heed to him, until she had jumped down to the ground, and even then she did not have a chance to speak. For he called out: "Jose!"

A man jumped out and stood beside him.

"Your mistress has just come home," said Don Alfonso. "Go open the windows of her room."

The moon hung an hour high in the west; four weeks had run since it was there last, at this time, when the sunset and the twilight were meeting.

And old Don Alfonso was saying: "It is better out here on the veranda. The air is sweeter and cooler. You can feel the river moisture in it, on an evening like this, and the mosquitoes are not so bad, this year, Mary. I think we may have to make a screened porch, one of these days.

"Mr. Steyn, will you take this chair on my right? I should live more and happier years, Mr. Steyn, if I could always look forward to having you here at my right hand. But I understand your point of view. A man's home is more than family, more than blood; it is a part of his soul.

"Now, then, Joseph, I think that other chair will bear your weight. And you, Mr. Pierson, try that canvas chair. You'll find your leg more comfortable, while you're in it. And now, I think, we are all together?"

Joe Wynne laughed faintly.

"All except fifty-one per cent of us," said he. "Speedy isn't here."

"Yes," said Don Alfonso, "even Speedy is here. He'll always be present, when we're together. He can't be absent. And just now I have a letter from him—a letter written to Mary, for me to read to her, and explain. But instead, I am going to read it to all of you because, my dear friends, in a certain way we are all members of one family. Danger and blood have cemented us together. So, then, if you're ready, I'll begin. Mary, sit there on the step, where I can watch your face.

"The letter begins:

" 'Dear Mary,

" 'Last night I talked things over with your grandfather. We reached an agreement. I'd better say he agreed with me.

" 'The things that make me happiest I can put first. One is that you're first, with me, and all the rest of the world is a bad second. The other is that, the other day, I think you were about to say that you are fond of me, too. The reason I wouldn't let you finish your sentence, that time, was that an instinct tapped me like a hand on the shoulder and told me that it was wrong.

" 'Since then, I've been thinking it over, for hours, and I've been feeling so sorry for myself that there have been tears in my eyes and dry bread in my throat. But what I see clearly, now, and what your grandfather agrees, is that a house and a life and a woman's happiness cannot be built on a rolling stone.

" 'This old house, and this whole fine old estate is enough to fill any sensible man's eye. But I'm not sensible, and when I look on the spot where I'm to spend the rest of my life, I feel as though I were already half in the grave.

" 'So I have to see other places, and roll here and there, and go my own way, which is a vagabond's way. I always thought that I was only killing time until a grand opportunity should come my way, but now that the opportunity has come, I see that the devil has been too careful a school-teacher, for me, and I can't forget his lessons.

" 'No, as I see it, a far better man than I ever will be ought to stand first with you. You love him already. And as soon as the tramp is out of the way, you'll see him more clearly. There's no spot on him. He's the one man to whom I'm willing to owe a certain sort of debt and leave it unpaid. There's still a very small bump on the back of my head, and every time I touch it, I'll think of the two of you. It will be a sad business at first, but after a while I know that I'll be happy about it.

" 'I haven't the courage to say good-bye to you, because if I looked in your eyes and saw the least shadow of happiness, I know that I would drop to my knees and beg you to let me try to make you happy the rest of your life.

" 'So, tonight, when the moon begins to shine, I'm going to take my guitar and start out. Tell Pierson that I know he'll be rich before he dies, and give my love to your grandfather and old Joe Wynne, and Mr. Steyn. Three like them never sat together in one room.

" 'Mary, good-bye; and now that I come to the end, I see that I never have given you any name to remember me by except one that will quickly run downhill out of your mind.

Speedy.' "

Now, as the old man finished reading this letter, a great silence came over all of those on the porch. And each one of them looked down, and studied his own thoughts.

So complete grew the stillness, that out of the distance a thin sound of music drifted to them, though so indistinctly that only those who already knew the words could have guessed them:

> "Julia,
> You are peculiar;
> Julia,
> You are queer.
> Truly,
> You are unruly,
> As a wild, western steer.
> Sweetheart, when we marry,
> Dear one, you and I—"

Here the music faded away.

The words of that song were not familiar to Don Alfonso. Besides, he hardly heard the song at all, he was so engaged, now, in watching the girl.

For on the high shoulder of wall beside the steps, she sat just a shade above him, and now the westering moon began to slide down behind her, first catching in a glow of light her hair, and then gliding the curve of her throat, and outlining with infinite tenderness her bowed face.

So it stood, at last, like a great golden shield, and her head the bright boss in the center of it.

She did not stir, and there was no voice along the dark veranda until the wind from the coolness of the river came up through the trees, hushing and whispering at every ear.

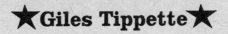